VOYAGES OF THE STAR HAWK

PRAXTON

#5

N.S. HOWARD

VOYAGES OF THE STAR HAWK
Copyright © 2020 by N.S. Howard

ISBN: 978-1-68046-993-6

Melange Books, LLC
White Bear Lake, MN 55110
www.melange-books.com

Published in the United States of America.

Cover Design by Lynsee Lauritsen

It's not easy to write a book on what-ifs and a possible future universe. I spent many hours sitting, trying to make an enjoyable story for my readers. So, I would like to thank the following for helping me make this story possible. In no particular order:

Microsoft Surface
My leather easy chair
Spell Check
ProWritingAid
Microsoft Word
Times New Roman font
Obra Prima Reserva Malbec
Maker's Mark Bourbon
Wiser's 15 year old Canadian Whisky
Kirk and Sweeney 12 year old rum
My apologies if I missed any alcoholic product.

GLOSSARY OF TERMS

▭

The Star Hawk series begins after the fourth Praxton novel, A Vote For Change. For those unfamiliar with the Praxton universe, I have listed below a few of the terms used in this book.

Alliance Worlds: The Alliance worlds comprised approximately half of the human worlds. The government is located on Mars, although Earth with its large population has the most voting power. Most of the Alliance worlds reside within fifty light years from Earth.

Rebel Worlds: Any world not part of the Alliance worlds. Some Rebel worlds formed a loose association with other Rebel worlds but most live independently. The Rebel worlds are located outside of the Alliance worlds boundary, although a few are in close proximity. There is only minor trade between the Rebel and Alliance worlds.

Praxton: Formerly a Rebel world. Praxton is known for requiring women to wear collars and obeying their male guardians. Alliance forces invaded Praxton to free the women from perceived slavery. The battle did not go as the Alliance forces expected, resulting in Praxton becoming part of the Alliance Worlds but keeping many of their unique culture and social customs.

Charter of Conduct Office: A bureaucratic Alliance world government department. The Charter of Conduct Office was created with the premise that human conflicts occurred because of differences in the social and culture of various people. If everyone spoke the same language and acted the same, conflicts would end. The authority of the Charter of Conduct Office increased to the point of ruling even on the alcohol content of wine and the caffeine in tea. The Charter of Conduct ordered Alliance forces to invade Praxton, a political disaster for the Alliance government. Afterward, the Charter of Conduct Office powers were sharply curtailed.

Pirates: Spaceships use hyperspace to jump to their destinations. It takes enormous energy to make a jump, such that most ships require a series of jumps to reach their final destination. Using advanced algorithms, pirate ships try to estimate where passenger and cargo ships will jump to between their destinations. Until the ship can recharge their jump engines, they can be attacked by pirates. Goods are the most sought-after commodity, although pirates will take women as slaves on occasion. It is generally accepted that if the spaceship does not resist the theft, it will be allowed to continue on its journey. If the spaceship is small and transporting wealthy passengers, it may be taken to a rebel world where a ransom has to be paid for the release of the passengers. Pirating is not considered illegal among the Rebel worlds.

The Wave: Earth and the rest of the solar system sent out many colony ships to habitable planets. All the planets agreed to have Earth as the governing body, sending representatives to vote on regulations and laws. Then an unknown phenomenon spread from the galactic core. The Wave destroyed electrical and electronic devices. Order was restored many years after. However, many of the planets that were the most distant decided not to rejoin the Earth dominated government, even though Earth agreed to move the governing body to Mars. Individual Rebel worlds, such as Praxton, deciding on their own laws they chose to adhere to.

Gene therapy: Advances in biology gave everyone access to gene therapy. Besides medical treatment, many people used gene therapy to improve their looks. The result was it became difficult to determine a person's age and many people appeared far younger than their years. For most people, gene therapy was very expensive due to the high tax.

Viewscreen: This device replaces mirrors and windows. For mirrors, cameras are placed so that the viewer can see their normal mirror image, plus sides and rear view. For windows, the viewscreen can give the same image as a window. The advantage is the thin membrane is mounted on a hard surface, making the danger of broken glass windows on spacecraft obsolete. The viewscreen gives the illusion of a three-dimensional image and can expand or shrink the image.

———

Star Hawk crew rankings.

The Star Hawk carries both military and non-military personnel. Civilians are permitted to wear civilian clothing, but most non-military crew wear a uniform that matches the military uniform in style but has a different colour scheme. Military ranks are listed below with the equivalent civilian positions.

Admiral- not based on ship
Rear Admiral- not based on ship

Military Personnel
    Captain
    First Officer (Commander, 1st class)
    Steermaster (Commander, 2nd class)
    Communication Officer (Commander, 3rd class)
    Lieutenant (1st, 2nd, 3rd class- includes Senior Female)
    Warrant Officer (1st, 2nd, 3rd class)
    Sergeant (1st Sergeant, Master Sergeant)
    Cadet (1st, 2nd, 3rd class)

Non-military personnel
    Senior Technician
    Food and beverage manager
    Technician (1st, 2nd)
    Maintenance, Hospitality

CAPTAIN JULIUS ELMWOOD STOOD, surveying the bridge of the spaceship, Queen Sophia. He checked with the steermaster. "Are we ready to orbit?"

The steermaster moved his fingers through the holographic display floating in front of him. "Yup, a piece of cake."

Elmwood stepped toward his next in command, Morgan Regan. "Everything appears normal."

"It does. Except for the second jump, most of the trip has been quiet." She looked up at Elmwood, taller than most men with a lean build of a hungry tiger. Sky-blue eyes dominated his strong facial features. He kept his dark hair short.

"Yeah, it's hard to avoid the rebels at every turn. Still, it was nice when they backed down."

"You did a nice little bluff there." Morgan kept her shoulder-length red hair neat. She was average height with a well-curved figure. Over the past four years, she moved up the chain of command for Terra Passenger Space Lines and her next position could be the command of her own ship. That was when a spot came open. New ships were not launched regularly. It depended on travel demand to justify new routes.

"I suppose so. But hijackers don't like to take risks. They want easy prey. I suggested they might lose part of their crew and they left us alone."

A sound chimed, alerting them that they were now in orbit around Praxton. Below the Queen Sophia, Praxton with red features dominated the view. Moving shuttles, two space stations and the new ship building facility passed by the viewscreens.

"What are you going to do with your time off?" Morgan referred to the twenty-five-day turnaround between cruises.

"It's Praxton and so there's lots to do if one likes adult entertainment. I know a pair of freelancers. It gives me a place to stay and I don't need to go and party every night. How about you?"

The freelancers Elmwood referred to were unattached women who wore collars but would obey a male guardian for a price. The freelancers were frowned upon by other women on the planet but served a purpose for Praxton society. Men arriving on Praxton, to reside for a short time and in need of female companionship, would contact freelancers. There were few independent women on Praxton. Because of social pressure and the difficulty in getting financial freedom, almost all women were under the guardianship of a male.

"There's not much for single women to do on Praxton other than in the tourist zone. But that ends up being just too much drinking. So, that being said, I've hired a freelancer." Morgan glanced at Elmwood, curious if his usual authoritarian expression would change. "I figured I would at least have a friend for a few weeks, paid for, but still a friend. Shopping, a few bars and just relaxing. And no, not for sex."

"That sounds fair enough."

"I know what you're thinking. I prefer men, but sometimes a warm friend, not for sex, is all I need."

"I get it. A woman on Praxton has few options. I think it's a smart thing to do to get a freelancer. It provides you with something to do and saves you the risk of being a single woman on Praxton."

"Thanks." She touched his upper arm. "See you in a few weeks. Maybe we can get together for a drink on Praxton."

"That would be great."

Elmwood was the last to leave the Queen Sophia. When he arrived at the waiting shuttle, the spaceship was busy with maintenance crews moving purposely. The Queen Sophia was a large passenger ship, and its twenty-four hundred metre length featured thousands of corridors, rooms, a myriad of machines and devices. All of which had to be checked, cleaned, repaired and certified for spaceflight.

A smiling hostess greeted him. She wore the standard dress for female flight attendants on Praxton, a dark blue, tight-fitting jacket with a deep V neck, a short, matching skirt, high heels, a dark green metal collar with identical wrist cuffs and a few gold glittering chains connecting them.

"Welcome aboard, Captain Elmwood."

He couldn't help but return a smile to the cheerful blonde and sat in one of the vacant seats.

She closed the shuttle door. "You're our only passenger."

"So much for efficiency." He chuckled. "I'm thrilled to have you to take care of me in that case."

She laughed. "What would you like? A drink or perhaps something to eat?"

"I'm fine." He shook his head. "Are you from Praxton?"

"Yes, born and raised." She nodded. "I'm so happy to be working on the shuttle team. I get to meet so many interesting people."

"Does your guardian approve of you being away days at a time?" He knew shuttle crews usually worked several days on and off. It was easier to keep the same crew for extended trips then just a few hours on a day shift.

"Yes, he's very good to me. He encouraged me to take the courses required to be on a shuttle crew when I expressed an interest in going to space." She laughed. "Maybe he's just wanting to get rid of me."

"If so, the man must be blind."

"Our captains are female, so we have an all female flight crew on this shuttle."

"I feel very privileged. Is it possible for me to meet them? I would like to say hello." He knew normally passengers didn't get to go into the control cabin, but he felt his rank of a captain of a passenger ship would carry sufficient weight.

"I will check." She smiled and walked up to the front, leaving Elmwood time to relax.

A few minutes later he felt a bump as the shuttle disengaged from the Queen Sophia and the starfield he saw through the window, actually a viewscreen that provided a high enough resolution as to be indistinguishable from a glass window, shifted. He watched as his passenger ship rotated in the view, dwarfing most of the other ships around her. The Queen Sophia receded as the hostess returned.

"The captain and first officer would be delighted to meet you. Please follow me."

Elmwood noted they used Alliance world terms for the shuttle crew officers. He recalled at one time Praxton called their officers below captain as commander, followed by lieutenant-commander. The ranking originated from ships that sailed oceans, and it seemed Praxton was now becoming more in alignment with Alliance worlds.

The door to the cabin opened and Elmwood stood at the doorway, waiting for recognition.

Each woman greeted him, then returned to their seat afterward.

"I suddenly feel old. Both of you look much younger than when I first became a pilot."

"Drug therapy," laughed the first officer named Marcie. "We're older than we look. Renix has been a pilot for two years now. I just received my shuttle pilot licence four months ago."

"Welcome to the pilot fraternity. Any plans in flying something besides a shuttle?"

"Eventually I'd like to fly a hopper," Renix answered. "I don't want to be away more than a few days at a time. Hoppers are usually gone for three to six days. I don't believe Marcie knows what she wants yet. She's still excited to fly a shuttle."

Elmwood understood about hoppers. The small passenger ships were well appointed and used by executives for short stays at close-by star systems. Often it would be a travel period of two days with a day long meeting. Then a quick trip back. "I suppose there's an increased demand for those now that Praxton is part of the Alliance worlds."

"There are a lot more business travelers and government officials coming to Praxton now."

"The spaceports here are busy. It looks like Praxton is doing well since they agreed to join the Alliance worlds."

"Well, Praxton wasn't given much of an option. Still, in the long run, Praxton is going to do just fine. Our government won the bid to build the new Explorer Space Fleet. I guess you know how much revenue that brings in."

Elmwood was aware of the Explorer Space ships. The newest military spaceships were made specifically to not only ensure peace in Alliance space, but to venture beyond the borders to establish a presence in rebel territory. He had applied for the position of captain of the first explorer ship, which would be commissioned within the month. He had already had two interviews, via video, and hoped to be short listed for the final interviews.

"If you're planning to be on hoppers, does that mean you've had military training?" Alliance Military Space Command required all pilots and other executives on spaceships to receive military training. In case of a military conflict, the pilots and crew could be pressed into service. In effect, all spaceship executive officers were on reserve, and could be called up in an emergency. Elmwood had served as a pilot for the military for several years, helping his career to be fast tracked when he joined a civilian space fleet.

"I served in the Praxton military for a short time, before obtaining a guardian. That means my training with Alliance Military will be reduced from eight weeks to four."

"Good for you. Serving on spaceships can be a rewarding career."

━━━

After the space shuttle landed at a ground port, Elmwood used a ground shuttle to reach his next destination, the apartment where his hired freelancers lived.

Grata greeted Elmwood at her apartment door. The large suite covered half of the thirty-third floor and afforded a great view of the city skyline. "It's wonderful to see you again, Master Julius. It has been a long three months since your last visit." She looked at Acacia. "You remember Acacia, of course. We have also added a new member to our household."

Elmwood looked at the woman waiting further back, her hands held behind her back. The tall brunette peered at him with a forced smile.

"Her name is Emmia. She has been with us only a few weeks."

"Wonderful to see Acacia and you. I look forward to being acquainted with Emmia."

Elmwood insisted on carrying his own luggage to the master bedroom and later settled in the living room on the couch. Acacia sat on his left as Grata passed around glasses of wine. With a hand on Emmia's shoulder, she directed the newest female to kneel on the floor in front of Elmwood and sat on Elmwood's right.

Grata initiated the conversation. "I know you just arrived on Praxton and you have a different view of local time. Let me know whenever you're hungry or tired."

"Thanks, I'm okay for a while." He felt the women on either side of him curl up close to him, resting a hand on his lap and arm. "So, Emmia, where are you from?"

"Provost, it's a small world and far from here."

"I'm familiar with it. You came to Praxton for fame and fortune?" He gave her a smile, letting her know he knew the reason most women came to Praxton as a freelancer.

"I wanted to visit other worlds and Praxton sounded so exotic." She nodded. "At least compared to Provost. So far it has been a good experience."

Elmwood relaxed with the women, sharing a few stories of life on a starship. As a captain of a passenger starship, it meant intimate relations with the junior crew members had to be done carefully. It wasn't forbidden, but Elmwood knew there would be consequences if problems occurred by his involvement with them. Executive crew members were possible, but he still needed to be cautious. Passengers were considered off limits, meaning his visit to Praxton presented an opportunity he had been looking forward to. Later, he would choose who he would share a bed with.

[2]

MORGAN MET Eleni in the apartment lobby, receiving a big smile and a hug from the freelancer. She felt apprehensive as she travelled on Praxton. Part of it included wearing the Praxton fashions. Women on Praxton only wore skirts or dresses and never pants. The tops were usually made of a light material, which she found flattering. However, females on Praxton rarely wore bras, and while Morgan found the freedom stimulating, she was aware of the extra movement under her shirt. One item Morgan needed to wear caused her nervousness, namely the famous Praxton collar.

The collar she wore was authentic, and not the imitation ones she had occasionally worn in Alliance space. She had discretely purchased it and matching cuffs in one of the ship's shops as they approached Praxton. When she put it on, she didn't bother adding chains to the wrist cuffs, but it still felt sensual. Morgan knew about Praxton and its customs, finding it intriguing. When she received the opportunity to spend time on Praxton, she wanted to experience their lifestyle. This included hiring a freelancer to help her understand the nuances of their society. It made her nervous, paying another woman for companionship.

"It's wonderful to meet you. I'm dying to learn what a spaceship officer does."

Morgan felt better when she had met Eleni. She felt it odd she had hired a freelancer for companionship, but she didn't want to stay by herself. She had considered joining up with another crewmember, but that could have future problems of friendship with subordinates on the ship.

"I'm afraid to say it's not all that glamorous." She followed Eleni to the elevators, pulling her suitcase behind her. The suitcase had gravity-neutralizer pads on the bottom, allowing it to glide easily over surfaces.

An elevator took them to the twenty-seventh floor where Eleni showed her around the suite, featuring two bedrooms and two washrooms, plus a living room, kitchen and dining room. "The smaller bedroom is for when we have more females, but I don't expect we will have extra guests."

Morgan looked inside the master bedroom with the large window. "Nice size and a great view, too." She looked at the adjourning washroom, which had a second enclosed area where the toilet was located. The rest of the washroom which included both a shower and a bathtub, had a full-length window to the outside. She knew of the Praxton custom to have females using showers and baths visible to the others. Still, it surprised her to see how open it was to the outside world. The suite also had a private washroom but that would be reserved for male visitors, who were not expected to show off their bodies. "It looks nice."

"Thanks, let's have a drink. There are two things I want to go over with you."

Morgan sat holding a glass of white wine on a loveseat with Eleni. "You really have a nice place here. It's larger than I expected."

"Thank you. You said you just wanted a companion for the time you were on Praxton. That's fine, but if you should want something different later, I'm open to that. If you want me more submissive, I understand. I can act who you want me to be."

"I really didn't want to be on Praxton alone. I hear it's tough to meet men here, and I figure a girlfriend might be the best route. A paid for girlfriend, but that's still better than being alone."

"Fair enough. I assume we're going to be sleeping together. Praxton custom is to avoid females sleeping alone. But if sleeping with me bothers you, I can sleep in the spare room."

"No, I've slept alone long enough on the ship. I figure I can sleep with a girlfriend here. I don't mean sex. I'm still after guys."

"That's okay. You may change your mind and I'm fine with that too."

Morgan looked at Eleni's long legs. *Yeah, if I drink too much wine, that may be tempting.*

—————

Eleni stood naked at the foot of the bed. "Okay, just a couple more Praxton customs. You don't have to follow them, but you should know about them. One is that females always sleep in the nude. The reasons for that are rooted when guardians were worried their females would try to escape at night. They believed keeping them naked would reduce that risk. For that same reason, females were cuffed by the ankle to the bed." She held up a wide silver coloured cuff attached with a chain. The chain went to the end of the bed had enough length to allow the wearer sufficient movement in the bed.

"Interesting." Morgan studied the ankle cuff. "Does it lock?"

"It does but has a quick release. All cuffs and restraints have a quick release thanks to the Charter of Conduct laws for safety reasons. Previous to the new law, a key was kept close by. That way a female could undo the cuff if she needed to do so rather than wake her guardian. The ankle cuff is only traditional, but all Praxton females still follow it, maybe out of defiance of the Charter of Conduct Office interfering with our way of life."

"I guess since I'm on Praxton I should follow the Praxton customs."

Eleni grinned. "That's great to hear."

Morgan undressed, aware of Eleni observing her. She folded her clothes, placing them on the same low table that also held Eleni's daytime wear. She placed a knee on the bed and slowly slid on the mattress. Eleni helped her into the cuff, then climbed in bed. The ankle cuff had a stiff exterior but was padded on the inside. Morgan heard the soft click of the lock as she closed the cuff on her ankle. *Okay, I'm naked, next to another naked woman, and both of us are cuffed to the bed. How am I supposed to fall asleep?* She pulled the light blanket up to her shoulders.

"Are you okay?" Eleni sat up on her elbows, giving her a smile. "Nervous?"

"Nervous. New bed. Naked and cuffed. I guess I'm out of my comfort zone."

"I understand. I'll be right back."

Morgan watched Eleni undo her ankle cuff and leave the bedroom. *Nice back and ass. She's gorgeous.*

Eleni returned carrying two glasses and a bottle of wine. She filled one glass with red wine and handed it to Morgan as she sat up against the padded headboard. She placed the bottle and the other glass on a table by the head of the bed on her side. After locking the ankle cuff, she joined Morgan with her own glass of wine. "Okay, let's talk about life on a spaceship."

Morgan talked about her role on the spaceship and the people in it. She relaxed, and the long day took its toll. She finished her wine and slid down into the bed. She was barely aware of Eleni fixing the blanket over her and the close contact of their bodies before she fell asleep.

JULIUS ELMWOOD DOUBLED CHECKED the message on his mobile and confirmed the interview time. "Grata, I have an interview tomorrow with the space agency." He walked out of the bedroom, fully dressed. Praxton customs required males to be fully dressed when they left the bedroom, including footwear. Females were expected to be barefoot and only partially dressed in clothes but were required to wear a collar and, preferably, matching cuffs and chains.

"That's great news. Is that for the new explorer ships?"

"Yes, it is." He looked at her standing in only her panties, a collar and a pair of wrist cuffs as she held a cup of tea. The other two females were sleeping in the spare bedroom. Elmwood earlier decided his first night should be with just the senior freelancer.

Grata went back to the kitchen and returned carrying a cup of coffee for him. "Did you wish for me to wake the other females?"

"No, let them sleep. I'm on vacation and don't mind the slower pace."

"What would you like for breakfast? I'm a skilled cook."

"I remember that. But let's go out. I'm looking forward to being outside."

She laughed. "Then I better get dressed."

"Damn, but not too many clothes."

[4]

MORGAN YAWNED as she eyed the inside of the shower. *This is odd, showering where people can see me if they had good eyesight. Mind you, sleeping naked next to another woman is odd. And the ankle cuff to the foot of the bed is one strange Praxton custom.*

"Good morning." Eleni reached around her and turned on the water. "Come on, eventually you're going to have to get wet." She took Morgan by the hand and pulled her into the mist of hot water.

"Oh, this is nice. Much better than the little closet I had to shower in on the ship." She stared out clear, full-length window at the city beyond. While all the buildings were tall, there were sizeable gaps between them that provided green spaces. She wondered if anyone was watching them as they showered.

Eleni rubbed her back with a soapy sponge. "The advantage of extra room. We both can take a shower at the same time."

Morgan relaxed under the water and the light touches of Eleni as she used a sponge. Morgan enjoyed the soap as she applied it to her front. *It has been too long between human touches.*

With the shower over, Morgan put on a blouse and wandered into the kitchen where Eleni had tea ready. She was nude, save for a collar.

"Oh, I forgot to put on a collar. I know about that Praxton custom, but my brain is still in a fog this morning."

Eleni laughed. "There aren't any fashion police here. No worries."

"I still want to follow the Praxton customs. I don't want to be the tourist who refuses to change what she is accustomed to doing."

"You're doing well. You even wore an ankle cuff in bed last night."

"That was a bit of a shock when you first showed it to me, but I didn't notice it afterward."

"Good. Now what about female touching? Praxton females do a lot of touching and cuddling with each other."

"I can do that. I knew what could happen when I hired a companion for my stay on Praxton."

"Okay, what do you want to do today? Breakfast and then shopping?"

"Sounds perfect."

Morgan learned to slow down her pace as she shopped with Eleni. The high-heeled shoes made her more aware of her walk, but she discovered Praxton females preferred a slow movement in everything they did. Morgan examined the jewellery in the display case, admiring a collar with gold interlaced in a S pattern. "That's pretty."

"It is." Eleni agreed. "It has matching cuffs. Do you want another collar?"

"I have the one I have now plus a fashion collar. You know, the kind that doesn't have a lock on it." Morgan, like many Alliance women, had purchased collars during the confrontation between Praxton and the Alliance worlds. It was a statement she and other women made to support Praxton. Most of the Alliance world population believed the women on Praxton had the right to choose if they wanted to live in a submissive role. Many women on the Alliance worlds showed that it might not be their lifestyle choice but wanted Praxton to be left alone. Alliance forces bowed to the political pressure and arrived at an agreement with Praxton as quickly as possible rather than enduring a prolonged struggle.

Morgan liked the look of wearing collars as a fashion accessory. Unlike the collars on Praxton, the fashion collars didn't have a locking mechanism. Wrist cuffs were sold but weren't as common.

"Then you should get another locking collar. A girl should have more than one, even if she doesn't live on Praxton."

Morgan nodded. Since Praxton joined the Alliance worlds, women were increasingly wearing locked collars. They didn't always see the locked collars as a symbol of being submissive, but rather as a substitute for a necklace or, in some cases, a ring. This latest trend on Alliance worlds annoyed the Charter of Conduct Office. They had expected Praxton would move toward Alliance customs, but it seemed the Praxton culture invaded the rest of human space. "I think you're right. I do like this one."

Morgan purchased the collar with the two pairs of matching cuffs. As usual, the set included chains of various lengths that could attach to the collar and cuffs. "I'll never get used to all those chains and how to attach them." She walked with Eleni to a nearby café in the shopping mall. They waited in line until the hostess escorted them to a table.

"Does every restaurant escort their customers to a table? On most worlds it's usually self seating."

"Praxton is conservative with change. They like to keep formality in business. I've been to a few restaurants where the hostess attaches a leash to any female without a guardian and leads them to a table. If a male was standing behind us in line, the hostess would have greeted him first, ignoring us."

"Wow, that's chauvinistic." She looked at the menu on her tablet, deciding on the soup and salad. She placed her new purchase on the table, examining the gold detail woven into the collar and the small rings used to attach chains. "I suppose I should attempt to use those chains. I hope I don't get tangled in them."

"It's not a secret." Eleni laughed. "Just put them where you feel like it. The chains should drape and not hinder you. Be more careful with a chain between ankle cuffs, obviously. Usually you wear those only at home or short walks."

Morgan opened a smaller package and took out two chains, attaching one each from her collar to the wrist cuffs. She grinned. "There. Now I look more like a Praxton female."

"You do, except your hair is shorter than most. Still, you pull off the pretty girl in a collar and cuffs well."

"Thanks. May I ask how you ended up being a freelancer? You look like you were originally from Praxton and therefore probably had a guardian before." Morgan heard you could always spot a Praxton female. Besides the obviously revealing dress, collar and cuffs, Praxton women had a grace to almost everything they did. A slow, seductive walk, the careful placement of limbs when at rest and the extra time spent on makeup and hair all led to a style unique in human space. Most women who migrated to Praxton never could master the feminism of a Praxton born female.

"Yes, I was born on Praxton and followed the usual route of being a female on Praxton. That included having a guardian. Then a few years ago, Praxton had an election where females not only could vote but could run for office. Terri Baxter won a seat. She inspired many females that we could do more with our lives, that we had a choice. When my guardian added a fourth female to our household, I decided I needed to explore life outside the confines of my guardian's rules.

"I couldn't have done this a few years ago, but new laws allowed females to have their own financial accounts and even own a business. It took a lot of effort, but I left my guardian and set up my own life."

"Excuse me for saying this, but aren't freelancers somewhat ostracised?"

"Oh, yes." Eleni touched her arm. "But it has changed in the past couple of years. At one time freelancers referred to females who were prostitutes. Now the definition includes any female without a guardian and runs her own financial affairs. I guess I fall under the prostitute category right now, but I'm putting money aside to open my own business. Maybe a clothing store or a skin care boutique."

"Good for you. No man in your life right now?"

Eleni shook her head. "But once I'm independent with my own business, I would like to have a guardian. I miss having a man in my life, but the next guardian will have to understand I'm not only a submissive female. I know I may have to share a guardian with another female, but not two or three others."

"You sound determined. I think you're going to be a successful business woman."

[5]

GRATA PUT ON HER SHOES, high heeled with thin straps that circled around her ankles several times. "Before we leave, I better tell the others we're going out. She took Julius's hand and led him to the smaller bedroom. The bed, designed for Praxton women, was long with the centre of the bed indented to encourage contact between bed partners.

Julius looked at the two women curled against each other with the blanket around their waist. At the base of the bed, he saw their ankles cuffed with a length of chain. The room had a small private toilet, and another contained a shower with transparent sides. One side faced the living room, allowing anyone there to watch the showering. Along one-bedroom wall, he could see various hooks and the ceiling had a bar with cuffs attached. With an assortment of whips on a rack, Julius concluded the bedroom also served as a discipline room.

Grata touched one woman on the shoulder. "We're going out and will be back later. When we return, I expect both of you to be looking your best."

"Yes, sorry," a sleepy voice answered. "I had a bit too much to drink last night." Acacia slowly sat. "Good morning, Master Julius. I apologize for still being in bed. Do you wish to discipline me?"

Julius looked at the bare breasted beauty. "Of course not. You look too beautiful to discipline."

"Too bad." She smiled. "I don't mind a nice spanking."

Grata wagged a finger at her. "You'll get us all into trouble with that attitude." She took Julius by the arm and exited the room. "She does like a bit of punishment now and then."

"And Emmia?"

"Hmm, I believe she likes spankings and has accepted a light flogging well."

"Much like yourself, if my memory serves me right. You also like being restrained with rope."

"You have a good memory." Grata laughed. "Just to be clear, I enjoy being tied up only when I'm with someone I trust. And I do trust you."

"Thanks. Tell me about Emmia. She's obviously still learning about life on Praxton."

"One of my clients said he knew of a girl who wanted to change up her life and move to Praxton. He asked me if we could help her settle down here. So now we're teaching her how to act like a proper Praxton female. She's doing okay. She likes both males and females and can take discipline. You may not like using discipline at every opportunity, but a lot of our male clients have a different attitude."

"Does that mean I'm the strange Alliance visitor?"

"No, you're one of my favourite clients. I like the fact you don't want to discipline for any minor infraction. It's fine in small doses, but too many males get carried away with that aspect of Praxton customs."

They walked down the street and Grata laughed at how he enjoyed the open air. "You must have felt cooped up in that spaceship."

"I didn't mind being on it, and it was big enough that one isn't cramped. But when you see the sky again, you suddenly realize how much you miss clouds and the sun."

They reached a café open for breakfast and Julius made a choice of pancakes, eggs and sausage. The eggs, which were factory grown, had a bright orange yoke.

"You must be hungry." Grata had a meal of just two pancakes.

"My body thinks it's supper time."

"We'll get your body straightened out soon enough."

"I have a question. Do you have many female clients?"

"No, just males. Occasionally we have taken in couples. An Alliance husband and wife will hire us for a special experience. Why do you ask?"

"My first officer, a woman, hired a freelancer for her stay on Praxton. I'm curious about that."

"I have heard of Alliance women hiring only a single freelancer before. A single female on Praxton could feel a little uncomfortable, and it makes sense to hire a companion who would know their way around Praxton and be familiar with all of our strange customs."

"So not necessarily for sex."

"No. However, if your officer is curious about being with another woman, a freelancer would be a safe way to explore that. If she is going to spending a few weeks with a beautiful woman who knows the art of being seductive, chances are sex is going happen. On Praxton, sex between females is no big thing. Does it surprise you that it might interest your officer in another female? Because females are complicated when comes to sex."

"No kidding about women being complicated." He laughed. "I guess when the ship's crew was given extended shore leave time, I didn't think how of how it would affect her. She is an executive officer, and that makes fraternizing with the crew, even on leave, more difficult. A male officer has more flexibility. He can just head to the Praxton surface and party or do what he wants. She may not believe she has that option. I should have approached her and see if she needed any help."

"It's still not too late to call her and ask. I'm sure she'll appreciate your concern."

[6]

MORGAN STROLLED with Eleni around the four-story mall, picking up another pair of shoes. "I don't want to buy everything at once. There's only so much room I have for personal items on the ship."

"That sounds reasonable. Do you have a list of things you want to do and buy on Praxton? Or is it more than just let it happen?"

"I do have a list of to do things. Buying stuff is a space issue, but I want to get more of those famous Praxton high-heeled shoes. Maybe a dress and a couple of tops. I'm intrigued by those wider collars. I mean, they really stand out. I like wearing something a little edgy. Those ship uniforms are conservative."

"I know a few shops that sell a wide range of collars and restraints. We can go there tomorrow as it's in a different mall. What is your other to do list?"

"I have a long list there." She grinned. "I want to spend time in the desert with all that red sand. I want to go to one of those wild night clubs where the women might end up naked. I want to take a hike in one of the rain forests where all the plants have strange colours and shapes."

"It sounds like you want to see a lot." Eleni laughed. "Our nightclubs aren't usually that wild. The wilder ones are in the tourist zone, but we can go there. How about other Praxton customs? Like I have friends who live in a traditional home and we can spend a night there. An all female party."

"That would be fun. If we have the chance, I would like to go to one of those fancy restaurants and try traditional Praxton foods. I don't normally eat a lot of meat, but I know meat dishes are fairly common here."

"That may be an issue. A lot of those fancy restaurants follow this strange Praxton custom of only accepting male guests and the females he's in charge of. If two females like us were to show up at a restaurant, we'd likely be turned away. Guardians and accompanying females only."

"Good grief. I don't know if I should laugh or cry."

"Laugh. Believe me, it's not the only odd custom on Praxton."

"Well, I guess no fancy dinner."

"Sorry, but I will check to see if I can get a male I know to take us to dinner. I'm sure it won't be too much of a problem."

Morgan's mobile chirped, and she answered it, surprised to see it was Elmwood.

"Captain Elmwood, sir. Is there a problem?" Morgan stopped walking, taking a deep breath and straightening her shoulders.

"I hope not." A pause. "Morgan, I wanted to check to see if everything is all right with you. In hindsight, I realize sending a single woman to Praxton on leave could be difficult for her. I apologize for not inquiring if you required support."

"Thank you, sir. I am doing fine. My hired companion is making sure I don't get into trouble with Praxton customs."

"That's good to hear. Since we're not on duty, please use Julius instead of a formal title. If you require any help at all, please contact me. In fact, I would be upset if you didn't make me aware if you ran into a problem."

"Thank you. I promise to do so, and…well, actually there's one thing you could help me with."

"What is it?"

"I would like to go to a fancy restaurant with my companion, but apparently females can only go there accompanied with a guardian. Would you be willing to take us? I would be happy to pay for the dinner."

He chuckled. "Now what kind of guardian would I be if I had a lady pay for my food? It would honour me to take you to dinner plus your companion. If you don't mind, I would like to take my own companions with us."

"That would be great."

"Then I will make a reservation at one of the better restaurants and contact you later with the details."

Morgan grinned as she disconnected the call. "I guess we're going to dinner."

[7]

"I'm glad I made that call like you suggested. Now I need your help in picking out one of the better restaurants." He smiled. "It looks like I'll be taking Morgan and her companion for dinner, plus our group."

"I know a few of the better places. It'll be nice to meet your officer. She sounds like an interesting female."

They walked back to the apartment and Grata spoke inside the elevator. "Now, I know you don't normally like to use too much discipline, but if you're not pleased with anything the females do, or don't do, discipline them. Spank them. Suspend them in restraints. Or just a light session with a flogger. This is the Praxton way to make sure females remain obedient. That includes myself."

"Are you hinting I should do so, regardless?"

"Master Julius, I recall you using discipline on myself last time you were on Praxton. Females like a powerful guardian, one who measures out discipline occasionally."

"I thought with Praxton becoming part of the Alliance worlds, some of those discipline customs would be disappearing."

"I hope not. I may not always like being punished, but I like the thought you would do so."

The apartment looked cleaned and Acacia and Emmia both wore short dresses with a full complement of cuffs and chains. They stood with their hands clasped behind their backs. "Hello, Master Julius."

He walked around them, admiring the bodies under the thin dresses. "I'm pleased that you two look presentable and have kept the apartment in order. I will warn you, I believe a discipline session may be in order in the near future."

"Yes, Master Julius," Acacia answered. "We understand that we should have been up earlier. We are sorry if we have disappointed you."

"Very well. For now, we can relax."

He sat on the couch next to Grata. "As much as I would like to do nothing, I need to take time to prepare for the interview tomorrow. I expect there will be some tough questions to answer."

"I understand." She pointed at Acacia and Emmia. "I suggest you go to the gym and exercise. Master Julius needs quiet, and this will give you time to do self-improvement."

"Of course." Emmia nodded. "Will you be coming with us?"

"No, I will remain here to attend to any of Master Julius's needs. Now go."

After he kissed Acacia and Emmia goodbye, Grata called out from the kitchen. "I'll prepare coffee for you and then leave you alone. If you desire anything, I will be available."

Julius focused on his tablet, studying questions they might ask him. He saw Grata walk nude to the washroom and slide into the bathtub, momentarily ruining his concentration.

Two hours later, Grata walked naked toward him. "Still studying hard?"

He looked up, startled. "Yes, I guess I am."

"Maybe it's time for a break." She glided on top of his lap on her stomach and he held his tablet above her glistening skin.

Julius looked at Grata stretched across and rested a hand on her ass. He placed the tablet on the arm of the couch. "I suppose I should take a break." He slapped her cheeks lightly. Grata twisted her head to look behind, watching him. He increased the smacks, causing her to release a small moan. He massaged her cheeks, stroking the skin between moments of squeezing the flesh.

"That feels good." She placed her hands behind her back, locking her fingers together.

Julius increased the spanking, watching Grata twist her fingers with each hit. He paused to stroke the pink skin. He heard her sigh. With one hand, he gripped her wrists while using the other hand to continue the spanking. He increased the strength of hits, occasionally slapping at her thighs. Her ass turned red and she let out a small cry after the last hit. "Spread your legs."

Grata quickly obeyed. Elmwood smacked each cheek twice more. He reached between her legs and felt her, pleased at the warm wetness. "Perhaps we could go to the bedroom."

"If that's what Master Julius desires," she gasped out. Grata moved off his lap and walked toward the bedroom with her hands still behind her back.

Julius walked to the bedroom, taking off his shirt by the time he reached the bed.

Grata dropped to her knees by the bed, watching him undress. "How does Master Julius wish to use me?"

He walked in front of her, his penis swelling. "I think I would like to have you on the bed, but first I shall take advantage of your position." He grabbed her hair, pulling her mouth toward his member.

"Of course, Master Julius." Grata rushed out the words. She used her fingers to guide him into her mouth and he slowly eased his full length into her. He held her against him as his erection increased and finally pulled out. She gasped for air as he slid his erection across her face. Grata slid out her tongue, licking at his testicles and shaft.

"Once more." Elmwood pushed his hard cock into her open mouth. He pulled at her hair to press her face against his stomach. He felt her work her tongue on him before sliding out. "Let's make use of that bed now."

She climbed on the bed, lying on her back with her limbs spread apart.

Julius suspected she was playing an expected role but looked convincing as a female wanting to please her guardian. They had developed an affection for each other beyond the payment of a freelancer. He took a deep breath and dived on top of her, placing his mouth on her swollen nipples. She moaned, arching her back. Julius kissed her skin, working his way up to her neck and back down. He licked between her legs as she cried out.

"Please, Master Julius, I need you inside me now!"

He moved quickly to oblige, panting as she locked her legs around him.

Afterward they sat on the bed with Julius putting his arm around her. "Thanks, I needed a break from reading."

"My pleasure, Master Julius. I'm looking forward to that dinner."

"Yes, it should be interesting. It has been a while since I've had dinner in a high-end restaurant on Praxton." He kissed the top of her head.

"I guess the restaurants on passenger ships are nice."

"Yes, but being a captain, I'm being scrutinized on whatever I order and what I eat. This will be more relaxing."

"Would you like me to get you something to eat or to drink?"

"Sure, a glass of wine would be good."

Grata rolled out of bed and exited the bedroom. As she walked away, she called out, "I'm looking forward to meeting your officer. I'm curious how a woman can work so closely with you. On Praxton it would be difficult to have such an arrangement."

She returned to the room carrying two glasses of red wine. He took the offered glass.

"It's different on ships. It's similar to military where there is a definite hierarchy and we don't cross lines from professional duties to personal issues."

"I see. Still, she must have a strong character." She sat on the bed facing him, curling one leg under her. "On Praxton it is difficult for females not to act submissively to males even if it is a business relationship. I understand that she is an officer. Does that mean she gives orders to males?"

"She does, and she is an excellent officer." He took a drink of the wine, and Julius considered how Morgan could snap out commands when it became necessary. *But she has that submissive side now that Grata mentioned it. It's hard to say exactly what it is, just some subtle body language.*

"That's rare on Praxton for females to give orders to males. Yes, I really want to meet this female."

[8]

"Okay, I now have a date of sorts to an expensive restaurant. I guess I'll need to get a new dress." Morgan grinned.

"I think you do. The stuff you're wearing is pretty conservative." Eleni tugged at the sleeve of Morgan's shirt.

"Really? I thought what I wore is much like I see around here."

"Not really, close. Like your skirt is short, but it's loose. Your tops are of a heavier material and don't show much."

"I guess that's true. Well, let's rectify that."

They browsed through various shops, examining the racks of clothes. Finally, Eleni lifted a dress. "Oh, I think this is it."

Morgan stared at the pale-yellow mini-dress, made of a see-through fabric. A spiral band of glittering stones from top to bottom presented the wearer with a bit of modesty. The top had a single shoulder strap, with the left side dropping well below the shoulder. "Oh, my gosh. It's beautiful." She held the dress up to the light. "Dare I wear this? I would feel exposed."

"Trust me. Women wear even less at restaurants and nightclubs. If you get this dress, we'll have to find a collar, chains and cuffs to match. And shoes."

Morgan smiled. "Okay, more shopping then."

Eleni helped Morgan carry the shopping bags back to the apartment.

"Good shopping. You have two new dresses, two collars and accessories, and two pairs of shoes. And I have a new skirt."

"I couldn't resist that red dress. It looked so cute and I can wear it somewhere other than Praxton."

As soon as they entered the apartment, Morgan pulled open the packages. She lifted out a wide, green metal collar. "This sure makes a statement. I'm surprised how light it was."

"Put it on with the cuffs. Let's see how it looks with the chains attached."

Morgan eagerly replaced her current collar and cuffs with the new set. "How should I attach the chains? Through the collar to my wrist cuffs?" She pulled out a long gold chain. "What about the ankle cuffs?"

"I have a solution." Eleni disappeared into the bedroom, returning with a chain belt. "Here, put this on."

Morgan added the belt, securing it in place with a small padlock. Eleni helped her connect chains to the belt, including those to her ankle cuffs.

"I like it." Morgan looked in a viewscreen at her image. "Thank you so much." She gave Eleni a hug.

"You're welcome. Now you just relax while I put dinner together."

Morgan sat in the living room, pleased with her purchases and how well Eleni was working out as a companion.

After dinner, drinks extended the evening as the two women shared stories. Morgan wanted to learn more on how Praxton women behaved, finding it fascinating that three females would often share the same male guardian.

"Wouldn't that lead to fights? I know how jealous some women can get."

"Normally it would. But the guardian would make sure the females didn't misbehave. Many homes have a discipline room and it's used to keep order. At one time they treated all females as slaves, and discipline would be quick and severe. Today the discipline isn't as harsh, but a good paddling, whipping or being placed in a cage will subdue even the most stubborn female. Many homes have a housekeeper charged with keeping the home in good order. She will punish females who are not acting properly. Females learn what the boundaries are. To avoid punishment, she will conform to her guardian's expectations."

"As I understand, one female gets to sleep with the guardian and the other females have to sleep together. That's not fair. Do women still get placed in cages?"

"Yeah, they still use cages. Perhaps not as much, but most females are subjected to being caged. If you want, we can look at a few."

"Sure, that sounds interesting. Overall, I think Praxton needs a lot more men so women don't have to share."

"I agree, but that won't happen overnight." She put down her empty glass. "Come, let's go to bed and we can look at cages in the morning."

Morgan felt the effect of the wine and agreed that sleep would be good. She undressed and slid under the covers. She considered the Praxton custom of females only sleeping in the nude, deciding it was comfortable if she ignored the fact another naked woman slept next to her. She waited as Eleni undressed and attached the chained cuff to her ankle, doing the same to herself.

Morgan rolled on her side, facing the outside of the bed. As her eyes closed, she felt the warmth of another body close to her, spooning her as an arm gently draped over her. She let out a sigh and drifted off to sleep.

Morgan woke up as her eyes slowly focused. Through the open bedroom door, she observed Eleni crossing the living room. She was nude, carrying two cups toward the bedroom.

"Good morning." Morgan struggled to sit, pushing a pillow behind her back. She allowed the blanket to cluster around her waist, not worrying about her bare top.

"Good morning. I made coffee. Do you drink yours black?" She handed a cup to Morgan.

"Black is good." She smiled. "Thanks. I guess I slept in a bit."

"No worries." Eleni grinned. "You rented me and this apartment so you can do what you want."

Morgan pulled up a leg, tugging on the chain following her ankle. She understood the Praxton custom for the chain to remain attached until she got out of bed. "I guess we can do some shopping today. I'm curious about those cages. I'm surprised they sell such things to keep women in, especially considering the Charter of Conduct Office influence."

"It's an old Praxton custom, and the Charter wasn't able to take that away from us. The truth is they're not used as much anymore, but it's traditional for homes to have one. Actually, there are a few females that enjoy being put in a cage. I know I did like being put in one occasionally. As long as it isn't for a long time, I found it arousing being naked and caged."

"I saw the restraints on the wall in the other bedroom and how the cage would fit in there. I think the sight of a naked female in a cage is kind of sexy."

"Yes, it is an alluring image." She laughed. "I don't have a cage, but I've thought about it. I think it might add to the room as a place where discipline takes place. Most guardians believe discipline is a necessary function in Praxton society. A cage might be preferable than a whip. Oh, I forgot to ask you about what you want me to wear around the apartment. Some guardians let me wear what I want, others insist I stay naked."

Morgan looked at the nude female sitting on the edge of the bed. "What you have on is fine." She smiled. "But whatever you want to wear is good too."

"Thanks. I usually stay naked until I have to go out." She finished her coffee. "Do you want me to join you in the shower or do prefer being by yourself?"

"You shower first. I'm still waking up." Morgan watched Eleni enter the shower, observing her through the open doorway as she casually used a washcloth over her body. *Lord, Praxton females even make showering sensuous.*

Morgan remembered to put on her collar before she left the bedroom as she carried her cup to the kitchen to pour a second cup of coffee. She hesitated a moment and slid open the doors to the balcony, observing the surrounding city. The reddish sun warmed her skin, and she enjoyed the sensation of being naked outside. *I doubt anyone can see me, but what if they did? Female nudity is common here. Besides, they can see me when I'm in the shower. I'm getting used to being naked. It's going to be hard to wear a ship's uniform at the end of shore leave.*

Morgan strolled with Eleni through the mall, a different one than before. She felt a little self conscious wearing a new skirt shorter than anything she had worn before. The large shop they visited had several styles of cages on display. A sign noted that all merchandise sold met with Charter of Conduct regulations.

"Just what are regulations regarding cages for humans?" Morgan asked Eleni.

"The doors are not fully lockable. In case of an emergency, they can open the door from the inside at the hinges, bypassing the locks. In addition, the height of the cage cannot be less than one point two metres and not less than two point four metres in volume. That way the cage isn't cramped."

Morgan was drawn to a round cage with a domed top. It could easily hold two people standing up. A salesman approached them, swinging open the cage door.

"Would you like to step inside?"

Morgan nodded, giving the medium height man a smile. He was slim, and with dark eyes and hair, giving an intense look to him. The cage interior didn't surprise her as her fingers clutched the bars.

"Of course, restraints can be added to the inside so you could be caged and held in a certain position as your guardian sees fit." He closed the door, making Morgan feel captured.

"Interesting," she breathed out. *It's like I'm in a giant birdcage. I just need a swing to sit on.*

The door opened and Eleni took her to another set of cages. Two rectangular cages were joined to form an L shape. The salesman swung open the door on one end.

"Please enter and see how you like this one."

Morgan took in a slow breath. She removed her shoes and lowered herself to the floor. *Okay, so I crawl inside. With my short skirt, everything can be seen. The cage is more than just making a female captive, it's also made to make her feel exposed.* Her skirt lifted behind her as she made her way inside. The padded floor made it easy on her knees and hands as she traveled the length of the cage. The salesman closed the door and she sat, allowing a measure of dignity to return.

Eleni dropped to her knees and smiled at her. "Well, what do you think? Do you like being in a cage?"

Morgan looked at the salesman who stood close by, and back to Eleni. "This one is not quite to my tastes, I'm sorry to say."

The salesman opened the other end of the cage and Morgan exited. She retrieved her shoes and joined the others at a corner of the store.

"This design is for areas with a lack of extra space." He pointed to the two doors joined to adjacent walls, forming a square cage. He opened one cage door and Morgan stepped inside. When he closed the door, she felt hemmed in by the walls and the cage doors.

"It doesn't take up much space. I do feel trapped inside here."

The salesman continued. "This is one style. We carry a similar model only with curved cage doors, so the cage is a semicircle. It has a touch more room."

Morgan thanked him and walked with Eleni to where an assortment of whips and restraints were displayed.

"Did you like that cage better?"

"I did. Actually, I didn't want to say anything with him standing so close, but it's kind of fun being in a cage."

"So, you do like them?"

"I can see the appeal. I think you should get one of those corner cages, maybe the one with curved doors.

Eleni looked at her. "If I purchased one, then I assume you would want me to put you inside it for a while."

"I think the experience would be interesting." Morgan blushed as she felt the strands on a flogger. "These are pretty soft."

"New Charter of Conduct regulations. It's hard to hurt anyone with these new whips. They do come in different grades. That is grade one, and they progressed to four. Grade four will hurt but still won't leave permanent marks on the skin. I have the grade two at my apartment."

Morgan followed Eleni to the sales counter. The salesman surprised her when he resisted selling her the cage.

"Normally we only sell to guardians. I had assumed you were looking for one for your guardian." He studied her credentials on the screen. "You have your own financial authority."

"Seriously?" Morgan spoke up. "What difference does it make who buys it as long as you get your money?"

"It's just a bit irregular, that's all. The transaction is complete."

Eleni made arrangements for the delivery and installation. She laughed as they exited the store, informing Morgan, "Welcome to my world. Females on Praxton just don't have the same privileges as males when it comes to finances or business. It's getting better but we have a long way to go just overcoming attitudes."

"I can see that. Now we have dinner to go to tonight. Is there anything else I need to know on how to act like a proper Praxton female?"

"I believe you have everything you need to wear. I'll go over a few social graces for you. It'll be fun."

[9]

MORGAN FOLLOWED the suggestions from Eleni when putting on makeup. There were several containers for her face and eyes, plus more for her neck and breasts. As Eleni summarized, there was a different makeup for each part of the body. After putting on makeup on her nipples, Morgan added nipple jewellery. She lifted her dress from the bed, still amazed at the lightness of the material. *It's going to be rather obvious I'm not wearing anything underneath. I wonder what Julius will think when he sees me in this dress with collar and cuffs.*

Morgan entered the living room, giving a smile to Eleni. "You look gorgeous."

Eleni spun around in her green dress. "Thank you, and so do you. Master Julius will be here soon to escort us." She held a leash in her hand. "We should attach these now."

"Another quaint Praxton custom." Morgan clipped the leash on her collar. "I'm nervous about this dinner. Julius…"

"Master Julius. Better remember that or you could get a spanking in that rather fancy restaurant."

"Oh, wouldn't that be fun? Okay, Master Julius is going to see me in this very revealing dress."

"Do you have feelings for him?"

"We're friends on the ship, and he is my commanding officer. I don't want him to get the wrong impression of me."

"I think the impression he will get of you will be very positive." She passed Morgan a glass of a dark liquid. "Here, this will help you relax."

"I need relaxing."

Shortly after she finished her drink, the door chime announced guests had arrived at the apartment and Eleni opened the door to Elmwood. "It is wonderful to meet you, Master Julius."

"It's my pleasure." Smiling, he looked past the open door and saw Morgan. His eyebrows raised. "Wow, Morgan, you look lovely."

"Hello, Master Julius. Thank you. I think Praxton dresses are different from ones in Alliance space."

Eleni handed the ends of the leash from Morgan and herself to Julius. "I think Morgan is appreciating some of the Praxton customs."

"There're many positive aspects to Praxton society." Elmwood led the two women out of the apartment and to the elevator. "Some parts are unusual compared to other worlds, but differences can be good."

Morgan let out her breath once she sat in the shuttle. Following Julius and Eleni filled her with apprehension as they left the apartment. He acted calm as he held the handles of the two leashes, only asking how they were with no reference to the collars and restraints.

Morgan and Eleni exchanged introductions with the other three women in the shuttle. She was pleased to see their dresses were as revealing as her own. She made small talk with the others, noticing Julius made numerous glances at her.

The shuttle landed on a platform that went directly into a building, where a band of elevators were located. They took the elevator to the lobby, chattering as they walked. Morgan looked for clues from Eleni and the other women on how to act. She waited at the entrance to the restaurant as the maître d' efficiently organized their escort to the table. Julius entered first while the women were escorted by three other female staff.

Grata was led by the leash first, followed by Acacia and Emmia. Morgan and Eleni were the last, and they received glances from the other diners who acted surprised to see a single guardian followed by five females. Morgan noticed the women in the restaurants wore dresses light on coverage. A few women were topless and wore breast and nipple jewellery, giving them an exotic appearance.

I feel like a sex slave. A skimpy dress, collar, cuffs and chains being led by a leash by another underdressed woman. It's embarrassing, and I'm so excited.

Julius sat at the head of the rectangular table. On one corner next to him sat Morgan, and across from her sat Grata. Morgan watched Julius be given the only menu. She waited in silence, although she heard occasional whispers from the other women. The end of her leash was placed at the top of the back of her chair. She understood she wasn't allowed to leave the chair without an escort, not even to go to the restroom. Morgan looked at Julius, curious what he planned to order for them. Then she heard his question.

"Does anyone here not want to have steak?"

Emmia answered, "May I please have a vegetarian dish, Master Julius?"

He nodded, and when the waiter returned to take the order, he gave instructions for the meal.

Morgan eagerly took a drink of the red wine, hoping it would help her to relax. She glanced between Julius and at Eleni.

"Are we just supposed to sit here and whisper comments?" she asked Eleni.

"No, we're waiting for Master Julius to start the conversation."

Morgan looked at Julius, who looked uncertain of the lack of conversation. "Master Julius, we are waiting for you to speak first."

"Oh." He looked at the length of the table. "Please don't wait for me to enjoy the wine, food and conversation. I'm lucky to have the company of five beautiful women that I'm too busy staring at to think of anything to say. Your beauty has left me speechless." He held up his wine glass. "To Praxton and its lovely females."

Morgan took a drink of her wine with the rest. She heard the chatter increase among the women and determined things had returned to normal for six people at a dinner. Morgan felt Eleni place a hand on her thigh, lingering her fingers across the skin. Morgan looked at Julius. "I understand you're being interviewed for a position on the new military ship."

He raised his eyebrows. "So, the rumour mill works even when we're off duty. Yes, as a matter of fact, I'm going to an interview tomorrow."

"Good luck. I hope you'll remember me when it comes time to look for the new crew."

"Don't worry, you're difficult to forget."

"I would love to know about how you work on a spaceship as an officer," Grata asked. "I understand you give orders to males. Isn't that difficult? Do they listen to you?"

The question surprised Morgan, but she considered how subservient women were to men on Praxton. "No, it's different on ships, particularly in Alliance space. There's a hierarchy of command, and gender doesn't matter. As long as everyone is treated fairly there aren't any problems."

"But what if you were on a Praxton ship and had to give an order to a male?"

"Then I would. I know you're accustomed to obeying your guardian on Praxton and that all males are respected, but things are different on ships. We make orders to ensure the safe operation of the ship and to refuse an order by a commanding officer is not acceptable."

"I see. Aren't you intimidated by the males on the ship? I mean, you're acting like a Praxton female and wearing a collar. Can you just turn off being submissive?"

"In a word, yes." Morgan was aware of the close attention by the others to her conversation with Grata. "This collar, dress and how I'm acting is fine here. This is my relaxation time and I'm indulging a bit of a fantasy of being the obedient female. But just like it's okay to indulge in a chocolate sundae occasionally, one has to remember it is just temporary. So yes, I can turn off being submissive when I'm on a ship and the men don't intimidate me."

Morgan saw Julius paid scrutiny to her words, giving her a slight nod as she finished speaking. They served the food, with Julius receiving his plate first. Eleni removed her hand so she could eat, and Morgan looked forward to enjoying the meal without being the centre of attention.

At the end of the meal, Morgan thanked Julius for agreeing to take her and the others to dinner. "I was looking forward to experiencing an expensive Praxton dinner, and I didn't realize women couldn't be by themselves in some restaurants. So, thank you for doing this for me and for paying for everything. I'm sure it cost a lot."

"It was worth it."

Morgan followed the others out of the restaurant with Eleni holding her hand.

"I have to say I found it interesting how you talked about being able to order males around. You must have a bit of a dominant streak in you."

"I suppose I do."

"However, it's your submissive side that I'd like to explore."

Morgan took a quick intake of air. "Perhaps we can but be aware I have that dominant side that may appear."

Conversation filled the ride home in the shuttle. Morgan saw how Grata made sure she sat next to Julius. The shuttle stopped at the apartment and Eleni invited everyone for a nightcap. Julius accepted, and the group entered the apartment building.

Morgan noticed Grata, Acacia and Emmia all walked unescorted to the elevator, but Elmwood took the leash of Eleni and herself as he led the way. "I guess we are still following Praxton's customs."

Elmwood turned around. "I thought you'd appreciate the experience. Do you object?"

Morgan swallowed, "Not at all, Master Julius." She followed him into the apartment where he released Eleni so she could obtain drinks. He still held Morgan's leash, and when he sat in an armchair, she hesitated and kneeled on the floor next to him. *What else can I do? I'm glad he can't easily see how high this dress has risen.* She took in deep breaths, wondering how she ended up being the only one still on a leash as she looked at the other women who sat on the furniture.

"So, Morgan, do you like being a submissive Praxton female?" Grata took her wine glass from Eleni.

Morgan blushed. *It's not as if I have a choice right now.* "I can play the role. It's okay sometimes."

Grata laughed. "I think you're enjoying it."

Elmwood accepted his whisky from Eleni and reached down to undo the leash from Morgan's collar. "My apologizes, I didn't mean to embarrass you by leaving you still attached to the leash."

"That's okay. When in Rome... I don't mind trying out the Praxton culture and I just have to accept some discomforts that it entails." She continued to kneel by his side, deciding it would be awkward to leave and sit in a chair.

Grata continued her questioning. "On Alliance worlds, do you ever find yourself to be submissive to males?" She leaned forward, focusing on Morgan.

"No." Morgan shook her head. "I'm equal when dealing with men in a relationship."

"How about on Praxton?" Grata grinned.

"Well." Morgan laughed. "As you can see, wearing this collar and cuffs has an effect." She looked up at Elmwood, hoping he was happy with her obedience.

"So, I see." Grata laughed with her. "How about with females?"

"I didn't have female relationships." She shook her head. "I had girlfriends, but never had a relationship with one."

"Really? Yet you hired a freelancer on Praxton." Grata eased back into her chair, taking a drink. She appeared pleased with Morgan's discomfort when answering.

"It was easier to hire a freelancer than to live by myself. I heard it can tough for a single female to do things on Praxton and thought I should get an expert guide." *And I was curious about sleeping with another woman.*

"Okay." Elmwood held up his hand. "Enough interrogation of Morgan. Perhaps we can talk about other subjects."

Morgan was relieved when the conversation turned to the meal and the fashions worn by other women. When it came time for Julius and his entourage to leave, Morgan said goodbye at the door. She gave him a kiss on his cheek. "Thanks again for dinner. Good luck on the interview. You'd be my choice as captain."

"Thank you for the vote of confidence. I'm sorry if Grata made you a little uncomfortable."

"That's fine. She just teased me a bit."

Eleni stroked Morgan's back after they closed the door. "That was a fun evening. Master Julius seems like he would make a very good guardian."

"I'm sure he would. But I see him as my ship's captain, which is a bit different."

"If you don't mind me saying so, you sure acted submissive toward him. Is it just the collar you're wearing or is there more to it than that?"

"I honestly don't know. Either as a captain or a guardian, he is a powerful man."

"Do you have romantic thoughts about him?"

"No, of course not. He's just a man I work with."

"Okay." Eleni undid Morgan's dress. "Let me put you to bed. I want to try a couple of things with you." She draped Morgan's dress on her arm.

"What are they?"

"Trust me." She led Morgan to the bed, leaving her collar and cuffs on. When they arrived in the bedroom, she pulled off her panties. "Lie on your back."

Morgan rested on the bed, watching Eleni join her ankle cuffs together and attached a chain to them from the foot of the bed. She didn't resist as her wrist cuffs were similarly attached to the headboard with another chain.

"Now relax and enjoy." She began by giving light kisses on her face and neck, slowly moving downward. She paused at her breasts, showering them with kisses before sucking on each nipple.

Morgan let out a small moan. The kisses, the touch of Eleni's tongue and gentle fingers were making her skin warm and sensitive. She tugged at her wrist cuffs, enjoying the restriction. A warm hand pressed between her legs as lips touched her stomach. "Ohhh."

Eleni moved back upward, leaving a trail of kisses. She kissed Morgan with an open mouth as a hand squeezed a breast. "Tell me again how you feel about Master Julius."

"He's very sexy."

"He would make a great guardian, wouldn't he?"

"The best." Morgan gasped out.

Eleni placed a pillow next to Morgan's waist. "Roll over on your stomach onto the pillow."

Morgan complied, twisting her body over the pillow. She felt Eleni run her fingers on her back. Nails scratched her skin. Then a smack on her ass, followed by another. The blows were repeated, harder and faster.

"Ow, ow."

"Hush, or I'll make it really hurt." Eleni increase the strength of her hits, causing Morgan to make fists as the spanking continued. "I'll bet you wish it was Master Julius giving you this spanking."

"Yes."

"Roll over on your back but stay on the pillow."

Morgan rolled over and Eleni slid on top of her, grinding her hips on Morgan's. "Close your eyes and think of Master Julius."

Morgan groaned, enjoying the sensation of skin on skin as Eleni rubbed her breasts against hers. "Yes, yes, Master Julius."

Eleni moved down, pressing soft kisses between Morgan's legs, before she focused on her core.

Morgan felt a wave of heat rush from her groin. She tried to lift her hips as Eleni dug her fingers into her ass. She cried out as her lungs expelled all the air and then took in ragged breaths.

A couple of minutes later, Eleni stroked Morgan's hair away from her face. "There, how was that for an end to the evening?"

"Very nice."

"Am I your first female experience?"

"Yes."

"So?"

"I hope it won't be my last. You made it memorable."

Eleni undid Morgan's ankle and wrist cuffs. Gently she placed Morgan's hands behind her back, locking the cuffs together.

"Hey." Morgan gave a smile.

"This is how you're going to sleep tonight. A little helpless and under my control. Okay?"

"Okay." Morgan turned on her side as Eleni pulled her close. She found her face placed against Eleni's breasts, kissed the skin and closed her eyes. "Goodnight."

[10]

GRATA GAVE Julius a smile after they arrived back at their apartment. "I was a little jealous of how you looked at Morgan. You even led her on a leash, and she looked very content to be under your control. Do you have special feelings for her?"

"No." Julius sat on the couch. "Although I've known her for a while, and I guess I enjoy her company."

"She's pretty and wore that Praxton dress to its full advantage."

"Good point, but I have you and your roommates for company."

"Okay, it just made me curious. Shall I send Acacia or Emmia to your bedroom, or do you wish to have both for company tonight?"

"Acacia would be fine. Do wish to join us?"

"I would like to, but I believe Acacia would appreciate time with you alone."

Julius gave her a kiss and entered the master bedroom. A few minutes later, a naked Acacia entered his room and sat on the bed.

"How may I please you, Master Julius?"

"I find you pleasing just the way you are." He reached out an arm and pulled her against him. They started with kisses and he took the advantage. He pinned her on the bed, touching and kissing her body. Acacia moaned and gave out a small gasp when he suddenly rolled her on her stomach. He spanked her, smacking her cheeks several times until he heard her cry out.

He pulled her away from the headboard and turned her on her back. Julius sucked on her nipples as he squeezed her breasts. A hand went between her legs, massaging the lips until they were wet. He inserted two fingers inside, working inside her as he sucked on her nipples in rhythm.

Acacia groaned louder. Julius moved up her body, rubbing his hard cock on her breasts. He moved over her, pressing his erection over her face before sliding it into her open mouth. He lifted his hips up and down several times, getting her to accept the full length of his shaft. He raised his hips again, and she licked at his testicles.

Julius moved down and inside her wetness. Acacia wrapped her legs around him. Her cries told him they reached a climax at the same time.

[11]

It surprised Elmwood when he entered the interview room, seeing four board members sitting across from an oval, black topped table.

"Please sit down, Mr. Elmwood." The lead interviewer spoke, an average weight woman with shoulder-length blonde hair. She appeared to be in her mid-forties, although the common use of gene therapy made age hard to determine. She sat next to a woman on her left and two men on her right. All of them wore Alliance military uniforms, with one exception. The woman sitting next to the lead interviewer had a shoulder patch showing she served in the Praxton military division. She wore a blue metal collar.

"I wasn't expecting a committee."

She gave a short-lived smile. "I'm Rear Admiral Rosetta Harley and I will conduct the final interviews. Mr. Elmwood, you are on a brief list for our final selection. We want to decide on the new captain as soon as possible."

Elmwood answered the questions posed by the lead interviewer, with his responses followed by the other three members of the panel, who added notes to their tablets.

"Mr. Elmwood, tell me about the latest trip you captained. I understand there was an incident."

"There was a situation with a rebel organization. They ambushed us when we came out of a jump. They demanded entry to our ship, intending to take as many valuables as possible from us. On occasions in the past, on other attacks of ships, they have abducted passengers to be sold as slaves. I informed them we were ready to make another jump. As you are likely aware, if one of their ships is docked with ours during a jump, it would be taken with us to the new location. The rebel ship would be stranded wherever we jumped to. The smaller rebel ships don't have enough power to make long jumps."

"What was their answer?"

"The leader of the rebels thought I was bluffing, that our ship couldn't possibly be nearly ready to make a jump. I informed him we had a new quick charging system to make jumps. It was up to him if he wanted to sacrifice part of his crew."

"I wasn't previously aware we had a quick charging system."

"We don't. I was bluffing. But I had a sense this leader cared about his crew. I thought he would weigh the risk of trying to board our ship. He cursed me but let us go."

"In other words, you lied your way out of danger."

"Yes, although I prefer the term bluff."

"Praxton has the view that females are submissive to males," Harley continued. "Do you agree with the condition of females always submitting to males?"

Elmwood looked at the interviewer. *She sure doesn't seem to be the submissive type.* "For Praxton, that works. It doesn't matter if I agree or not. What is important is both genders accept those conditions on Praxton."

"For the new Explorer Class ships, Praxton women will be required to be in positions of decision making. In some cases, it will be in command of men. How would you resolve this conflict of a submissive female being in charge of a male?"

"Any crew member under my command better be ready to obey any orders given by a superior. Gender will not be an issue. There is a time for personal life, but when on duty each person better follow the chain of command."

"Do you believe the Praxton cultural aspects can be integrated with an Alliance run military vessel?"

"Yes. If we have a trained crew, it shouldn't matter what their social background is."

"Thank you, Mr. Elmwood. Please wait in Conference Room Two for a short time. We may wish to discuss additional details with you."

Elmwood waited in the second conference room with a warm cup of coffee. He occasionally gazed at the bland paintings on the walls, observing they were not meant to be a distraction for any meeting taking place in the room. The chairs around the oval table were comfortable, but he would have preferred to pace about. Unfortunately, that may have given a poor impression of his emotional state. He continued to sit as his coffee cooled.

A brunette receptionist tapped on the door frame. "The selection committee would like to see you now."

He followed her back to the main board room, facing the four members again.

Rear Admiral Harley spoke, "Mr. Elmwood, after conferring with the rest of the selection committee, we have concluded that you would be best choice to captain the Star Hawk. Therefore, we would like to offer you the position of captain for the first Explorer Class ship."

Elmwood thanked the committee for their choice, accepting the position and declining the offer to think it over.

"Excellent. Please remain here so I may go over a few details with you." She turned to the rest of the committee. "You are now dismissed. Thank you for your input." After they left the room, she spoke again. "I trust you understand your appointment required many factors to be considered. One of which was political. As you are aware, Praxton contributed a large portion of the finances to enable the construction of the new spaceport which is essential to build the new class of Explorer ships. The Explorer Class ships are the new flagship of the Alliance Forces and Praxton obtaining the privilege of building them was quite a coup."

"I understand the Office of Charter of Conduct supported the building of the Explorer ships here."

"Yes." She nodded. "The Charter of Conduct has considerable influence. That brings me to the next point. The Charter of Conduct believes the women on Praxton are still subjected to second class status on Praxton and lack of financial independence. The Charter of Conduct's support hinges on the Star Hawk accepting a large portion of Praxton women as crew members, with a set minimum percentage as officers and senior positions one solar year after launch. There are other political considerations, such as having political observers and a diplomat on board."

"I understand. I will work within those parameters."

"There are other details. Your ship, while fully capable of military action, will be primarily for diplomatic and information gathering. We should extend an olive branch before we use military persuasion. Besides, your ship will be ready much sooner than the next series of Explorer class ships and thus will be working alone.

"In addition, we are gong to have difficulty in filling all positions of the Star Hawk with military personnel from other Alliance ships. We will supplement positions by using non-military staff in areas of maintenance and technical expertise such as food preparation.

"A second complication, with the large number of inexperience personnel you will have on the ship, is we need to avoid using weapons during these confrontations."

Elmwood agreed. "Diplomacy is the best course in most situations."

"Let's focus on your ship's particular character, since a large portion is to comprise of Praxton women, you may find it advantageous to instill Praxton social customs." She frowned. "I'm certain this is not what the Charter of Conduct Office had in mind when it pushed for a large contingent of women from Praxton, but it seems the best course of action."

"Understood. We need to make the new recruits feel comfortable in their new environment."

"I'll be frank with you. The choice of you being appointed captain is partially due to your interaction with the Praxton population and being able to navigate around the nuances of their culture. With a large female contingent coming from Praxton, and how they revere male leaders, it made the choice of having a male captain almost essential." She frowned. "This is not a negative comment about you, but my personal annoyance at eliminating many fine women candidates from this position." She continued. "This is the most significant promotion in many years, yet our choice of the best candidate was restricted by political ramifications. Captain Elmwood, I have no doubt you will make a fine captain. I just wish our choice could have been made on merit alone. Having said that, it seems likely you would have been the best candidate, regardless."

"I will do my best to make sure the Alliances forces are proud of the Star Hawk."

"I know you will. Congratulations, Captain Elmwood. Report for duty at oh-nine-hundred tomorrow morning at Spaceport Centurion, bay one. You will have the opportunity to visit your new ship."

[12]

Elmwood used his mobile to contact Morgan, telling her the news of his promotion.

"Oh, wow! Congratulations!"

"Thank you. Now I've got a lot of work to do, which includes hiring officers. Are you interested in joining the Alliance-Praxton armed forces?"

"Are you offering me a position on the new explorer ship?"

"Yes. We need a top-notch Alliance officer familiar with the Praxton lifestyle. I believe you more than qualify."

"I think I better sit down. I can't believe this. Yes, I want to work with you on the new ship."

"Excellent. I will have a contract and information sent to you. It will be great to work with you on the Star Hawk."

Elmwood returned to his apartment, informing the women of his promotion to captain of the Star Hawk. "However, that means I'll be spending less time here. There are a thousand details to look after, and it's going to take a lot of my time to get the ship ready."

Grata sounded disappointed. "I suppose you have to do a lot of things to prepare for."

"Yeah, I'm going up to the ship in the morning. It's still under construction, but I need to get a feel of the ship. There is a lot to take care of."

"Until then, we better make use of your time here." She took his hand, leading him to the master bedroom. "The other females will have to wait another time to please you."

———

Morgan felt too excited to eat dinner, and instead consumed several drinks. She grinned, chatting about how it was a chance of a lifetime and how she knew Elmwood was going to be a great captain on the new ship.

Eleni laughed at her. "I'm seen no one so excited to leave me to go to work."

"Well, I still have a few days before I have to report for duty. Maybe I can make that time more memorable by squeezing in additional activities." She pointed at the spare bedroom where the wall cage had been installed. "I want to test that cage out."

"Okay, I will be glad to give you a demonstration." She stood and pointed a finger at Morgan. "Strip."

The tone of Eleni's voice surprised Morgan. *I guess she has taken control.* She stood and took off her clothes and faced Eleni, placing her hands behind her back.

"I'm going to discipline you, understand?"

"Yes."

Eleni used her fingers to comb Morgan's hair. "You will feel a bit of pain, helplessness, and you will want to cry out, but you won't. Or there will be additional measures taken."

Morgan nodded. Her nipples became swollen and warmth spread to her groin. She felt a push at her back, and she made her way to the spare bedroom.

Eleni placed Morgan facing a wall with hooks attached to the wall. Each wrist cuff was placed to a wall hook placed above her head. She twisted her head to see Eleni take a flogger from a tall cabinet with two decorative doors. Morgan tried to see what else was kept inside, but Eleni blocked her view.

The flogger struck her from her neck down to her feet. She heard the swish of the flogger as it travelled across her skin, back and forth. The strikes didn't vary in intensity but moved everywhere across her body. Morgan tried not to groan too loud, but her skin tingled from the multiple strikes. Occasionally, strikes were at the inside of her thighs. When she tried to close her legs, she received several hand smacks on her ass.

"No. Keep your legs apart or I'll get tough on you."

Morgan complied, and she felt the flogger work on her body again, including between her legs. The hits became gentle but still came close to touching her vagina. She gasped. The whipping continued up and down the length of her body, stopping only after Morgan felt her skin was burning. Suddenly, Eleni spanked her. Morgan pressed her body against the wall, but the spanking continued until she thought her ass had blisters. She cried out, "Mercy. Please."

"No, we're not finished yet." Eleni undid one wrist cuff and turned Morgan around, attaching the cuff to a new hook. She squeezed her breast and kissed Morgan on the lips, broke apart and kissed her again. "There's more to come. Keep your legs spread."

Morgan widened her stance and watched Eleni wave the flogger across her skin. The first few strikes grazed across her ribs. The light hits merely caused her skin to prickle. Eleni increased the intensity of the hits. She moved the strikes up to her breasts, whipping them back and forth several times.

Morgan let out a long groan.

"If you cry out, I will gag you."

The flogging continued from her breasts down to her feet and back up. When the strands hit her between her legs, Morgan let out a cry. "Oh, oh, oh!" Morgan breathed out in gasps.

Eleni stopped and stepped to the cabinet, returning with several items. Morgan watched as Eleni held a pair of nipple clamps held together by a chain. She first put her mouth on each nipple, sucking on it until satisfied the nipple was as erect as it could be. Then she attached a gold metal clamp to each nipple, causing Morgan to let out a moan. She held up a gag. "I think we need to use this now."

Morgan looked at the black gag, with the end shaped like a short, thick penis. She parted her lips, her tongue feeling the gag as it pressed inside her mouth.

After the gag was secured behind her head, Eleni used the flogger again, lightly brushing the sensitive skin. She tugged at the chain holding the nipple clamps. "Your skin is a lovely shade of pink. Maybe it's time I placed you in the cage."

Morgan nodded, hoping for the ordeal to be over soon. She felt too warm and aroused to the point of frustration. Her skin tingled everywhere, and her swollen nipples ached against their clamps. She meekly followed Eleni to the cage where her wrists were secured above her.

Eleni closed the cage doors. "I'll be back in a while."

Morgan sagged, feeling exhausted. Slowly, she recovered and stood straighter. Long minutes passed when she heard Eleni return.

"How are you doing? Enjoy being in the cage?"

Morgan nodded.

"Are you okay with the gag? Nipple clamps?"

She nodded again.

"Good, I think you've had enough torture." Eleni removed the gag and the nipple clamps.

Morgan let out a cry when the blood entered her nipples again.

"Let's take you to bed and finish you."

"Please." Morgan stepped out from the cage. She didn't object when her wrist cuffs were joined behind her back. Morgan weakly made her way to the master bedroom, dropping on the bed. She rolled on her back and closed her eyes. Eleni began to lick her pussy. Morgan didn't last long and let out a long cry as the orgasm hit like an ocean wave over her.

It took several minutes before Morgan could sit again. After her wrists were released, she went to the kitchen for a drink and a bite to eat. She saw Eleni smile as she entered the kitchen.

"That was almost too much. Thanks."

"You're welcome."

"I'm going to sleep like a log tonight."

"Good. I know we have only a short time together before you need to go to the Star Hawk, so I wanted to make sure you have a memorable experience tonight."

Morgan laughed. "No problem there. My ass still hurts."

"Good."

Morgan returned to the bedroom, ready to have a good sleep.

"Good night. Let's cuddle up."

Morgan wiggled into proximity of Eleni. She exchanged a few kisses with her and fell asleep.

[13]

JULIUS ELMWOOD COULDN'T SEE all of the Star Hawk from the lounge window. The elevator opened to a spacious lounge, and the windows afforded a grand view of Praxton and ships parked at the space station. However, the front part of the ship went past the edge of the viewscreens. What he saw was impressive. The flat-black body of the ship had numerous cut-outs, bulges, antenna, doors dominating the outside. Flood lamps lit up most sections where robots and humans in spacesuits continued to inspect and work on various components.

After getting his fill of the scene beyond the lounge viewscreens, he made his way to the secured entrance to the Star Hawk. He had two sets of identification checks. One from electronic screening and the next by a human. The MP didn't smile or show any emotion while inspecting his documents.

Finally, the police officer gave a salute. In a flat voice he announced, "Welcome aboard, Captain Elmwood."

Elmwood proceeded inside the spaceship. A whistle sounded. "Captain on board." The declaration came from a speaker hidden inside a wall but without sounding muffled.

A man in a dark green and blue uniform came to greet him.

"Captain Elmwood, welcome aboard. We've been expecting you. I'm Commander Kelly Walling." He saluted.

Elmwood appraised the dark-skinned, muscular looking executive officer. The officer looked about Elmwood's age and almost as tall. Ribbons and medals decorated his chest. He returned the salute. "Kelly Walling. You're in charge of the Star Hawk armaments?"

"Yes, sir."

"As such, we will be working together a lot."

"Yes, sir."

"Then you better call me Julius." Elmwood stuck out his hand. "We can save a lot of breath if we keep to our first names."

"That sounds great." Walling grinned. "How about I show you around our new girl?"

Elmwood walked with Walling, turning toward the main command centre. A secondary command centre was near the central area of the ship. The tall hallways had a dome ceiling and were wide, allowing for numerous personnel to move rapidly through the ship. Walling described the military advantages of the one-point-four-kilometre long ship. Walling listed the armaments.

"We have eighty-four small to medium sized gun turrets mounted on the outside of the ship. These are protected by covers that conceal their location until they're ready to be deployed. We also have two large gun turrets, one each at the bow and stern. The gun at the bow is mounted on the bottom of the ship, while the one at the stern is on top. Neither have covers. This enables them to be activated without warning."

"What type of armaments do the guns use?"

"Most of the small guns use masers as a primary weapon, although a few use projectiles. The medium size weapons all use pulse plasma energy. The large guns use continuous plasma energy supported by delta missiles."

"Delta missiles. Those are battle changers." Elmwood knew each delta missile contained four non-identical missiles. The four missiles each had a unique way of attacking a designated target, making defence against a delta missile extremely difficult. "I understand the Star Hawk carries a contingent of smaller ships."

"Correct. We have twenty-four micro drone ships, four ships capable of seating five that are capable of limited military action. These are named

Falcon One to Four. We also have a pair of shuttles that hold ten crew each called Eagles. The latter has light armaments and can land troops on a planetary surface."

"Pretty impressive."

"Julius, this ship has the power to defend itself against a fleet of enemy craft all by itself. It is the ultimate war machine." He gestured at an open door. "Captain's quarters."

Elmwood looked around the suite. One wall in the sitting room featured several viewscreens, with all of them currently in the transparent mode and showing the star littered space beyond. The rest of his lower level suite was divided among the kitchen and dining room. There were doors to a washroom, closets, and to the executive meeting room next door. A spiral staircase led to an upstairs level. "Very nice."

"Two bedrooms, a den and exercise room are upstairs." Walling continued. "So far, the furnishings are a bit sparse. An interior decorator will come in to finish it as you would like."

"Good. Let's check out the command centre."

Early spaceships placed the command centre at the front of the ship. One advantage of a forward location included windows to see immediately in front. The location also made it vulnerable to attack.

With the use of viewscreens instead of windows, it allowed the command centre to be placed in any part of the ship. In the Star Hawk, it was placed under the recreation decks, which gave it protection. Although viewscreens largely replaced windows for viewing, the command centre had windows located behind the viewscreens along the side portion of the ship's hull. In case of an emergency when the viewscreens were not operable, they could be moved aside to reveal the windows.

The control centre was currently occupied by technicians setting up the various consoles. Command from the consoles to other parts of the ship used different methods. Normal operation used wi-fi as the primary method. In the event of such communication failure, encrypted radio became the next option. Finally, wired connections could be utilized.

"It looks like it's coming together." Elmwood remarked.

"Yes. Although there are workers everywhere around the ship, we're right on schedule for launch."

"That's something to look forward to."

A tall, blonde woman with short hair approached them. She wore an Alliance military uniform, her patches showing she had reached the position of lieutenant. Her tailored dark navy jacket was fitted over a lighter blue shirt. The skirt's hem rested just above her knees. The Star Hawk had not issued new uniforms, with those from the Alliance and Praxton military wearing the uniforms of their previous position.

"Captain Elmwood. I'm Janice Madison and have been appointed to serve you as your communications officer, pending your approval, sir." She saluted, her face passive of any emotion.

"It's good to meet you." Elmwood returned her salute. "Please call me Julius. We can save the formal titles for when other crew members are present."

"Very well." She gave a forced smile. "It is good to meet you as well, captain. I mean, Julius."

"Have you met Commander Kelly Walling, our weapons officer?"

"No, not yet." She stuck out a hand. "Good to meet you, sir." She turned her attention back to Elmwood. "We have a meeting scheduled for oh-eight-hundred tomorrow morning. I have forwarded the agenda to you, for you to review. We will be seeking approval of the ship's new uniforms, including issues specific to the female crew's sleeping quarters. General Noreen Howler has asked to sit in on the meeting, but you will be the chair."

"Good. We need to have a few meetings to introduce our personnel to each other and to resolve any issues before we launch."

Madison left the two men and Walling quietly spoke. "I hope she learns to relax by the time we get underway."

"She just met us. It would be stressful coming from an Alliance Forces ship to one run by Praxton social standards. For an Alliance woman, I can understand how there would be some apprehension."

"I agree. It might be a challenge for her to adjust to the Praxton customs."

———

The following morning, Elmwood finished his cup of coffee and walked over to the executive meeting room. It was fully functional while the rest of the ship still had areas of work to be finished. Elmwood sat at the head of the oval table with several other ship officers present, along with General Noreen Howler.

Elmwood moved through several agenda items, most of them dealing with the ship's interior design schedule. On the next agenda item, he referred to Warrant Officer Sheri Richards to report on the new ship uniforms.

"Thank you, Captain Elmwood. Our proposed ship's uniforms are a departure from the Alliance uniforms in style, although we have kept the colour scheme. One parameter we were under required Praxton females to be comfortable with the new uniforms. The recruiting office stressed the Praxton population would be hesitant to join a military organization that looked like the same Alliance Forces that invaded Praxton.

"So, we leaned heavily toward the fashions of Praxton to design the new uniforms. Besides the male and female military uniforms, we have designed uniforms for the non-military crew on the Star Hawk. These are similar to the military style but are of a different colour, emphasising dark blue-grey. For our demonstration we will review the military uniforms. First, we will show the male uniform." She clicked a control and a rotating holographic image of a male model appeared in the centre of the table. The model wasn't full size, reaching approximately two-thirds the height of a normal male.

"As you can see, we used a dark blue with a red trim. The blue is similar to the Alliance uniform colour shade, while the red trim is an acknowledgement to Praxton and its red soil. The shirt has a small collar and is loose fitting. The jacket, as you can see, is open at the front and held by a single brass button."

Elmwood studied the holographic image. The shirt and jacket were similar to Praxton formal wear. The pants were also of Praxton design; loose fitting with a high waist. The fly was conservative by Praxton standards, a dense weave that hid mostly what was underneath. The footwear was a black, boot style. The jacket had an epaulette, with the model's shoulder mark indicating the rank of a corporal.

"Are there any questions?"

"The uniform appears to be loose fitting," Kelly Walling observed. "That should allow easy movement in case of a military operation. I like it."

"That is quite a departure from Alliance military uniforms," Janice

Madison commented. "Do you believe they lack some professionalism? For example, they are rather loose fitting and I question the need of an open weave fly."

"We believe the uniforms are very professional in appearance." Richards voice changed in pitch. "The style is loose fitting in design to *reflect* what is worn on Praxton, which helps to make the male body appear larger. The fly is not as open as conventional Praxton pants, although it is a departure from Alliance customs. It is a style that those from Alliance worlds will have to be get accustomed to."

"I believe that is sufficient discussion on the male uniform," Elmwood stated. "I understand new uniforms often get differences of opinion. However, these uniforms have already been studied by the committee, and have been determined to be the best choice for the Star Hawk. While there may be minor changes made later by the design committee, let us accept Warren Officer Richards' report on new uniforms. Can you review the new female uniforms for us now?"

"Yes, thank you, captain," Richards replied. "The female uniform leans toward the Praxton style of dress. We decided a skirt with pleats along the side would allow for greater movement, something that may be required in an emergency. For the same reason, the shoes have a lower than normal heel, at least by Praxton standards."

A few low comments were made as the holographic female model rotated around. Elmwood thought the short skirt, complimented by a chain belt, wasn't a significant departure from Alliance fashions, although shorter than the military style. The sleeveless, light fabric top was cut like a vest. The vest had an open oval at the back with buttons at the top and bottom. The upper arms were bare, but the forearms were covered by 'phantom sleeves', where the fabric at the elbow was held by an elastic. What would cause a reaction, Elmwood thought, was the blue metal collar with a ring at the centre. The wrist and ankle cuffs matched in colour but were of stiff fabric material. The collar and cuffs each held a red metal ring.

Richards added a few details concerning the uniform. "Not shown on our model are the optional chains that can be attached to the cuffs and collars, or the lead that can be attached to the collar or wrist cuff. The collar shown here is the basic style. Higher ranks will with have a more elaborate design and be slightly wider. We are open to the ankle cuffs being optional, but the wrist cuffs are a traditional part of Praxton female attire."

"I am wondering how set this design is." Madison spoke up. "I believe that the collar and cuffs should be an option. Not all women would be comfortable wearing them. I understand that the Charter of Conduct Office has officially ruled them to be jewellery, but some of us still see them as a symbol of submission."

"But," Richards countered. "As you pointed out, the Charter of Conduct Office recognizes the collar and cuffs as jewellery. Therefore, our committee is reluctant not to include them as part of the uniform."

"Do you have an image of the model wearing the chains and leash?" Elmwood asked.

"Yes, of course." Richards changed the holographic image and the model now had chains draped between her wrist cuffs and belt. Another a chain went between her ankle cuffs. A leash clipped from her collar to her left wrist that held a strap.

There were several quiet comments made as the model rotated above the table.

"The chains come in different lengths." Richards continued with a description. "For example, the chains at the wrist cuffs can be changed to longer ones that attach to the collar. The chains, regardless of where they are attached to, are meant to hang loose and not impede movement. The leash, as you can see, is not too long but still won't impede arm movement when it is held at the wrist."

Another officer, a senior weapons officer, Rickey Spelling, added her opinion. "My thoughts are that the uniform is slightly too revealing. However, I understand that it does fit within the Praxton norms. Concerning the collar and cuffs. I have worn a fashion collar occasionally and have never considered that it made me submissive. I'm fine with the uniform with the collar. Perhaps the cuffs could be made optional. I don't have a problem with the chains. I think they add a degree of elegance to the uniform. I'm uncertain about the leash."

"Perhaps a collar doesn't make you feel that way, but I believe it represents control over the wearer. My objection to the collar and cuffs remains." Madison raised her voice.

Elmwood spoke, aware those at the table, in particular General Howler, would evaluate how he handled the dispute. "I understand how something new can be exciting and frightening. Everything on this ship has the ability to give us pause. The Star Hawk is an amazing ship, a military ship that will force us to work and depend on each other. A uniform must make us feel as part of a team. To have part of the personnel not wearing a portion of the uniform defeats its purpose. The collar and cuffs, both wrist and ankle, will be part of the uniform and there will be no exceptions to wearing them. The chains and leash, for the time being, will be optional. The discussion is now closed concerning the uniforms and specifically the collar and cuffs."

[14]

ELMWOOD LOOKED up at the approach of Senior Technician Derik Holton as he checked progress reports at his workstation in the command centre. The dark blue-grey uniform Holton wore showed he was a non-military employee.

"Captain Elmwood, you wanted to see me?"

"Yes, I wanted to let you know we are going to bring in a consultant to help improve the flavour the food and beverages. I've noticed that the food formulas have not deviated from when I first served on military ships. As we will be away from any ports for long periods of time, I believe we need a better fare in our dining rooms. I know your responsibilities are to only ensure the food processing equipment is functioning, but I wanted to keep you informed you will work with a food consultant in the future. I don't know who or when that will happen."

"I see. As long as he, or she, doesn't get in my way that's fine with me."

Elmwood watched Holton leave. *He doesn't look happy about this.*

A few minutes later, Communication Officer Janice Madison approached Elmwood.

"Captain Elmwood, I have verified the communication systems are fully operational, including the redundant network."

"Excellent. It looks like we'll be ready to do testing of the Star Hawk in space soon. Will you be ready for simulations?"

"Yes, sir."

"I see you're still being very formal with titles, Janice."

"It seems to be my nature to be conservative when addressing others in the forces."

"That can be an attribute. However, if we're going to work together as a team, we need to be comfortable with each other. Do you agree?"

"Yes, sir."

"Comfort with each other implies that there is a personal connection. The easiest way to such a connection is an exchange of names without titles."

"Point taken." She frowned. "I felt nervous about my new position on the Star Hawk, and I guess I want to hide a bit."

"You're not comfortable with your position?"

"No, not entirely. I applied for the position on the Star Hawk, not because I expected to get it, but to show the Alliance forces of my interest in moving up in the ranks. It seemed during the interviews I was being offered the promotion because I was a woman in the Alliance forces. To be honest, I wasn't sure if I deserved to be promoted as Communications Officer other than being of the right gender."

"That's not the reason why you have been made the Communication Officer."

"I wish I could be sure of that."

"I read your personnel file. I saw your qualifications and attributes. You, Janice Madison, have all the requirements to make a great communication officer, and I have no doubt you're going to do a fine job here. To be honest, I investigated you as I do with all my senior officers. The fact is you're here is because you deserve it and it has nothing to do with you being a woman. No one else is better for the job."

Madison blinked. "Thank you, sir."

"You're welcome, Janice."

She smiled. "Julius."

"Hello Morgan, welcome aboard the Star Hawk." Elmwood extended his hand in a greeting.

Morgan grinned. "It's great to be here." She looked around the command centre. "I understand we're going to be at the spaceport for a few more days."

"Yes, everything is on schedule and I'm optimistic we can launch right on time. How were your final days on Praxton?"

"Fantastic. I didn't have time to see all I wanted to, but it was still great. Yesterday we spent a day at a resort nearby sand dunes. The sand was red, and we slid down them on these plastic carpets. It was so much fun. I want to go back and visit more of Praxton."

"It is a unique planet. Now we have a unique spaceship, and it's time to get her ready to visit deep space."

She took in a deep breath. "I just have to say, it's like I'm dreaming. Thanks for including me in this."

"No, I have to thank you. As a captain, I need to have absolute trust in my second in command. To have someone like you available is critical to the successful operation of the ship. I'm lucky to have a second in command such as yourself."

She smiled. "Okay, now I'm embarrassed and as an attempt to change the subject, I hear the new uniforms are available. I believe we need to integrate them as soon as possible. Right now, we have the Alliance uniforms dominating the dress style here."

"Good point. Why don't you organize the distribution of the uniforms?"

"I'll do that. I can have the uniforms delivered to those who are currently on the ship. As other personnel arrive, they can pick up their uniforms from the central distribution and storage facilities."

"We have another meeting scheduled for executive officers tomorrow morning in the executive meeting room. Please inform the officers I expect them to be in our new uniform. I'm not going after all the ship's personnel if they're slow to change to the new uniforms, but I expect officers to lead by example."

"Yes, sir." She smiled. "I'm looking forward to wearing the new uniform."

Morgan walked around the ship, introducing herself to the personnel.

Near lunch time, she entered the officer's lounge, obtaining a bowl of soup and a tea. She recognized Janice Madison and asked if she could join her at her table.

"Of course, Morgan." She gave a restrained smile.

"Thanks. It's exciting being part of this new ship. I can hardly wait until we launch."

"It certainly will be an experience."

Morgan tilted her head. "Is there something bothering you? I don't mean to pry, but perhaps I can be of help."

"I'm nervous about the new ship's uniforms."

"What is it that bothers you?"

"I can get accepting the revealing nature of the uniform. After all, this ship is gong to have a large population from Praxton. However, I just don't like the thought of wearing a collar and cuffs. I'll feel like I'm a slave. I'm not looking forward to tomorrow when I have to wear them."

"I understand. Maybe I can help you with this. First, the uniform is just that, a uniform. It doesn't change who you are. Second, a collar alone doesn't make you a slave. It is the inside of you that determines if you're a slave or not. Third, on Praxton the collar does not represent being a slave. It is a symbol of being a Praxton female. It is not a symbol of being a slave or of weakness. Rather it means fulfilling the role of a Praxton female which may include being submissive to her male guardian."

"Okay, I hear what you are saying, although I don't know if I fully appreciate the difference between a slave and being submissive to a guardian."

"Simple. A slave cannot leave and does not control their lives. A female wearing a collar, while being submissive to her guardian, may leave him if she doesn't like the conditions she is living under."

"Okay. That makes it sound better. Still, I have apprehension about the wearing of a collar and cuffs."

"Let's tackle that right now." She stood. "I'll meet you in your quarters in fifteen minutes."

Morgan changed into the new uniform. She added the collar and cuffs and attached chains from the collar to her wrist cuffs. She checked her appearance in a full-length viewscreen, pleased with what she saw. The viewscreen showed her sides and back from concealed cameras. It could also reverse her image of left and right, giving the same image others saw.

She made her way to Madison's suite, located near to her own. All the higher ranked officers had their quarters in the same area, including the facilities reserved for senior officers. Madison opened her suite door to Morgan, looking surprised at what she wore.

"Hi, Janice. Let's get over this uniform situation right now. I'm wearing mine and, as you can see, I'm still the same person. Put yours on and let's go for a drink."

Janice took a deep breath and held it as she stepped back into her suite. She scrutinized the uniform as she released her breath. "Somehow it looks different from what I remember during the meeting."

"Better? Or worse?" Morgan grinned as she spun around.

"I guess I have to say better. It is a rather revealing uniform, but it looks really nice. And the collar isn't as noticeable as I thought, like it just matches the rest of the uniform."

"Try yours on."

"I suppose you're right." Janice departed to her bedroom. "I better get used to wearing this uniform now rather than tomorrow."

"I'll bet after a couple of days you won't notice the collar and cuffs. It'll feel natural wearing them."

"I'll take that bet." Janice called out from the bedroom. "But since I don't have a choice, I might as well get on with it." She emerged from the bedroom. "I'm not comfortable with these chains. Do I need to wear them?"

Morgan looked at the pair of chains dangling from Janice's hand. "Just part of the uniform, nothing more." She took the chains and attached them to the collar and cuffs. "There. You look great."

"Thanks."

"Now, let's go to the forward lounge and get a drink." She pulled on Janice's arm, taking her out of the suite and down the hallway. The ship still hadn't obtained its full complement of a crew, but there were still people passing by. Because the new ship's uniforms were only now just being released to the personnel there was a mixture of dress. For those just joining the military forces, civilian clothes were worn. It wasn't uncommon to see civilian dress on the ship, though most of those on the ship that had military training wore their previous uniform.

There were Alliance uniforms seen, but there were several women wearing Praxton style civilian clothes. Everyone looked at the two women wearing the new uniforms, giving approving glances.

They entered the lounge, selecting a table in the sparsely populated room.

Janice observed, "I guess not many people drink in the afternoon here."

"It's probably not normal procedure, but since we haven't left port yet, I don't think anyone will pay attention."

"Excuse me."

Morgan and Janice looked up at the brunette wearing a Praxton forces uniform.

Morgan wasn't surprised at the Praxton military uniform; a short black and green camouflage skirt, knee high black boots with a heel, and a tight-fitting jacket with a deep V neck. "Yes?"

"I don't mean to intrude, but I noticed you're wearing the new uniforms. I think they look wonderful. I can hardly wait until I get mine."

"Thank you. I'm Morgan Regan and this is Janice Madison." She didn't bother mentioning their rank on the ship, which their collar indicated by the width and colour bands.

"Khloe Levit. I'm in charge of the female quarters." She saw the puzzled looks from the two women. "On Praxton, females are used to having a guardian to inform them of correct behaviour. Many households have housekeepers and senior females to help enforce rules. On the Star Hawk we have a lot of females who are suddenly without a direct authority to tell them what they can or cannot do. So, my job is to act like that senior female or housekeeper, only at a higher level."

"That's interesting," Janice replied. "I never thought before about how much we are putting these women in a different world than they were used to."

"Since you're an officer, will you be at the meeting tomorrow morning?" Morgan asked.

"Yes. I understand it will have all higher rank personnel attending. I have to give a report." Khloe smiled. "Agenda item number eight, which I believe is the last one."

"I look forward to hearing your report and seeing others wear this new uniform. Why don't you join us?" Morgan gestured at an empty chair at their table.

"Thank you." She sat. "I'd love to talk to someone about the ship. I find the size of it rather intimidating."

"I didn't find the size of the ship intimidating. Just this." Janice laughed and pointed at her collar. "Fortunately, Morgan has helped me over come my fear."

"I guess we all have a fear of something. What's the trick of not being scared of this monster of a ship?" Khloe asked.

"The thing to remember is, no matter how big the ship is, you can only be in one part at a time. You'll find that a lot of the floors are duplicates of another. And a big ship means you're better protected," Morgan replied.

"Like a big and powerful guardian." Khloe grinned.

Yeah, just like our captain. Morgan sighed.

[15]

DIANA ADORIA CLOSED her small luggage bag for a one-night stay on the planet below the space station. A second message she received last week surprised her, requesting a meeting to discuss a new position. The message, sent by a recruiter, indicated it was for an executive position.

She wasn't looking for a new job. Her career had a steady progression where she was now the executive food and beverage programmer on a private luxury space liner. The La Bella was owned by the extremely wealthy Nella Louis, who hired her to prepare the meals and drinks for herself, guests and the complement of crew. There were less than two hundred people at any given time on the ship, although that didn't make her job much easier. Nella was a fussy eater who always wanted to try something new, not satisfied with the same main dish she had a month ago.

Diana had university training on how to program the stored food packages into edible dishes. The food packages contained basic organic foods, such as soybean, carbon mash, starches, protein strings and various other ingredients. Most graduates could easily program the food packages into a simple meal. To make the same into a meal that excited the senses was difficult and required more art than science to accomplish. Where Diana excelled was to pair such food with wine. Her palate allowed her to make a wine taste like a rare vintage. At a relatively young age, she had obtained peer recognition and financial security. Several of her wine creations were patented, and she received a licensing fee from those who used it.

When Paula Nixon contacted her and asked her to come to Praxton for an interview, Diana politely turned her down. A second message requested where the La Bella was going to stop next, and if Diana could meet her there. A paid for hotel room, dinner and a promise the interview would pique her interest won her over for the meeting. It would also give her a chance to explore the city of Neteliek on the planet Risus. The city was known for its waterways that wove around parkland on the main continent.

Diana checked her appearance once more in the viewscreen of her well-appointed suite. She saw the image of a slim, medium height woman wearing a pale-yellow skirt and a matching jacket open to reveal a green satin blouse. Cat-like hazel eyes gave her a mischievous look. The blouse used a single button just below her rib cage, revealing the cleavage of medium sized breasts. She fixed her dark hair and exited to the hallway outside.

A crew member saw her guide her floating suitcase and immediately took it from her, insisting he would place it personally on the private shuttle. She thanked him, even though the gravity-neutralizer pads made the guiding the suitcase effortless. A few minutes later, she climbed into the shuttle. The six-person shuttle held only the pilot and herself. The pilot, a man whose age was hard to determine, was there only for emergencies in case the autopilot failed. He was an expense most ships didn't bother with.

She did converse with him, finding out his primary interests were just visiting other worlds and the La Bella allowed him to do so. He never married, enjoying a solitary life. He informed her that his sister had several children, and he liked the role of being the uncle that brought them exotic gifts when he made his rare appearances.

The shuttle landed on the roof top terrace of the Chateau Montreal and the pilot carried her bag inside to the front desk located one floor below. He bid her a pleasant day.

The hotel lobby gave the appearance of an upscale hotel. She signed in, declining help in carrying up her bag. The elevator used tracks on the outside of the hotel to take her to her floor, giving her a view of the city beyond the curved glass exterior. The elevator doors opened on the seventy-second floor. She was met with three doors to different suites and used her thumb print to open the one on her right. The suite inside was larger than her own ship's quarters and included several luxury amenities. *It looks like they're trying to impress me.*

Diana changed into a dark blue dress. It was more conservative than she normally wore, but decided it was more appropriate for a business dinner. She expected Paula would likely wear conservative attire as well. The dress did have a slit that slid up to mid thigh and the back had a deep scoop, but the front had a high neckline. Anyone facing her would see just the dress, although those behind her would have a better view.

The Blazon Dining Room was in the hotel, a dozen floors below her own suite. As soon as she entered the room, the maître d stepped forward.

"Ms. Adoria, welcome to the Blazon. Your companion is already present at your table." He led her to a table that could seat four in a booth where the rear half consisted of a window, giving an unobstructed view of the world beyond.

Paula Nixon stood to greet her. As they exchanged handshakes Diana observed the tall, dark-skinned woman. She appeared to be only slightly older than herself and carried the effortless grace of a woman comfortable in any situation. She wore an expensive looking maroon gown that featured a small cape to cover the bare shoulders. She was well endowed and the dress with its wide U neck accented her assets. Besides the glittering wrist band, what held Diana's attention was a red and black banded collar she displayed around her neck. The large silver ring in the centre left no doubt it of it being a Praxton style of collar.

They sat and made small talk as the waiter brought bowls of gin and tomato soup. Paula finally moved to the subject at hand.

"As you know I'm a recruiter. I have an exciting opportunity for you I want you to seriously consider.

"I will, but I'm happy where I am. I'm well paid and I have no desire to move elsewhere. Let me put it this way. I don't want to be stuck on a planet preparing food and beverages for whatever restaurant you might have in mind. I enjoy travelling on a spaceship and seeing different worlds. The ship I'm on is first class, and I enjoy the crew and engaging visitors that travel with us. What could you offer that can rival that?"

"May I assume you're very comfortable where you are?"

Diana nodded. The conversation paused during the salad preparation at their table and placed on the plates. Sparkling water with a hint of raspberry flavour was poured into their glasses.

"Then what I have to offer you is to take you out of your comfortable job and put you where you'll be challenged. As far as compensation is concerned, we'll double your salary. But that is not what will drive you to take our offer. You need to push your abilities again. We can offer that."

"Okay, now you have my interest. What, and where, is this challenging place?"

"A spaceship with a crew of twelve hundred. Meals from the very basic to the most elaborate."

"Twelve hundred...what kind of ship is that?"

"The newest military vessel, the Star Hawk."

"Star Hawk? Isn't that the Praxton ship being built?"

"It is. If you want adventure, this ship is going to visit the rebel worlds hoping to establish peace. You would design meals for the visiting head of states. It won't be easy, even with the thirty staff working with you."

The next course appeared along with a pinot noir as a softer wine to start with. Diana approved of the pairing with the slivers of meat nestled among the seasoned potato cubes and the yellow beans.

"You must have studied up on me to know what foods I enjoy."

"Of course. We need to know everything we can about a person to whom we are offering such an incredible job."

"Fair enough." Diana smiled at the sales pitch. "Let's talk about you. I notice you're wearing a collar, the type one associates with Praxton."

"I married about a year ago. It isn't my first, nor was it Miguel's. The reason our marriages didn't work before is because of the travelling each of us did put a strain on our previous relationships. A few months ago, he presented to me with a gift. I opened it and it held this collar and an assortment of cuffs and chains. I just stared at the collar as he told me he didn't want to just be married to me, he wanted to own me. He slowly picked up the collar and placed it around my neck. I heard it lock, and I knew that was what I wanted too."

"What does that mean? How does that make things any different?"

"Right then and there, I knew he became my protector and that if I obeyed him, I would always be his. There is security in wearing his collar. I don't know if you can understand that."

"Well, I guess I've never had a reason to wear someone's collar. The fashion collars I've worn were just that, jewellery. But I can understand what you're saying. How does the collar help when you spend time alone?"

"When I wear his collar, I feel safer going to places by myself. For example, if I sit in a lounge by myself, men may approach me, check that, they do. But when they see the collar they're not as aggressive, understanding I'm already taken. A few ask if they can buy me a drink and sit with me, but they don't assume I'll go anywhere with them."

"Okay, I can see that as an advantage. But you still have given Miguel control over you."

"Men like thinking they're in control." She gave a grin.

"Are you saying it's an illusion?"

"It depends on the viewpoint. Occasionally he has ordered me to spend the day without any underwear."

"Did you?"

"Let's just say I try to work within his orders."

"How about when you're spending time together? Does he still exert control?"

Paula looked down and used her fork to play with the remains of her salad. She lifted her head. "To be truthful, he has put me over his lap and spanked me. Does that shock you?"

Diana shook her head. "I have heard of the Praxton customs and don't have a problem if both the man and woman want to follow them. I don't know if it's for me."

"If you get to be spanked by a man you care about, you'll enjoy it. I'm certain of that."

Before Diana could answer the next course arrived, consisting of steak, yams and vegetables. The wine, a sauvignon cabernet, merlot, malbec blend picked up the soft white pepper sauce used to marinate the steak.

"I would put forward that there are a lot of women who like the man being in control. It helps define relationships." Paula insisted.

"Interesting theory. Does that mean you believe wearing a collar and obeying your husband helps your marriage?"

"It does, because it defines our responsibilities. I like the thought he wants and has taken control. However, as you can see, I can be submissive but still be very good at my job."

"Okay, that may be good for you. But I don't have a man in my life. If I were to accept this position, would I be part of the crew and have to wear a collar? If you had studied me as much as you claimed, you would know I'm not the type to be collared."

Paula finished swallowing a bite of steak. "We did a thorough study of you." She took a sip of her wine, gently placing it back on the table. "You are a strong, determined woman. Damn smart, too. Which, perhaps ironically, indicates that you want powerful men around you. Weak people are scared of those who are strong. You aren't."

"Clever words."

"They're true. What's also true is you understand that the interplay between men and women works best if one or the other takes the superior position. You, being who you are, are strong enough to wear a collar and do your job. In fact, your profile suggests wearing a collar and cuffs and being submissive is part of your character."

"I don't believe that."

"I'm only repeating the information given me." Nella gave a slight shrug. "Intelligent women often enjoy something other than a vanilla relationship."

Diana took a drink of wine and almost put it back on the table before deciding to take another drink.

"What I told you is a computer assessment of your personality, traits and intelligence." Paula smiled. "Is it that bad to have a submissive side? Tell me, do you think less of me because I let my husband have control?"

"No, of course I don't."

"Then you shouldn't think less of yourself for having submissive feelings."

"I don't have those feelings." Diana waited as the waiter refilled her wine glass. "Okay, maybe part of me does." She gave a momentary smile. "I guess I do like the thought of a guy having of control over me. Mostly when I've been drinking. But you didn't answer my question if I would be part of the crew and be required to wear a collar."

"You would not be part of the crew, but be a civilian contractor. Some of the crew would work under you and you would have control of your department. You would report to the Star Hawk executive officers but still have a degree of independence. Concerning the collar, you would be expected to adhere to a Praxton style of dress and behaviour."

"That means I would be required to wear a collar."

The waiter brought over a wheeled cart filled with desserts.

The two women picked a dessert each, plus a coffee and a dessert wine.

"May I ask if you agree being on Star Hawk visiting the rebel worlds is a fantastic opportunity?" Paula asked.

"It is."

"Does wearing Praxton style fashions really bother you that much?"

"I don't know how to answer that. It is quite a change from what I'm used to wearing."

"I thought you liked a challenge."

Diana laughed. "I do, but this is definitely different from what I'm used to."

"Different can be good. I would like to get a yes from you. What else can I offer you to take this position?"

"You've offered me a lot already. I need to think about this."

Paula nodded. "Would it be all right if I called you in the morning?"

"Of course."

"Thank you. I have sent a package to your hotel room. I'm hoping it will help convince you to take up on our offer."

Diana departed to her room, light-headed from the wine and the after-dessert liqueur. She was curious about the package Paula had sent to her room and spotted it on a metal and plastic coffee table in the living area. She slipped off her shoes and sat on the loveseat by the table.

A small white box, tied with a red ribbon, sat on top of a larger box. Both were wrapped in a soft pink plastic film. She eagerly opened the wrap and saw a note on top of the first box. As soon as she touched the plastic membrane note, words glowed.

Diana, I hope you will enjoy these small presents. I trust it will help you make your decision easier. Thank you for meeting me for dinner and we will talk soon. I highly recommend you put on these gifts while nude—it will enhance their appeal and show them off better.
Paula

"Really? Nude?" She opened the first box and wasn't surprised to see a soft, white metal collar with a decorative band of blue and red in an alternating pattern. Three blue rings were attached to the collar; one in the centre and the other two rings on the side. *That's rather pretty.* Diana lifted it out of the velvet cushion and turned it in her hands. She lifted it up and put it around her neck. A quiet click indicated it was locked.

She stood in front of a viewscreen to examine it. *Okay, it does look nice. Rather exotic.* When she returned to the box, she found underneath the velvet cushion a matching set of four cuffs with several chains in a small round box set in the centre. Diana licked her lips. She reached behind her back and undid the zipper, allowing her dress to drop to her feet. She placed it on the loveseat along with her panties and began the task of adding the four cuffs. She sat on the loveseat and examined the chains, determining which chain attached where. She connected one chain between her ankle cuffs and used two more to go from her wrist cuffs to her collar, choosing the outside rings. There was a long chain with a strap on the end that she ignored. *I'm not adding the leash to the collar.* The small box contained one more chain with a clip on each end. *It's been a long time since I wore a set of these.* She gently placed a clip on each nipple, finding her nipples immediately reacted to the light pressure by swelling.

She opened the second, larger box. Inside were a pair of red stilettos with thin straps. On the sole, a marker showed they made the shoes in Praxton. Diana knew of the reputation Praxton had for women's shoes, claiming to be the most comfortable anywhere. *Okay, let's see how these fit.*

The shoes fit perfectly. Diana stood and walked to the viewscreen, testing the shoes for comfort. They felt light without any pressure points. Something else that made them easy to stand and walk in and she discovered the heel compressed a millimetre with each step to give a cushioned feel.

The viewscreen showed her image wearing the collar, cuffs and chains. She swallowed. *Lordy, that is sexy. Naked me in cuffs and chains. I would never have thought this is how I would look dressed as a slave.* She smiled at herself. *I like the look. Dammit, I have a tough decision to make.* She moved her hands around, testing the freedom of movement and deciding the chains didn't hinder her at all. The light chains draped along her bare skin, tickling at the side of her breasts when she moved her hands together. She strolled around the room, aware of the chain trailing between her ankle cuffs. *No wonder Praxton women walk slowly. These chains make sure your steps are conservative in movement.*

After her walk around the room, she returned to the loveseat and coffee table. She reached inside the smaller of the two boxes and lifted out the leash. She stared at the long chain, let out a long breath and attached the clip to the centre ring of her collar. She held the strap in her left hand and returned to the viewscreen. Her jaw dropped, parting her lips. Her right hand touched her breast, sliding it down to her vagina. She stood transfixed at her naked image, suddenly aroused.

Diana returned to the loveseat and began removing the cuffs and chains. The last item she removed were her shoes. She left her collar on.

Touching a device located behind her right ear, she spoke, "Message for Paula Nixon. Thank you for the exquisite gifts. I appreciate what they represent and promise to try them on later. Warm regards, Diana. Send message." Diana decided against telling her she had tried them on. That may show she was ready to accept her offer, and she still wasn't sure about that.

Still nude except for the collar, Diana slid into bed. Sleep didn't arrive immediately as she thought about her choice to remain on La Bella or join the Star Hawk. *Safe or adventure?*

She woke in the morning, the fragments of a dream still floating in her mind. In her dream, she was naked, wearing a collar and cuffs. A short chain joined ankle cuffs, and another chain went between her wrist cuffs, holding them behind her back. Paula pulled on a leash attached to her collar, taking her up a ramp that led to a monstrous spaceship. Diana climbed the walkway barefoot and reached the top. Paula passed the leash to the captain of the ship, a tall man with dark features. He stared at Diana, taking his time as he examined her body.

"Welcome aboard. You have made the right choice."

After her shower, Diana contacted the La Bella, informing them she would not be returning in the morning, but would spend the day as a tourist. She opened her suitcase, taking out a short skirt, white with a flower pattern. Her top was a simple t-shirt, although it featured a scooped back that bared half her back. The silver material had a small image of a bikini'd woman that appeared to walk across the front of the shirt to anyone she passed by. She put on a pair of flat shoes, wishing she could wear the red stilettos instead. *A little impractical for where I'm going, and they don't match my outfit.*

After a moment of hesitation, she decided to wear her collar. The hotel readily agreed to store her suitcase for her later return, providing a shuttle to Neteliek's famous beach and island area. The small islands had walkways that passed over the narrow waterways. Each island had beach areas and various amenities. Tall buildings were prohibited, and shuttle crafts were restricted, resulting in quiet, open areas. Even though it was a popular tourist destination, the large number of islands and beaches made for uncrowded conditions.

She left the shuttle and joined the other vacation goers walking along the stone pathways. The warm, humid air made it comfortable to stroll around in the minimum of clothing. She took notice of what other women were wearing. Most wore what one expected at the tourist area, although there was also a variance there. She understood Risus, with the planet relatively close to Praxton in the neighbour of stars, received a lot of visitors from the former outlaw world.

Diana found the Praxton citizens were easy to spot. The women wore collars, and often cuffs and chain accessories. Their clothes were less modest, and they walked behind their male guardians. The Praxton males had a definite, confident stride in their walk. The men that wore clothes purchased on Risus looked unsure about how they fitted. Their bare arms, legs and torso showed the signs of previously low exposure to the sun. Praxton males were normally expected to be fully dressed at all times, with the result of few opportunities for skin exposure. The opposite was true for women, who had ample opportunity to wear few clothes or even sunbathe nude.

She continued to stroll along the flat stone and sand pathway, passing various vendors selling goods in temporary kiosks. A woman wearing a collar but without cuffs, gave her a brief look that Diana translated as a look of approval of a kindred spirit. The momentary glance made her feel better about her choice to wear a collar even though she didn't have a partner.

A small coffee shop set off the main path caught her attention, and she decided she could use a coffee and a bite to eat. Service was a walk-up counter, then the purchaser would take their purchased goods to the scattering of tables around the café. She ordered a latte and a coffee cake and took the items to one of the identical tables that held four chairs. Soon after she sat, a group entered consisting of one male and four females. One female looked to be about fourteen Earth years old. The group also looked to be from Praxton with all females wearing collars, cuffs and various chains. Two of the older females were topless and the rest wearing short skirts and see-through tops. The male wore dark shorts and a colourful short-sleeve shirt. His pale limbs made it obvious they rarely saw any sun.

The new group sat at the next table and asked if they could borrow one of the chairs. Diana obliged, striking up a conversation with the young blonde woman.

"You must be from Praxton."

The topless, pretty blonde laughed. "I guess that's rather obvious. We're here on a vacation and trying, rather unsuccessfully, to fit in with the locals. How about you?"

"Just a one-day stopover. I work on an independent spacecraft."

"That sounds wonderful, travelling between planets."

"It has its perks." She pointed at the girl sitting at the end of the table. "Is she yours?"

"No." The blonde grinned. "Although she looks like my younger self. She's Kystal's daughter. We took her out of boarding school for this trip. It's important for her to see what other worlds and cultures are like." She laughed. "She was shocked to see women without collars on, a big no-no on Praxton. And for the first time she saw a male without a shirt on. She had a fit when she saw Master Daniel bare chested and wearing shorts. She almost ran back to her room."

Diana laughed with her. "On most worlds men without shirts on are common."

"Please don't remind me. I am having my eyes filled with undressed males. I wish I could see that on Praxton. Instead, Master Daniel gets to choose which female has the privilege of his company that night. The other females get to sleep together."

"That doesn't sound too good."

The blonde lowered her voice. "On Praxton I get to walk around barely dressed, I don't have to work, Master Daniels protects and provides for me and I have a family that includes two other females. All things considered I wouldn't trade that for whatever most Alliance females have. I live very well, and I'm loved."

"Maybe that's all we all really need. The idea of belonging."

The blonde nodded. "You got it."

Diana continued her journey toward one of the beach islands. She stopped at a kiosk that sold swimsuits. The swimsuits were either a bikini thong bottom without a top, or for the more conservative, a suit that had an additional two thin strips that came down from around the neck. The semi-transparent see-through material crossed over her breasts and joined at the waist, going between the legs and back up the back. The design, efficient on fabric, became a thong before going around the hips to circle to the front and attaching to the material at the front. The swimming suit came in a choice of colour and material, with the result a body on full display. She had already seen enough topless women to know that she looked overdressed.

The owner of the kiosk directed Diana to the rear of the shop where a curtained off area gave her privacy to change. The clerk provided her with a small bag to use for her garments. Diana thanked her and emerged wearing only her skirt and the abbreviated swimwear after placing her other clothes into the bag. *At least I fit in with the rest now.*

Once she crossed a small footbridge to an island, she saw clothes were only an option. She saw many naked women and a few naked men. With the men it was clear which ones were nude in the sun for the first time, with pale skin appearing from the waist down. It the case of Praxton men, they were without tan lines anywhere. *I do hope they are using sunscreen, especially on those sensitive areas.*

Her mobile announced a caller and Diana answered. "Hello, Paula."

"Hi. How is your day?"

Diana told her of her decision to walk around Neteliek and take advantage of the island beaches. "It's been fun so far."

"Nice. Are you wearing any of the gifts I sent you?"

"Yes, the collar. I thought it was beautiful, and it wouldn't look out of place here."

"It wouldn't look out of place on any Alliance worlds." A pause. "The reason for my call is to ask if you've arrived at a positive decision regarding working on the Star Hawk."

"It's a big decision for me. I'm still working out my feelings."

"I don't want to put more pressure on you. However, earlier I told my superior I believed you are leaning toward yes, and to stop interviewing other candidates until we hear back from you."

"I see."

"Diana, I think you want to take this challenge. What's holding you back?"

"I'm just not sure about this Praxton society on board of a spaceship."

"They're just people who grew up in a different environment. Yes, there are differences on how they see and do things. But they're human beings just like yourself. You'll have an adjustment period, but soon you'll be focusing on the job ahead. And that job is everything you'd ever want. Don't let fear stop you from stepping forward."

Diana thought about the Praxton family she met in the coffee shop. "You're right. I can't thing of a good reason why I shouldn't accept your offer. But give me until tonight. I need to be sure."

She ended the call with a promise to call back later. Diana crossed over to one of the islands and took off her skirt. Thoughts whirled around in her mind. She stopped to have a drink and lunch in a bar, observing people from different worlds intermingling. The Praxton natives were easy to spot, but she saw how they didn't have any difficulties interacting with anyone around them. *We're all still people.*

Diana arrived back to the La Bella and requested an immediate meeting with Nella Louise. The older woman frowned at Diana's news but in the end gave her a smile, a handshake and her blessing.

"I didn't get where I did by sitting around and playing it safe. You have a chance for adventure. Better grab it while you can. If it doesn't work out, contact me and I'll make sure you have a place to work."

Ten minutes later Diana called Paula. "I'm in."

[16]

MORGAN REGAN STEPPED out of the control centre, studying a tablet as she walked down the wide hallway.

"Excuse me, I'm looking for Captain Elmwood."

Morgan looked up at the tall, dark-skinned man wearing civilian clothes. "He's not available right now. Who would you be?"

"I'm Chris Novak, the administrator of the ship's interior design and esthetics. I've been trying to set up an appointment with the captain to finish the design of his quarters. Unfortunately, he seems to be busy every time I try to contact him."

"I assure you he really is very busy."

"Of that I have no doubt, but I do need to finish off the design."

Morgan took a liking to the polite, well-dressed man. "I'll contact the captain and see what I can do."

She used her mobile to call Elmwood. "Captain, the interior designer is here and wants to make an appointment with you."

"Damn, I don't have time for this."

"It has to taken care of soon." She hated reminding him of something he knew needed to be done.

"I know. Morgan, you know my tastes. Can you take over on this?"

"Sure, I'll get it done."

"I'll grant you access to my quarters."

She spoke to Novak. "You're in luck, we can take care of this right now. Come with me."

"Thank you. By your uniform, I see you're one of the executive officers."

"Yes, I'm second in command. First Officer Morgan Regan." She offered her hand.

"Pleased to have met you, First Officer Regan." He shook it.

"Chris, best call me Morgan. We don't need to be formal."

They walked down the hallway to the captain's quarters and soon arrived at the entrance. Regan used her thumb print to open the sliding door.

"Here we are." Regan took off her shoes, the custom for females entering a place of residence.

Novak entered and looked around. "This is really quite spacious, but seems rather empty." He made a few notations on his tablet.

"Yes, he hasn't had much time to add anything personal yet. Basically, this is how the captain's quarters looked before anyone lived in it."

"Do you know what Captain Elmwood's preferences are?" He moved around and continued to take notes. "His favourite colour? Type of furniture? Would he be leaning toward Alliance or Praxton interior style?"

Morgan laughed. "That's a lot of questions. Let's see... he likes dark colours in shades of blue or green. Furniture, nothing too fancy, I would guess. And let's go with the Praxton style." She smiled. "He has shown an interest in that lifestyle."

"We can incorporate that. The present furnishing here seems very functional. There's a lot of possibility here." Novak made additional notes. "Praxton design usually encompasses strong, clean lines, with lots of space between furnishings."

"That sounds like what he'd like."

"Praxton furniture has subtle designs to increase the male's dominance in the household. Every common room has an armchair reserved for the guardian. It's usually oversized and slightly higher from the floor than the rest of the furniture. That's also true of the chair he sits at during meals."

"That would make the guardian appear even larger."

"Yes." Novak gave a shrug. "Praxton has a unique culture, to say the least."

"It does indeed." Morgan laughed. "You aren't from Praxton, are you?"

"Heavens, no. I wouldn't be able to survive there. As you may have guessed, I'm gay. And while I can appreciate the female form and personality, acting as a guardian is not my style. I have managed to meet a few like-minded men on Praxton, but it is not like it is on Alliance worlds."

"You're just here as a design contractor?" She walked with him up the spiral staircase.

"Yes, I've been here six months and will be working on the next two explorer class ships." He gave a sigh. "It will be a long two years." He stopped in front of the master bedroom. "Oh, this needs to be redone. This room has much personality as a showroom."

Morgan peered inside the room. "I agree completely." She looked at a three-dimensional print of a mid-sized spaceship, recognizing it as the model he captained in the Alliance Forces. "And change that picture."

"A spaceship in a bedroom is not what one would expect to see. What should I change it to?"

"I don't know. Anything. Maybe a nude, or a Praxton female wearing cuffs and chains. A Praxton desert."

"I hear you. A picture that isn't a spaceship."

"Since this is the master bedroom, I believe the wall should have hooks to hold restraints. That's fairly basic in Praxton bedrooms."

"Yes, and we should have an ankle cuff added to the foot of the bed in case he has visitors."

"On my visit to Praxton, I noticed they sell small cages attached to the corners of a room. I think one will look appropriate here."

"I've seen those too. We could have one installed if you think that's what he'd want."

She recalled Elmwood leading her by a leash on Praxton and his desire to control her. "I think he'd appreciate it."

"Okay, let's look at the study."

Unlike the other rooms, Morgan saw the study did look like it was being used. The desk held two monitors and a temporary table held another. "What do you think can be done here?"

"Not too much. This is obviously a place for him to work. I shall install a longer desk so he can use multiple monitors. We can place the print of the spaceship in here. It won't look out of place. It needs a different colour scheme in here. These white walls are a little too sterile."

Novak stepped into the next room, a bedroom with an ensuite.

"Obviously this room has not been used yet." He raised his eyebrows. "A lot of potential here."

"I agree. Let's change that bed for starters. I want it to be the Praxton style of bed with an indent in the centre."

"A long narrow bed to sleep two females." He added a note. "And, of course, two ankle cuffs."

"Naturally. I think a cage that could hold two females would be a nice touch. The rectangular kind that keeps the females on their knees."

"I can make a special order for those. We should add more wall hooks, of course. Do you think he would like a rack in here that can hold whips and other discipline devices?"

"I'm sure he would." Morgan stood at the doorway that led to the shower room. "This is a nice shower, but just has walls around it. Do you know what is on the other side of this wall?" She pointed at the back wall of the shower.

"I believe that it faces the living room, only a floor above."

"Good. Can we replace the wall with a transparent one? Females should be seen while showering according to Praxton customs."

"I'll have to check with structure engineers, but I don't see a problem doing that."

"I think the captain will be surprised and pleased at the changes of his quarters."

"Are you good friends with him?"

"I've known him a long time. I can say with certainty he likes the Praxton culture."

"I don't mean to pry, but are you one of his females?"

"No." *I wish.*

"Okay, thank you. I've a plan for implementing a style for him. I appreciate your input."

"Glad to be of help. It was great talking to you. Perhaps we can meet again."

"Actually, you're on my list of quarters I need to work on."

"If you want, we can take care of that now."

Regan escorted Novak to her quarters a short distance from Elmwood's.

"As you can see, it is smaller than the captain's, but it also has two levels." Regan again took off her shoes.

Morgan Regan saw Novak glanced around the room. He noted the two prints hanging on a wall. One, a three-dimensional image of the Praxton desert, and the other a painting of a tall Praxton male leading a nude female by her leash across a room.

"I'm going to assume a Praxton style here as well. First, this plastic furniture has to go. We need soft fabric lounges, ones comfortable for bare skin. The floor has a pleasant shade to it with a touch of topaz in the design. But it is hard, so we need floor mats that will match with the furnishings. Praxton females often need to kneel on the floor, so soft floor mats are a must."

"I hadn't thought of that."

"We can add wall hooks and one or two in the ceiling." He checked out the study next to the living room. "The desk has hard edges to it. Let's change that to one with a larger surface but with gentle curves. Perhaps kidney shaped."

"That sounds nice."

"You need a photo or print here to break up the wall. Anything would work." He smiled. "Even one of a spaceship."

"No, thank you." Regan laughed. "Maybe a nude man. No, that would be too distracting."

"I'm sure you'll come up with something." Novak chuckled. He moved upstairs to her bedroom. "This is better than the captain's quarters. You have at least made it look like you live here and not as if it was a hotel room. Your bed needs to have another ankle cuff added. One is insufficient if you should have a female guest sleep over."

"Can I have restraints added to the headboard to hold wrists?"

"Of course." He made another note. He checked the washroom and next the shower room. "We could change the wall to a transparent one so the occupant of the bedroom can see the person showering."

"Do it. It'll make the shower seem less confining."

Novak examined the spare bedroom. "This is smaller than the spare bedroom in the captain's quarters. If you want a cage in here it would have to be a vertical one. This is a single bed, but we can change it to a Praxton style of bed with an indent in the centre. However, we couldn't have it as long. I know the purpose of the longer Praxton beds is so the female could have her arms secured above her head but that won't work here. I can add restraints to the sides of the bed, but that's the best I can do."

"That'll be fine. I don't expect to have guests here. I just wanted the look of a Praxton bedroom."

"Fair enough. I can add a rack to hold whips, additional chains and restraints. The shower for this room has a wall that overlooks the kitchen and dining room. I suggest we make that transparent as well."

"Good. I think this will work really well." Regan said goodbye to Novak and returned to her own thoughts. *Now how can I get Julius to be my guardian?*

[17]

MORGAN REGAN TWISTED in her chair as she watched Elmwood hurry into the meeting room and grab a cup of coffee. She knew the coffee was actually part of the agenda items on the list to discuss. She studied him as people entered the room, acknowledging as many as he could before the meeting started. The Senior Diplomat officer and the Charter of Conduct officer were among those joining the meeting.

Both wore Alliance forces uniforms, a sign of where their loyalties lie. He first greeted the diplomat, Tiffany Harris. Morgan listened as the average weight blonde responded with a genuine smile.

"Captain Elmwood. You have quite a ship here. I'm looking forward to our journey to other worlds."

"I as well," said Elmwood. "It will be nice to know we have an experienced diplomat to help overcome any challenges when we visit non-Alliance worlds."

"Thank you. When you have time, I would like to meet with you informally, perhaps over dinner."

"I'll make a note of that and send you possible meeting times."

The Charter of Conduct officer, Paul Thyssen, seemed less enthusiastic with his handshake. The tall, overly slim man had an intense look in his blue eyes. "I'm disappointed that you did not see fit to give me time to speak at this meeting. I believe the Charter of Conduct laws are to be taken seriously, and that should be brought to the attention to the officers *before* we launch."

"I'm aware of your opinion. However, I had to make hard decisions on what agenda items were to be a priority. I decided I don't want to make the meetings overly long, where those attending lose concentration. I'm sure you can appreciate the constraints I'm under."

"I thought the Charter of Conduct laws would be considered a priority."

"I have made my decision on today's agenda items. I studied your request, but it appeared to me little more than to recite policies of the Charter of Conduct. This meeting is not the place for such a lecture. If you wish to pursue an opportunity to discuss this later, we can talk about this another time."

Morgan was glad she didn't have to deal with Paul Thyssen often. The Charter of Conduct Officer took his position on Charter polices far too seriously, never failing to mention any slight perceived infraction.

Elmwood took his seat at the head of the table, waiting briefly for the last of the attendees to sit down.

Khloe Levit sat at the corner of the table next to him, wearing chains attached from her collar to her wrist cuffs and a leash from her collar with the lead end wrapped around her left wrist.

Elmwood cleared his throat. "I assume everyone has read the agenda. We will keep to the time allotted to each item, so questions will be limited. The first agenda item is additional guidelines for safety procedures during a power outage. Lieutenant Dr. Roberta Dorsett, the officer in charge of medical and safety, will address this issue."

Elmwood was the lead on the next item. "This isn't meant for discussion, although comments are welcome. Prior to serving on the Star Hawk, I have worked on both military and civilian ships. The last passenger ship had excellent food and beverages. I have noticed the food and the coffee on the Star Hawk are not any better than the military vessels I served on ten years ago. I decided that since we will be in deep space for extended periods of time, we need better beverages and food. I received authorization to hire a civilian contractor who specializes in food chemistry. This is not in any way a slight on Senior Technician Holton, who is doing a remarkable job of maintaining the food and beverage processing equipment. However, he can only use the formulas given by the military forces. It seems those formulas have been changed little in over a decade."

The announcement generated several vocal agreements. Holton crossed his arms without speaking.

Morgan checked the time, noting each agenda item didn't go over its allotted time. Questions were precise and fitted within the time frame. The break time came exactly as planned. Eventually, the last agenda item was reached.

Khloe Levit gave a smile before speaking. "I suppose everyone is glad we have reached the last item on the agenda. I just have a few items to go over. First, on a personal note, I'm very pleased with our new uniforms and how quickly they have been distributed through the ship. It will be nice to see almost everyone wearing the same uniform on the Star Hawk. As everyone is aware, we have a large contingent of women who will be assigned to a spaceship for the first time. These women, who are native to Praxton, have to make a major adjustment in their lives. I want to stress that we all need to give them allowances for any minor mistakes they make.

There have been challenges earlier, but we are making progress. In case some haven't seen the crew quarters, each section contains four to eight cabins, depending on whether they are single or double occupancy. Each grouping of cabins has a common area for socializing. This works well, as we can place the women from Praxton together and they will be able to support one another. Now the ship regulations state that couples wishing to share accommodation must make a request to do so. However, a few women are sharing beds without requesting permission. Part of the culture on Praxton is for females to share a bed. It is uncommon for a Praxton female to sleep alone. Thus, while each woman has her own cabin, it is likely she will choose a partner to sleep with."

One of the male officers interjected with a question. "May I ask if the sleeping together is of a sexual nature?"

"Not necessarily. Praxton females are comfortable with nudity and touching. When sharing a bed, the females may have some touching and kissing, but not normally much more than that. I should point out that Praxton females sleep in the nude, so touching may be considered intimate. This should be noted when we do our test drills and all personnel are required to be ready. Any female in bed at that time will probably exit their rooms naked and not be uncomfortable by it." She smiled. "I'm just letting you know in case there are reports of naked women on the ship."

Janice Madison obtained the attention of Elmwood and permission to speak. "That may help explain reports I have heard that there are women exercising in the nude in the common exercise facilities. It is proving to be, shall we say, a bit of a distraction. Although, it should be noted that it has increased the male precipitation."

Levit waited for the chuckles to die down. "Duly noted. I will have exercise outfits made up and have them distributed. Thank you for bringing that to my attention. If I may, I do have one more point to make regarding the uniforms, at least for the women. The collar and cuffs have optional chains, as well as a leash." She raised her left hand to show off the end of the leash. "The leash wasn't ordered originally as part of the uniform, but it seems the supplier of the collar and cuffs added the leash automatically. I would like to see the executive officers lead by example by wearing the chains at least occasionally. I'm comfortable with the leash attached to my collar or wrist cuff, although I understand not all females feel the same way. However, regarding the chains, it would make the personnel from Praxton a little more comfortable here if they saw officers adopting more of their customs."

Morgan Regan agreed, "I think it would add more flair to the uniforms. I'm willing to wear chains if it helps the Praxton women feel more included. I could also wear the leash occasionally."

The discussion continued, and Elmwood listened to those who supported wearing chains to those it made the wearer look too subservient. Thyssen tried to add his opinion.

"Captain Elmwood," Paul spoke up. "I most strenuously object to any pressure to women wearing chains with their uniforms. Chains represent the slavery…"

"That is quite enough." Elmwood cut him off. "I am certain we know your views on this matter. I believe both sides have expressed their thoughts. At this time, I will not impose any requirement on adding chains to the women's uniforms. I trust the senior women officers will all try adding chains to help make the new members of the Star Hawk feel comfortable.

The chains will be voluntary for now, but I will review making the chains and leash mandatory if the situation warrants it."

Elmwood wrapped up the meeting and tried to leave before Paul Thyssen could approach him with Charter of Conduct Office concerns.

"Captain Elmwood. I demand to speak to you immediately about exactly what transpired at this meeting." He hurried after Elmwood as he exited the room.

Morgan stepped out of the room after them.

"Then send me a message outlining your concerns. I'll review them as soon as I can, but I will not debate you here about the Charter of Conduct Laws." Elmwood never broke stride, leaving Thyssen muttering at the exit. He looked at Morgan. "Perhaps your influence with the captain will help persuade him to take the policies of the Charter of Conduct Office more seriously."

"I think he has taken due consideration of your concerns," said Morgan. "The problem is, he has an entire ship to look after, and cannot use all available time and energy working on what you see as a problem."

"As a woman, I would have thought you would want more freedom from the enforcement of wearing cuffs and chains for the women on the Star Hawk."

"And as a man, I would have thought you wouldn't pretend to know what Praxton women want to wear." She found his attitude annoying. "Mr. Thyssen, the cuffs and chains are part of the ship's uniform for women. This discussion is over with."

[18]

JANICE MADISON APPROACHED ELMWOOD. "Captain, all departments reported compliance within the parameters of the fire drill."

"Excellent." Elmwood spoke as he checked monitors in the command centre, confirming her report. He turned to her, pleased with how relaxed she had become since the first time they were introduced. "Anything else concerning the drill I should know about?"

"No, other than accounts of naked women in the hallways. It seems the safety monitors are still surprised by that event." She gave a smile. "Considering what the women uniforms cover, one would think nudity wouldn't be an issue."

"It would seem some are slower to adjust to change than others."

"Are you pointing a finger at me?" She touched her collar, a blue band with three gold rings that showed her rank. "I believe I have done well there. Besides the uniform, I wear a collar and cuffs without feeling like a slave. I even tried adding chains yesterday."

"Good point. No, I wasn't pointing a finger at you. You're doing an admirable job and not showing any concern with the uniform. You're to be commended for the change in your earlier misgivings."

"Thank you. Morgan helped me get over my anxiety. I realized if I make a big deal about the uniform, I'm not helping the rest of the crew. As an officer, I need to lead by example. And yes, that includes adding chains occasionally. Besides, I didn't want to risk that other Praxton social custom of female discipline." She gave him a grin. "I heard you have spent time on Praxton and no doubt you're familiar with that aspect."

"Yes, on Praxton." He chuckled. "On the Star Hawk, I may take a different approach to discipline." He gestured to the exit of the command centre. "Shall we go for lunch?"

"That sounds great."

The lounge for the ship's officers was fully staffed and, unlike the facilities for the unlisted crew, received table service. Elmwood had an option of having meals served at his suite, but he preferred to eat with the rest of the officers.

Madison continued to probe Elmwood with questions as they continued to the lounge. "Did you live on Praxton for an extended period?"

"No, I stayed there only on leave. There are a couple of freelancers I stay with when I'm on Praxton."

"Oh, so you have disciplined women before."

"Yes, but that's not the reason I stayed with them."

As they made their way to a table, Madison asked, "So what type of discipline did you administer?"

He laughed. "No comment."

"Someday I will have to get a few drinks into you and loosen that tongue. No comment? Then I must speculate instead."

Two other officers joined their table, Weapons Officer Kelly Walling and Nicole Redding, who had the title of Steermaster and was in charge of navigation and facilitated the hyperspace jumps. She had the final say on where and when a jump occurred.

"Speculate on what?" Redding asked. The dark-haired woman looked to have Asian heritage.

"I'm trying to speculate more on life on Praxton," Madison responded. "But the captain didn't want to discuss it."

Walling grunted. "To tell you the truth, I think there are a bunch of us who are tired of hearing about Praxton. Don't misunderstand me. I like the planet and its people just fine. But between that Charter man pestering everyone if any of his precious laws have been broken and Praxton women running around half naked, I just want to get off into space and leave this behind us."

Elmwood laughed. "So, Kelly, you think going into space will make our problems disappear?"

"Maybe not, but once we're in space, maybe everyone's focus will be on the job at hand instead of Praxton or the Charter laws."

"Good point." Elmwood nodded. "I'm looking forward to taking the Star Hawk out in three days' time."

They finished eating and Walling stood. "If you'll excuse me, I need to check on one of the weapons."

"A problem showing up?" Elmwood asked.

"No, I'm checking the weapon synchronization mode when the sensors are facing the sun. They worked perfectly when facing away from the sun, but this is a final check. They should work fine," he paused. "They better work or there'll be a lot of work to do."

"Can I go with you? I'm interested in what the weapons look like," Janice asked.

"Of course, I'll be happy to have your company."

"Have you ever lived on Praxton?" Janice asked as they walked toward a bank of elevators.

"No, not really. I've served in the Alliance forces for pretty much my adult life. I was part of the battle to free Praxton women and spent a few weeks on the ground. I didn't get to do any of the tourist things."

Janice was silent as the elevator dropped several floors. "I don't mean to argue with you, but the general view today is that the Praxton women didn't want to be freed from the perceived slavery. Praxton just has a different culture."

"I suppose that may be true. But after the conflict the Praxton women finally were allowed the right to vote, run for office and can now have financial independence. Perhaps they weren't slaves before, but they weren't free either."

"Good point. I agree that the women on Praxton are better off than before the invasion. But I've talked to many of the women from Praxton that are now on the Star Hawk. Most of them really do like having a male guardian." She held up a wrist cuff. "It's funny. I really was scared to put these cuffs and the collar on at first. But I can see the allure of wearing them. Psychologically, I feel protected, especially when I'm around men. Does that make sense to you?"

They stepped out of the elevator and walked down the wide corridor. "I suppose it does. Mind you, considering what the women wear for uniforms, perhaps they do need protection." He gave a smile. "Not that I'm complaining."

"Yes." Janice laughed. "The men must enjoy seeing women wearing the new uniforms. I tried wearing chains the other day, and I enjoyed the feel of them, kind of like decorations."

"I do admit it adds a touch of elegance to the uniform." Walling slipped a finger around the collar of his shirt. "Ah, here we are at the weapons station." He used his thumb to open the restricted access door.

Janice followed him and observed him as he checked a monitor. He then did a physical check around the black housing that held the weapon array.

"All looks good."

"That looks like a rather complicated piece of machinery."

"It can be at first glance. But in reality, it can be broken down into components, and individually all the components are rather simple. The tricky part is making sure they work together."

"Just like the people on the ship."

"Very true."

[19]

MORGAN REGAN LOOKED up as Khloe Levit hurried into the receiving line at the ship's main entrance. All officers were required to make an appearance for an unscheduled visit from the vice-president of Praxton, causing a disruption in the final preparations for launch. A chime sounded and a Praxton general marched in, leading the way for the vice-president, Terri Baxter. She stood next to Elmwood as the vice-president stopped to say a few words to some officers.

Terri Baxter wore the traditional Praxton attire for women, which included a collar and cuffs with an appropriate number of chains. Her blue skirt was shorter than the ones on the ship uniform, matching the colour of her stilettos. The cream top was thin enough to show she wore a pair of nipple clips with a chain attached between them. Her walk was slow and graceful, yet confident as she made it past the receiving line.

The blonde woman gave the officers a warm smile as she approached Morgan. Morgan was taken back by the beautiful woman. She had seen her in news reports, and knew of her rapid rise in Praxton politics, but seeing her in person gave her a new perspective of her.

"It's wonderful to see a female with the rank of first officer on this fine ship. You are serving an inspiration to other females here."

The vice-president stepped forward and looked up at the captain.

"Captain Elmwood, thank you for taking time to greet me on your extraordinary ship."

"The pleasure is all mine."

"I understand you have many issues to deal with, captain, but perhaps you can indulge me in a brief tour of the Star Hawk."

"Of course."

Morgan saw him turn to her.

"Perhaps you can accompany us. Ms. Baxter may have questions that a female officer is best qualified to answer."

Elmwood led the way, being customary for the male to be in front. Morgan conversed with Terri, with positive comments being made about the ship's uniform. After a stopping at the command centre, the weapons control station and the women's quarters, they returned to the main entrance.

"Is there anything else I can show you, Vice-president Baxter?" Elmwood asked.

"Perhaps a short meeting, just with you, to discuss a few items."

"Of course." Elmwood arranged for coffee and pastries to be sent to the captain's meeting room.

Terri stood at one end of the table, waiting for him to sit first.

Elmwood smiled as he hesitated before sitting down. "Sometimes it's hard to switch over to the Praxton culture in every aspect."

"I understand. After a while it becomes second nature. However, in your case, there is a mixture of Praxton and Alliance customs on the Star Hawk. I appreciate you have to adjust to different situations rapidly."

"Thank you for that observation."

Terri selected a blueberry turnover. "I haven't had one of these in years. On Praxton you rarely see turnovers or blueberries." She took a small bite. "Captain, I wanted to speak to you privately concerning the Star Hawk. These are strictly my views and not the official Praxton government's."

"Understood."

"When talk began of building the new Explorer line of ships, I pressed hard for Praxton to be awarded the contract. There were a number of financial reasons for wanting the new ship building facilities, but what I really wanted was for Praxton to gain a say on the future of Alliance space. As a concession, I proposed filling as much of the crew responsibilities as possible with females from Praxton. The Charter of Conduct jumped at that offer and pushed for Praxton to be given the contract. They believed that would help free the females from guardians and the submissive lifestyle on Praxton." Terri gave a hint of a smile. "Of course, the opposite may be true. The Praxton lifestyle may be allowed to spread past the planet itself."

"I believe you would like to see Praxton values reinforced on the Star Hawk." Elmwood took a drink of his coffee. He knew she didn't have direct command of him or the Star Hawk, but understood she had a powerful position on a planet with considerable influence due to Praxton's wealthy position among the Alliance worlds.

"I would. During the time of selecting the captain for the Star Hawk, I made it clear to the selection committee that Praxton would veto any candidate who wasn't sympathetic to Praxton culture. I believe you are exactly what we wanted to see in a captain, one that is familiar with Alliance world and Praxton values." She paused. "I'm sure you feel you're balancing on a tight rope at times."

"Well put. It is a situation that can have complexities at times." Elmwood took another drink of his coffee.

"The Charter of Conduct Office wants to see Praxton females become more independent, becoming more of the ideal woman in the Alliance world. I believe their philosophy is naïve. Men and women are more interdependent on each other than independent. Men and women are equally intelligent but think and reason differently. That's a positive. We need different approaches to a problem." Her voice changed, becoming stronger. "What I see as problematic in the Alliance world culture is that for women to succeed, they have to emulate male behaviour. It shouldn't be that way. Women need to be recognized for their own contributions."

"You believe women's method of accomplishing tasks should be on their own merits, and not on how a man would have done so." He nodded.

"Essentially, yes. I do not see a conflict in a woman being submissive and able to make the best decision anymore more than expecting a dominant to make the best decision every time. In the case of the Star Hawk, the Praxton style of uniform will allow the females to be more at ease and that helps to make better choices. I have fully embraced the role of a submissive, but I also have to make hard decisions for the government. They are not in conflict with each other."

"I have to say you make a convincing argument there." Elmwood grinned.

"Thank you. I would wish to ask you to consider making sure the Praxton culture is adhered to on the Star Hawk. Don't be afraid to add other refinements such as a discipline room. I can speak from experience that Praxton females require discipline occasionally."

"Thank you. I will consider your suggestions carefully."

"Thank you for your time." Terri stood. "I wish you and the Star Hawk a successful mission."

Morgan approached Elmwood in the command centre after Terri Baxter had left. "May I ask what you talked about?"

Elmwood felt his second in command should know what the conversation entailed. "She wanted me to ensure the Praxton customs were followed on the ship. She made an interesting point about decision making. Essentially, sometimes we don't pay enough attention to submissive people because they normally don't speak up. However, their decisions could be as accurate as those of a more aggressive stance. She remarked women should not be judged on how well they emulate men in the decision-making process, but if they arrive at the correct decision. I have to agree with her. When we consider promotions, we need to be aware that there is more than one way to view problems and see a solution."

"Good. I believe a woman can be submissive and still able to handle complex tasks."

"I think you're an excellent example of that."

She laughed. "Well, you have seen my submissive side."

"And your second-in-command side."

[20]

KHLOE LEVIT STEPPED past the open doorway and surveyed the common area. Several women sat around on the furniture. Most barely looked up at her entrance. She frowned. "Who's the senior female here?"

"I am," a tall, dark-skinned brunette announced. She immediately stood with her hands behind her back.

Levit looked at her name tag. "Narcel Cannith." She pointed at a garment lying on the coffee table. "What's going on here? This place looks awful. The females here don't appear to have spent much time on their appearance."

"I agree, Warrant Officer Levit. I have tried, but we have several females from Alliance worlds in this area. They don't seem to understand proper behaviour, and claim since we aren't on Praxton, they won't act like Praxton females. It is very frustrating as the females from Praxton are following their example."

Levit had heard and seen similar problems from other female quarters. At first, she blamed the senior females for not enforcing correct behaviours, but it became apparent that the problem was beyond their ability to control. "I see. Well, I believe we need to change the way this ship is run and increase your authority in this common area."

Levit headed to the location of the ship's common centre. Twenty minutes later she found Captain Elmwood briefing the communication officer, Janice Madison. She waited until they finished their conversation and requested a private meeting with him.

"Of course, come to my office." He led the way to the captain's office and sat in one of the armchairs rather than behind his desk. After she sat, he asked, "Now what's on your mind?"

"Sir, we are having a problem with the attitudes with many of the females on this ship. They are not addressing their appearance through makeup and exercise, not listening to the senior females, and usually not wearing chains and leashes when going about the ship. There are more issues, but it seems the females believe this is an Alliance ship and the Praxton culture no longer applies."

"That is discouraging to hear. Do you have any suggestions?"

"Yes, sir. We should make senior females an official promotional position so they have the means to enforce their authority. Currently, senior female is just an informal title. We have restraint holds already in the common areas, but I think we need to add a flogger for use by the senior females. I would also like to see a cage put in each common area."

"I see. You believe there's a need to increase female discipline."

"Absolutely, sir. Females, if a guardian isn't present, will misbehave, become lazy and start fighting among themselves."

"That is the traditional way of Praxton thinking."

"I admit I'm conservative in my beliefs. I believe females should be submissive to their guardians. They should strive to look their best and act properly at all times."

"I will consider what you have told me and make a decision later."

"Thank you, sir."

Levit left Elmwood, glad she had made her case to him. She hoped he would act on her suggestions, feeling otherwise her authority had little weight.

"Khloe."

She turned to sound of the weapons officer, Kelly Walling. "Hello, sir."

"Just Kelly. Where are you off to?"

"Nowhere in particular. I have some free time. Yourself?"

"I'm going to check on a weapons crew. Would you care to accompany me?"

"I would like that." She slipped the handle of her leash off her wrist and handed to him. She saw his surprised look. "It's a female Praxton custom. If I'm wearing a leash and collar, then I should allow the male to have control, Master Kelly."

"Very well." He walked down the hall toward the rear of the ship. "Are you enjoying your time on the Star Hawk so far?"

"I am, although I'm frustrated some female crew personnel are not acting properly."

"This is an unfamiliar experience for many of them, so it may take a bit for them to feel comfortable."

"How do you find the female crew working under you? Are they meeting your requirements?"

"Yes, from the reports I've seen, they've performed well."

Walling stopped to take an elevator; it dropped two floors, and they continued their walk. "May I ask if you're seeing anyone? On or off the ship."

"I'm without a guardian. That's a Praxton term for personal relationships. May I inquire if you are currently a guardian of a female?"

"No, I'm a confirmed bachelor. I like the ladies just fine. I just don't like being tied down."

"On Praxton, a male may be a guardian to more than one female."

"More than one?" Walling laughed. "That sounds like trouble to me."

They reached a weapons room and entered the secured area. At the far wall, the controls for the individual medium sized guns were mounted with a small access door to load ammunition and to do repairs. In the middle of the room, personnel occupied desks with monitors. At a side wall, supplies and tools sat on different shelves. The shelves were an open frame made of heavy gauge metal.

Levit watched Walling look uncertain with his leash end. "Just attach it to the shelving or order me to kneel on the floor and wait."

Walling looked uncomfortable as he led her to the shelving and looped the leash around on a support pole. He approached to those working at the desk, asking questions, pointing at different graphs.

Levit stood with her hands behind her back, observing him explain a portion of the graph. She noticed of the six personnel, two of them were women from Praxton, judging by their long hair and the subtle signs of their movements.

Walling returned for Levit and took her out of the weapons room. "Thanks for waiting."

"I'm glad to do so, Master Kelly."

"The women from Praxton in the weapons room weren't wearing leashes, or chains. Is that a personal choice? Or is there another Praxton rule?"

"Right now, that's a personal choice. But I would like all females to wear chains and occasionally a leash."

"What should I do if they wear a leash? How should they be treated in the weapons room?"

"If they have the end of their leash around their wrist, nothing has to be done. If they remove it from their wrist, they may hand it to the person on charge. That may be a male or female. In most cases, they would place the leash at the back of the chair. The chairs should have a hook at the back for the leash."

"Does that mean she can't leave that chair?"

"It does unless it's an emergency. If she wants to go anywhere, she must ask for an escort."

"Okay, that helps explain some Praxton social nuances to me. Anything else I may want to know?"

"Yes. If we have the same rank, you, being a male, have authority over me under Praxton rules. For example, it wouldn't be uncommon for you to join my wrist cuffs together to assert your authority over me." She smiled. "A little more control for you."

"Are you hinting I should?"

"That's your choice. But, yes, I guess I am."

Walling stopped, and Levit extended her hands toward him. He joined her wrist cuffs together. "There, how's that?"

"Much better, Master Kelly." She followed him down the corridor.

"I'm nearing the end of my shift. How about yourself?"

"I'm finished."

"Shall we go for a drink in the executive lounge?" Master Kelly asked.

"I'd like that."

The lounge was quiet, with only a few patrons. Walling placed the end of her leash on the hook at the back of her chair. "Now I know what those are for. Would you like me to uncuff your wrists now?"

She shook her head. "I can hold a glass this way."

The waitress came to take their order, and Levit and she exchanged a smile. The waitress looked to be from Praxton, wearing a complete collection of chains, including between her ankle cuffs. She walked with a graceful movement.

"I love that you're wearing ankle cuff chains," Levit commented. "Few on the ship do so."

"I do like the look of wearing chains. However, the lounge manager also insists we do. She's from Praxton and understands the importance of appearance."

"That's good to hear."

"There's a lot more to these Praxton customs than I thought." He sipped his beer as he watched her use both hands to lift her tumbler filled with a clear liquid.

"Oh, yes. For example, I can't go to the washroom without an escort because you leashed me to the back of the chair. Either you or the waitress will have to take me there."

"Interesting. Do I have any special responsibilities with you leashed?"

"You have to protect me from any danger." Levit grinned. "And if I misbehave, you need to take action by using some discipline."

"Ah, the famous Praxton discipline for females. I understand that often includes a spanking."

"Yes. It can also be a flogging, standing in a corner, or being caged."

"Now, may I ask, do you have a preference?"

"I like to receive a spanking, and occasionally I admit I do like a bit of humiliation, such as being displayed naked in restraints."

"That sounds most interesting. Do you think that social custom will be carried on the Star Hawk?

"I hope so. Females need discipline or they will misbehave."

Walling tilted his head. "Are you saying you may need discipline as well?"

"Yes." Levit giggled. "I believe I do. On Praxton, a guardian will occasionally discipline his females even if they're not doing anything wrong."

They finished their drinks and Walling escorted Levit to her suite.

"Thank you for escorting me, Master Kelly."

"I enjoyed our conversation and learned a lot more about Praxton customs." He undid her wrist cuffs and slipped the end of her leash on her wrist.

"I hope we can get together again soon."

"Yes, I look forward to it." He smiled.

[21]

"THANK YOU FOR SEEING ME, Captain Elmwood, although I would have appreciated an earlier meeting." Paul Thyssen seated himself in front of the captain's desk. The office was located as an extension of the captain's suite.

"I apologize, but timeframes are tight, and my schedule is rather full."

"Very well. However, I shall point out that the Charter of Conduct Office has the authority to intervene in matters it considers in violation of its laws. Further, denying access to the Charter of Conduct officers to remedy such offences is considered a violation. Captain, by refusing to arrange a timely meeting to address my concerns, you could be cited."

Thyssen leaned back in his chair, looking satisfied.

"Interesting information, but there isn't any official record of you wanting to speak to me on any alleged specific violation. True, you requested a meeting on several occasions, but you didn't indicate the exact nature of any deviation of the Charter of Conduct laws."

"You are merely trying to avoid addressing issues that you know full well would be of concern to the Charter of Conduct Office."

"Mr. Thyssen, I am responsible for the operation of the Star Hawk. Do not suggest that I do not take every issue concerning the safe procedure of this ship seriously. I will not entertain these vague accusations from you or anyone else." He stood. "Am I clear on this?"

Thyssen gasped, looking smaller in his chair. "I didn't mean to accuse, or imply, you of any dereliction of duties. Please, can we discuss the issues at hand?"

"Very well." Elmwood sat. "Proceed."

"I have noted that the women on this ship are treated differently than the men, which is a violation of the Charter of Conduct Laws. One issue is the uniform, which shows a great more detail of the female body than the male. Collars and cuffs are required for female crew members, while the male uniform has no such requirement. The Charter of Conduct Law requires similar, although not exactly the same, uniforms for the different genders. I am prepared to say that the uniforms for the women do not meet that criteria."

"Seriously?" Elmwood let out a long sigh. "I see nothing wrong with either uniform. The women's uniform may have less coverage, but it is within the norms of fashion on Praxton and Alliance worlds. The collar and cuffs are there because the Praxton women told us they are comfortable wearing them. They have spent their lives wearing collars and don't want to be without them. If this is your chief complaint, you have wasted our time."

Thyssen tightened his jaw. "The Charter of Conduct Laws are not to be ignored just because that is the way it *used* to be done on Praxton. Change is coming on that planet, and I would hope that the uniforms of the newest spaceship for the Alliance worlds would reflect that. I would suggest that perhaps you should consider that you have spent too much recreation time on Praxton."

"For your sake, I'm going to ignore that last accusation. Yes, change is coming to Praxton. And to the other Alliance worlds. Are you aware that the sale of collars for women on Alliance worlds has tripled since the end of the conflict between Praxton and the Alliance worlds? That means they sell more collars on Alliance worlds than on Praxton itself. Your argument against collars as part of the female uniform, I believe is moot. The women wanted the collar and cuffs, and that is the end of it." He stood. "Good day, Mr. Thyssen."

"But I have other issues."

"At this point, I don't care to hear them. Send them to me and I'll review them when I have the time."

⬛

"Captain, if you're free now, I would like you to accompany Janice and myself to look at the women's quarters. I believe it would be beneficial for you to see what they look like now. Later things may be too busy for a review of them." Khloe Levit approached Elmwood as he worked in the command centre.

He glanced at a couple of monitors, noting the series of green symbols, and returned his attention to Levit. He noticed she wore a complement of chains from her wrist cuffs to the belt around her waist, plus a leash from her collar with the end looped around her wrist. "Sure, I'd be glad to accompany you. He saw Madison standing behind her. Her chains only included a pair of chains from her collar to her wrist cuffs.

"Good. It'll be nice to show how the quarters are set up."

As they exited the control centre, Levit handed Elmwood the loop from her leash. "I believe it would be appropriate for you to hold this. It's a Praxton custom for a male to hold a leash attached to a female."

"Very well, this may be a good example to show the others we respect Praxton customs." He took the end of the leash, receiving a curious look from Madison.

Elmwood escorted Khloe and Janice to one of the women's quarters. The rooms were grouped together along a wide corridor identified as the entrance to the women's quarters. Unlike other spaceships, the men's and women's sleeping quarters were separated. Because the women from Praxton were likely to be in various states of undress, signs indicated that men were to enter the area only if invited to do so. Each of the crew's quarters were made into separate sections surrounding a common area. The corridor ran by the entrance of each grouping, which was located along the perimeter of the ship. On the interior side of the corridor were the cafeterias, lounges and exercise areas.

As soon as Elmwood entered, the women in the common area stood at attention.

"As you were. This is not an inspection, just a visit." He noted that two of the four women were wearing only panties, but their state of undress didn't surprise him. The women didn't appear to be nervous about their state of undress.

"I have mentioned to the women that they need to be aware that men will occasionally visit here." Levit smiled. "However, it seems they are rather unconcerned about being seen in a natural state."

"That is fine. Perhaps we may need to review the policy for when men visit. We don't want to cause a stampede of eager males."

"I agree." Khloe laughed. "There's also the quaint Praxton custom of touching and spanking among females."

"I believe we should ensure that the men know that they need to receive permission first before entering the quarters," Janice added.

"I agree." Elmwood glanced at the women crew members, and the subtle sign of their posture told him they viewed him as a guardian. "The onus should be on the men to ensure there isn't a problem here."

Khloe pointed to a door to one of eight private rooms for the crew. "This room is unoccupied. I don't believe you have seen a furnished suite yet."

Elmwood looked at the equally spaced doors, giving the impression the rooms were all identical inside. Between each of the doors a glass window showed the interior of a shower, except for the one next to the room they were approaching. That opaque window showed a dark surface. He entered the suite, observing the fixed closets, desk and other furniture. The bed was modified from a Praxton style, not including the indented centre that normally ran along the length of the bed. He noted a cuff attached at the end of the bed.

"I see there's the traditional ankle cuff."

"Yes, although it is the quick release type that does not require a key," Khloe replied. "We need personnel to respond quickly in case of an emergency. As a matter of safety, all restraints can be undone easily." She pointed at hooks on one wall. "Those hooks, for example, will pivot from the wall when sufficient pressure is applied."

Elmwood inspected the shower. The rectangular stall held two shower heads at opposite ends. One wall showed the black window.

"The glass can be made clear, or opaque, by whoever is using the shower. So far, most of the females have chosen the clear mode."

"I'm not surprised," Janice said. "It appears the Praxton women don't want to give up the customs of their planet. I suppose these cuffs and visible showering makes them feel like home."

"It seems the rooms are well designed." Elmwood couldn't detect from the tone of her voice how she felt about the Praxton customs on the ship. "As Janice pointed out, it has a Praxton presence to it."

They left the crew quarters and Janice commented to Elmwood. "I'm glad we took time to visit the female crew quarters. It seems they have made it more like home on Praxton."

"It would appear so. I don't mind that, and I trust they will focus on the ship's needs when we launch."

"I'm sure they will."

His communication device chirped. "Yes?"

A male voice spoke calmly. "Captain, we have an issue in the engine room that may require your intervention."

"What sort of situation do we have?"

"The engine calibration process is being delayed due to a dispute on who has priority."

"I'll be there immediately."

He spoke to Janice and Khloe. "I'm sorry, I need to go to the engine room. Apparently, there's a dispute." He held the end of Khloe's leash for a moment and passed it to Janice. "Perhaps you can escort Khloe back to the command centre."

Janice and Khloe exchanged looks. Janice spoke, "Please go ahead. We'll catch up with you later."

Elmwood took long strides down the hallway, barely acknowledging those he met. He fumed at the thought of any crew member, especially the executive officers not acting professionally. He reached the elevators and took it down to the seventh level, where he passed through the secure access doors. The enormous room housed the four main motors, plus an array of wall mounted equipment. Elmwood expected to see a dozen technicians and officers working to get the engines ready for operation. Instead, he was greeted by almost fifty officers. In the middle of the smiling group, a cake shaped in the form of the Star Hawk stood on a table.

Kelly Walling shouted, "Happy birthday, captain!"

"Very, very clever." Elmwood broke into a grin. "Here I was prepared to tear into the parties involved for a supposed disagreement and instead I walk into this."

Drinks and slices of cake were passed around. Janice and Khloe joined him, admitting their job was to provide a diversion so the party could be set up. It wouldn't do to have him check on a monitor for the engine room and see people setting things up.

Elmwood shared a drink with Morgan and determined she likely organized the surprise party. "You did a fine job putting this together."

"I had a lot of help."

"I'm sure you did." He finished his drink as Khloe came up to join them.

"Why do I have a feeling you're wanting to go back to work?" Khloe rolled her eyes upward.

"There's a lot of work to do before we launch."

"I guess we have to accept our captain is a man who takes his job seriously. We wouldn't want it any other way. I have work to do too. We're still getting transfers to the ship, and I need to make sure they all have the proper uniforms and accommodation."

"Morgan, thanks again for the surprise party. I really appreciate the time and effort you did to put this together. Now, I need to take my leave but please stay here and enjoy yourselves. There's still a lot of cake."

"I'll go with you, captain. One more drink and I won't get any work done," Khloe said.

Morgan watched Elmwood and Khloe leave. As they approached the exit doors, she saw Khloe take the end of leash from her wrist and pass it over to Elmwood.

What the hell? Is there something going on between them?

[22]

MORGAN STOOD with her fellow officers when Captain Elmwood introduced her as the first officer, weapons officer Kelly Walling, Steermaster Nicole Redding, and Alliance Worlds Diplomat Tiffany Harris, to Rear Admiral Rosetta Harley as they sat around an executive room table.

"Thank you, Captain Elmwood, it is good to meet your officers in person. The Explorer class of ships are a dramatic departure from our previous military vessels on several fronts. This is our largest and most heavily armed ship to date. It has enough armaments to engage a fleet of ships by itself, and thus we're confident in sending the Star Hawk outside of Alliance space to give presence of our resolve of ensuring the piracy and kidnapping of Alliance citizens ends.

"The second unique aspect of the Star Hawk is the large component of personnel of women from the planet Praxton. If the Star Hawk is successful in its missions, and I'm confident it will be, then credit must be shared with these women who left the confines of their planet."

Morgan didn't expect Harley to make a political statement. She did know a lot of people were curious how well the women from Praxton would do on a military ship.

"Well put, Rear Admiral Harley," said Elmwood. "The Star Hawk is poised to make history and it will be done with a combination of personnel from diverse backgrounds. I assure you we won't disappoint you by our efforts and results."

"That is good to hear. I want to outline, in broad terms, what is expected of the Star Hawk during its missions to worlds outside the sphere of Alliance Worlds. First, the intent when entering rebel territory is one of diplomacy. We want to start positive communications with these worlds, and give them an opportunity to avoid being isolated from the Alliance worlds. While the Star Hawk has more than sufficient weapons to counter attacks, the preference must be one of restraint.

"One thing we have learned from Praxton is that having overwhelming military strength is not a guarantee the population will accept your victory." Harley paused, acknowledging the difficulties Praxton has given the rest of the Alliance worlds. "That being said, we will not back away from a military attack. We expect the Star Hawk to defend herself, and to ensure that the enemy vessels understand we will be victorious in any confrontation.

"It is paramount that we establish an understanding with the rebel worlds without initiating a war. I understand these are difficult conditions to adhere to, but we need to proceed with re-establishing the Alliance world's influence without undue military deployment.

"Are there any questions?"

Morgan watched as Elmwood looked at the frozen lips of his officers.

"I believe the direction has been made clear to us," said Elmwood. "We understand the importance of what we need to do on our missions."

"Excellent. I know the Star Hawk will not let us down."

———

"I have to say Harley doesn't sound like she is tolerant of failure," Morgan commented after the Rear Admiral had left the ship.

"Believe me, when we move into rebel territory, we don't want to have any failures either," Elmwood replied. They shared a drink in the officers' lounge with Janice Madison and Kelly Walling.

Walling added, "I would rather blast a hole in an enemy ship, and say we failed, then to risk having the Star Hawk destroyed."

"Good grief, didn't you hear what the rear admiral said? We can defend ourselves, but we better not go overboard in fighting. This is a diplomatic mission," Janice responded.

"Tell that to the enemy wanting to blow us up." Walling threw back his straight whisky.

"Really, you need to understand *the enemy* only wants to defend their planet from an invasion. Try talking first and shooting second." Janice rolled her eyes upward.

"When the fire fight starts between us and your friends who only want peace, you'll be glad we have the bigger guns." Walling signaled the server for another round of drinks.

"As if bigger guns solve everything." Janice shook her head.

Morgan leaned over and whispered in Janice's ear. "If we were on Praxton chances are Master Kelly would put you over his knee and give you a good, hard spanking."

Janice was silent for a moment, smiled, and whispered back, "Interesting thought. I wonder how big his gun is?"

Morgan giggled.

Walling looked annoyed at the whispered comments and grunted, "When we get in a damn battle, perhaps you'll reconsider your comments."

"All right, I see your point." Janice licked her lips. "I didn't mean to cause an argument between us. I respect your position."

Elmwood watched and listened to the argument deescalate, noticing whatever Morgan whispered to Madison caused a change in her disposition.

Walling relaxed back into his chair. "I guess I overreacted. I take the defences of Star Hawk very seriously. I apologize for my strong words."

"It's good to see we have passionate people on the Star Hawk, and I'm glad to see we can accept other positions." As Elmwood spoke, he looked at each of the other officers. "Now that our differences have been settled, let's move on to lighter subjects, such as the reason Janice has a tattoo of a dragon on her left leg."

"I wasn't sure anyone had seen it, although this skirt is pretty short. The dragon is from a time I spent in Japan on Earth. I have a few stories about my experiences there, but that's for another time."

"Are you sure? We could use a change in conversation," Elmwood prodded her.

"No." Janice laughed. "I'd need a couple more drinks first."

"Fair enough." Elmwood stood. "I need to check on few things before I call it a night."

Morgan watched him leave and quickly stood. "I think I better go, too. I'll catch you guys later."

Janice looked at the departing Morgan and Elmwood. "Well, I don't need to turn in yet. I hope you're not planning to leave right away. I hate drinking alone."

Walling grinned. "How about another round of drinks, and you can tell me a story about Japan?"

"Okay, I'll tell you this story, but you can't repeat it to anyone. I was in Japan for almost an Earth year. I really liked their traditions and wanted to explore as much as I could of their nature." She took another drink. "I wanted to have a tattoo. A real ink one, not one of those that fade away after a couple of years. I searched for this artist that could draw this dragon I wanted. I found him, but he was reluctant to do the tattoo."

"Why didn't he want to?"

"He believed too many people didn't appreciate his art, and some even wanted the tattoo removed later. If he agreed to ink a tattoo, it would be of a dragon, and he wanted it on forever, therefore, it must be carefully chosen. So, this artist asked me to prove I wanted this tattoo by agreeing to be tied up in this ancient Japanese rope bondage. I think he called it shibari."

"Did you agree to this rope tying?"

Janice giggled. "I have the tattoo, don't I?"

"I have yet to see this tattoo."

"That's true. Perhaps later."

"Tell me more about this rope tying."

"I was naked, and the rope circled around me everywhere. My arms were tied behind my back at first, and I was suspended by all this rope. When I say it went everywhere, I mean *everywhere*. He changed the position of the rope several times and had my arms and legs held in different ways. It was a very erotic experience. Then he finally agreed to do the tattoo."

"That sounds very interesting."

"Thank you, Master Kelly." Janice briefly looked down before lifting her head and meeting his gaze.

"I want to see this tattoo even more now." He tossed back his whisky and signalled for another round from the server.

"It is very high up on my leg, Master Kelly. I would be willing to show it to you privately."

"I see. I would like that very much."

The server brought the drinks and Janice carefully took a drink.

He watched as she consumed her drink. Kelly finished his whisky. "Janice, as much as I would like to continue our conversation and see your tattoo, I do not believe this is the time for it. You and I both have consumed a fair bit of alcohol. I do not want to be thought of as taking advantage of the situation." He stood. "However, I would be honoured to escort you back to your quarters."

"Thank you, Master Kelly."

Janice felt his big hand on her arm as he led her out of the lounge. "I'm sorry, Master Kelly, if this is making it difficult for you."

"Not at all. I shall bid you good night, and perhaps I can have a look at your dragon tattoo next time." They reached her room and Walling stood at the edge of the doorway.

Janice was sorry to see him leave but saw the nervousness he displayed. "Thank you for walking me to my suite." She reached up and kissed him on the cheek.

"My pleasure. We will see you in the morning." He stepped backward to the door, looking unsure on what to do next before walking away.

After he left, Janice sighed. *I can't hint much more than that.*

[23]

NARCEL CANNITH GAVE A THIN SMILE, clearly relishing her new status. She addressed the seven women seated around in the common area. As the senior female, she was in charge of her unit, besides her regular position in supply management.

"I assume everyone here understands the new status of senior females. Captain Elmwood has agreed that we need to improve the behaviour of females. For those who ignored my suggestions earlier, understand there will now be consequences. I will not be receptive to any complaints concerning what is fair and not fair." She moved around the common area, looking at the nervous faces. "There are new rules to follow as of now. One, no one shall wear shoes in the common area. Females will carry their shoes to their rooms upon entering the common area. All females will sleep in the nude and wear ankle cuffs at night. Your room will be kept tidy and clean, and I will do inspections to ensure compliance. I expect a better attitude by everyone concerning exercise, applying makeup and wearing appropriate chains and jewellery." She pointed a finger at an athletic-looking redhead. "Teela Mezcal. You are an Alliance female who thought she could ignore my requests. These aren't requests anymore. Do you understand what's going to happen to you?"

"I think so," Teela replied in a quiet voice.

"You actually have no idea." Narcel smirked. "Pay attention everyone. Starting tomorrow morning, I expect a *much* better effort made in making yourself presentable."

Teela frowned as she made her way to her bedroom.

"Teela."

"Yes, Ms. Narcel."

"I want you to be ready early tomorrow morning. I will be escorting you by a leash to work."

Teela nodded. She closed her door and reflected; *I made an enemy with Narcel. Not good. Not good at all.* She undressed for bed and reluctantly attached the ankle cuff for the first time. She closed her eyes. *Damn.*

Her door opened and Narcel stepped inside her room. Teela didn't react when her blanket was removed, and the ankle cuff inspected.

"Lucky for you you remembered to add the ankle cuff." Narcel looked at the naked form lying on the bed. "I'll see you in the morning."

━━━

Teela woke up earlier than normal. She undid her ankle cuff, climbed out of bed, yawned and prepared for the day. After her shower, she took extra time to apply her makeup, following the Praxton style to add colour on her eyelids. She put on her uniform, adding the cuffs and collar. For the first time since she arrived on the ship, Teela added a chain between her wrist cuffs. Finally, she attached a leash to her collar, slipping the end strap around her left wrist.

The viewscreen showed a non-smiling woman of average height and slightly higher than average weight. The shoulder-length red, wavy hair outlined a pretty face. She was getting more comfortable with the revealing nature of the uniform, although she still didn't like how her breasts moved under the lightweight fabric. *It seems so obvious I'm not wearing a bra. Although none of the other women wear any, and I guess they don't draw extra attention.* She left her room and saw Narcel waiting for her, her hands on her hips.

She stared at Teela for several seconds before speaking. "That's a better effort in preparing for the day. However, when you took your shower this morning, you kept the outside wall dark. I prefer it to be transparent so you are visible showering in the morning. I also want you to add nipple jewellery occasionally in the future."

"Yes, Ms. Narcel."

"Put your shoes on. I'll escort you to your workstation." Narcel took the leash strap from Teela and led her out to the hallway.

Teela walked in silence, noticing the slower pace all women walked in the Star Hawk. She expected a few stares at being escorted by a leash but didn't receive undue attention. There were two other women being led with leashes, making her feel less conspicuous. She recalled studying the Praxton culture before accepting a position on the Star Hawk, but the reality of it applied to herself was something she now had to get used to.

The wearing of a collar, cuffs, revealing clothes and being submissive to males didn't cause her too much concern. What she hadn't expected was the hierarchy nature of the female group she was in, and the social rules of how a female was supposed to act. She resisted the senior female telling her what to do and how to behave.

"Ms. Narcel, I am sorry for any distress I have caused you."

"Your apology is accepted, but it will not deter me from disciplining you. I will make you behave as a proper female should. Someday, you may even thank me for teaching you this."

They arrived at Teela's work area, a room with six workstations to monitor incoming signals from the array of sensors on the outside of the ship. Narcel approached the shift leader, a dark-skinned woman.

"Corporal Karlson, Teela is required to be on a leash. Please ensure she follows the proper procedure. I will pick her up at the end of her shift."

"Of course." Karlson smiled, showing off a pleasant disposition. She took the leash lead. "Come with me, Teela."

Teela sighed as she walked to her workstation. She hooked the end of the leash at the back of the chair.

"Remember, you may not leave your station without an escort."

Teela nodded and began her work. *Great, I can't even go pee without an escort.*

———

"Coffee break time."

Teela looked up, seeing a tall, dark-haired male. She recognized him as Mitch Gallow.

"I've been assigned to be your escort today." He took the end of her leash.

"Okay. This is rather embarrassing." She stood.

"It could be a lot worse. Believe me, I spent two years on Praxton. Having a leash attached is nothing."

"Maybe to you." She followed him to a dining room across the hall that served as a rest area for the ship's personnel who were in the area. She sat at a table, accepting Gallow's offer to get her a coffee and a pastry.

"Thanks." She took a sip of her coffee. "You said you lived on Praxton for two years?"

"I was with the Alliance Forces during the conflict with Praxton. After the war ended, I stayed with a peace keeping contingent. It was a good experience."

"Does that mean you lived the Praxton lifestyle?"

"No, we lived separate from the general population. I made a few friends on Praxton and occasionally visited them in their homes. I observed their culture, and overall, it impressed me how well everyone got along."

"It seems the men have all the advantage on Praxton. Don't the women get annoyed at having to share a man and always obey him?"

"I guess that happens, but all the women I met appeared to be content. They were relaxed, not appearing stressed at all."

"Did you think of staying on Praxton to live?

"It was tempting." He gave a grin. "But a male on Praxton has to provide for all women living in the household. If there are any problems, he has to take care of them."

"Yes, the famous discipline of women on Praxton. That seems so backward."

"It works for them." He stood. "Time to return to work."

Teela continued her work, comparing the readouts on her monitor to expected values. Her excellence at doing the measurements was the reason for her invitation to apply at the Star Hawk. With apprehension, she took the step to the new spaceship, believing it would help advance her career. She was focused on her work when Gallow interrupted her for lunch.

"Time to eat."

"I guess it is." She added, "Master Mitch."

Once more he escorted her to the dining room. She was grateful when he chose a secluded table, not wanting to explain to her co-workers why she was on a leash. He went to the front counter and picked up the food for their table.

She ate her salad and commented his soup and sandwich looked better.

"I didn't think I was that hungry, but that looks tasty."

"It's pretty good. Want me to get you a soup?" He started to rise, prepared to go to the order counter.

"No, I'm fine with just the salad. Thank you, though."

"How long have you been in the forces?" Mitch asked.

"Just over five years. Previous to that I worked on passenger ships. I like the forces better. There's more urgency in everything we do."

"Were you on the patrol division?"

"Yes, trying to keep the rebel ships from attacking our transport and passenger ships," she responded.

"Is that why you applied to work on the Star Hawk? So we can enforce the boundaries better?"

"Definitely that's one reason. This is a new ship with new technologies. Plus, I received an invitation to apply. They wanted more experienced women for the Star Hawk."

"Yes, I heard the Star Hawk is mandated to have a large contingent of women on the ship, but there aren't enough experienced Praxton personnel to choose from. Were you worried about the Praxton environment on the ship? Some Alliance women are shocked by how Praxton women are treated."

"It didn't bother me at the time. I thought the women's uniform was different from what I was used to wearing, but that wasn't a big deal. I've spent time on worlds where women can walk around topless without anyone looking twice. I've worn collars before. Like most Alliance women, I've got a couple of collars I would wear occasionally. I even have a pair of wrist cuffs. They're just fashion accessories as far as I was concerned. What I didn't comprehend at the time was how women on the Star Hawk have to act, even off duty. I said a couple of nasty things to the senior female when she told me how to sit and walk. Now I'm in trouble." She touched her leash.

"Have you tried apologizing to her?"

"Yeah, she accepted it, but told me I was still going to be punished."

"I hope it won't be too harsh."

"Me too. I've learned not to argue with her about anything."

———

Corporal Karlson approached Teela after she returned from her second coffee break. "Teela, I've been reviewing your work today. You have done a fine job in isolating signals from the ambient noise."

"Thank you."

She placed a hand on her shoulder. "You appeared very stressed when you arrived for your shift. Despite that, you did first rate work. I will mention this to Senior Female Cannith, and request she relax conditions on you. I don't like seeing anyone looking as worried as you when they are at work."

Teela's shift ended, and she waited at her station, knowing she couldn't leave until Narcel arrived. It surprised her when Gallow came by.

"Come on. Let's go to the dining room and wait. You look uncomfortable just sitting here."

"Thank you, Master Mitch." She followed him out of the room after he informed Karlson where they were going.

"That's a good plan. The next shift will require her station."

"Thanks." Teela was glad Mitch thought of taking her to the dining room. "Waiting here is less awkward."

"No problem. After your probation is over with, maybe we can get together for a drink."

"Sure, I'd like that." She held up the leash. "It'll be nice to go around without this."

"I think it's part of your charm." He laughed.

"Oh, you would." Teela grinned. "I think you were on Praxton too long."

When Narcel arrived, she found Teela and Mitch enjoying their conversation.

"Okay, Teela. Time to return to your room. Thank you for looking after her, Master Mitch."

Teela followed Narcel back to the women's quarters. "Ms. Narcel, is it possible for me to go out for drinks with Master Mitch soon?"

"Perhaps in a few days. You need to be properly trained first. Your discipline is far from over. Depending on your attitude, I may grant you permission to go out socially."

Teela frowned but didn't dare say anything in return.

All the women looked up at Narcel and Teela as they returned to the common area.

"Teela, go to your room and remove your top. Then return here."

"Yes, Ms. Narcel."

Teela quietly carried her shoes to her room and removed her top. *Damn bitch.* When she returned, she saw Narcel point to the floor next to the chair where she sat. The chair was at the end of the seating arrangements and Teela kneeled on the floor at the outside edge.

"Back straight. Hands should be on your lap or held behind your back. Knees must be a fist apart."

Teela shifted position to comply. Her leash dangled from her neck to the floor.

Narcel raised her voice. "I will check for compliance on a number of issues. First, I expect everyone to spend more time in getting ready in the morning and looking presentable. All of you will make better use of the supplied chains. I don't like seeing wrist cuffs without chains attached. You can order breast and nipple jewellery from the ship's stores. I wish to see more use of those. I have checked the records of the exercise area, and I'm disappointed in the lack of attention given to physical exercise. That will change. If anyone is not exercising on a regular schedule, then there will be consequences."

Teela heard only silence, but the look on the faces of the other women told her none were happy with the lecture. The attention gradually returned to the viewing screen highlighting celebrities and new upcoming shows. She felt Narcel brush her hair away from her face and give a short stroke along her head. *Maybe she's starting to forgive me. That better not be an attempt to seduce me. She's the last woman I'd go to bed with and I'd go to bed with a woman only after all the men are gone.* She watched the news feed, promoting a new program featuring music, a political satire show, and a breaking story on a celebrity breakup. None of it seemed important when she thought of her own situation.

Teela observed two other women sitting next to each other on a couch. Tess, a pretty brunette, occasionally rested a hand on Julia's lap. After a few seconds, Julia would brush the hand away. Julia, a petite redhead, appeared comfortable wearing the Praxton style of uniform. She was one of the few women who did wear chains and spend time in the morning getting ready. Tess on the other hand looked to be an Alliance woman who was still adjusting to the nuances of the Praxton style of dress. The action of touching and rejecting repeated itself several times, with the hand on the lap remaining longer each time. By the end of the news video, the hand remained on the lap.

"Okay, Teela, let's go for dinner."

"I don't have my top on."

"You need to get used to being undressed in front of others."

Teela grimaced.

"I recommend that you obtain nipple clips and other fasteners. As far as exercise is concerned, I have enrolled you in a class of fille d'affichage."

"Fille d'affichage?"

"It means female on display. It is a special type of self bondage using strips of cloth. Loose cloth is tied to a horizontal frame the size of a bed, and a nude female wraps and unwraps the cloth around her limbs. Experts twist around to different positions. It takes endurance and a good core strength to do this. I think you may enjoy it."

Don't I get a say in this? "I don't know if I'd be any good at this sort of thing."

"Perhaps you'll surprise yourself. Regardless, this is to ensure you are getting proper exercise, and not merely going to the recreation area to socialize with males. You will start tomorrow after dinner."

The dining room was reserved for women only, and Teela didn't feel too self-conscious on her state of undress. There were two other women topless, but both were wearing nipple jewellery. *Okay, I need to get some of those. I may be forced to be topless more than I like with Narcel in charge.*

After dinner, Teela walked with Narcel back to the common area for her group. She saw Tess take Julia's hand as they strolled away from the common area. Julia would break free of the handholding briefly, only for Tess to reach out moments later and hold it again. *Tess is out to seduce Julia.*

Teela kneeled on the floor in front of Narcel when she sat on the couch. She watched the viewscreen but didn't have much interest in the movie. *Tomorrow's another day. At least I get to see Mitch.*

The other women came back, some going directly to their room. Julia pushed away at Tess, resisting her attempt for a kiss. Instead, they sat close together and engaged in whispered conversation.

Teela yawned and decided to go to bed. After she had attached her ankle cuff. she rolled over on her stomach. She wasn't surprised Narcel came in to inspect the ankle cuff but didn't expect the two quick smacks on her ass.

"Remember, get up early enough to put on makeup and get dressed properly."

"Yes, Ms. Narcel." *Now why couldn't that have been Mitch giving my ass a smack instead?*

[24]

KELLY WALLING JOINED Khloe Levit at the executive lounge, acknowledging the captain and Morgan Regan sitting at the table.

"You were working late again," Elmwood stated. "We've already had a couple of drinks."

"It couldn't be helped. One of the medium-sized guns was giving a false indication it required servicing. It was a program error, and I wanted to make sure it was just an isolated incident."

The conversation changed to other topics, including the improved behaviour of the female crew personnel.

Elmwood suggested a lot had to do with Khloe's suggestion on empowering the senior females. "You seemed to have identified the problem and a solution very well."

"Thank you, Master Julius."

"The Praxton custom of addressing males formally stays strong." Wailing laughed.

"On Praxton, if a female fails to use the phrase master in identifying a male in a public place, she could find herself over his knee in a hurry." Khloe grinned. "Some females may enjoy that."

After another round of drinks, Elmwood and Morgan bided the others goodnight.

"I'll stay with you." Khloe sipped her drink. "A man shouldn't drink alone."

"Thank you, but you shouldn't feel obligated to do so."

"It's no obligation, Master Kelly. I like to spend time with you."

After they finished the drinks, Walling offered to walk her back to her suite.

"That would be nice. Perhaps you can come into my unit for a drink or a coffee." She stood and passed the end of her leash to him.

He took the leash handle, asking, "Do you wish to have your wrist cuffs joined again like last time?"

"That is your decision, Master Kelly." She held her wrists in front of her. "You could join them behind my back instead if you prefer."

"If that's what you prefer, then let's do that." He waited as she turned around, holding her wrists together. He joined the latch between the cuffs.

Khloe followed Walling out of the lounge. "Thank you for taking care of me, Master Kelly."

Walling walked her to her suite. "I enjoy learning about the Praxton culture, but I'm a conservative man regarding relationships."

"Does that mean you wish to avoid intimacy? That's fine. I enjoy being with you, regardless."

They reached her suite and Khloe had to twist around to use her thumb to open her door. She laughed. "Maybe I need to add voice or face recognition for entry for situations like this. Will you come in for a refreshment?"

"I would. Just for a coffee, mind you."

Khloe entered her suite and immediately removed her shoes. "You, as a male, should leave your boots on. Females should be barefoot inside homes."

"Oh. Another odd Praxton custom." He undid her wrist cuffs. "I don't want to see you try to serve coffee with your wrists cuffed behind your back."

"Thank you, Master Kelly. Please relax in the living room. The armchair is normally used only by males."

"I see." He walked into the living room, noticing wall hooks along one wall and a tall cage set in a corner. The cage with twin semi-circular doors when closed could hold a person captive. He raised his eyebrows. *So this is a typical Praxton style of quarters.* He sat in the higher than normal armchair and looked around. He saw circular stairs, leading to a second level like his own suite. Unlike his suite, he could see through the clear wall into the bedroom and shower.

"Your coffee, Master Kelly. I recall that you take it with a small amount of cream." She held the mug in front of her, and he accepted it with thanks. She placed a cushion on the floor in front of him and kneeled.

"Don't you wish to sit too? I can move to the couch."

"Oh, no, Master Kelly. You are my guest. On Praxton, until one is familiar with the male, a female should defer to his status." She smiled sweetly and took a drink from her own mug.

I won't ask what she means by familiarity. I suspect that means being in bed with him. "Correct me if I'm wrong, but Khloe isn't a Praxton name. Were you born on an Alliance world?"

"You are correct. I was born on Costair. When I was two years old, my parents moved to Praxton. So, while I was given an Alliance name, my upbringing was entirely Praxton."

"You seem to promote Praxton values very strongly."

"Yes, I do. I have been to other worlds, and I have to say I appreciate Praxton more each time I come back."

"In what way?"

"It isn't easy to explain unless you understand women."

"I truly do not." He laughed.

She bit her lower lip for a moment. "Gene therapy allows for men and women to correct body flaws. Even for mental issues. It's expensive on most worlds, but many people have gene therapy done. On Praxton, gene therapy is rather inexpensive. The government doesn't tax gene therapy, where on Alliance worlds they want to restrict its use by high taxes. So, on Praxton all women can enhance their looks as much as they want, within reason. Master Kelly, women want to be thought of as being pretty. If we are pretty, we want to show it off."

"Fair enough. I guess in the same vein men want to be big and strong."

"True. On Praxton I can wear as much or as little as I want. I can show off my body. I can walk around practically naked. As long as I have my collar on, it means I have a guardian, and no one will bother me. I feel protected. On Alliance worlds, even if I wear normal clothes, males will often harass me. There's unwanted intrusion in my space and comments. I don't mind them staring, but I don't appreciate their attitude. On Praxton, males are supposed to protect females. On Alliance worlds, males don't understand boundaries. My collar doesn't always protect me there."

"That is sad to hear."

"Master Kelly, I have a confession to make. I think of you as my guardian. I have a sense of being very safe with you around."

"Oh, well, I don't know…"

"I'm sorry. I don't mean to embarrass you. I'm not asking you to be my guardian. I just mean I feel comfortable when you're around. How did you end up being the weapons officer, Master Kelly? I noticed you have a strong opinion on the rebel worlds."

He nodded. "I will make a long story short. Many years ago, I was a young lad travelling with my parents and my sister to New Cordinia. My mother was a professor and was offered a position of dean in a university there. We decided to move everything we had and start a new life on that planet. My sister was an older, beautiful young woman, and she was always teasing me, making my life miserable." He stopped speaking for a moment, and when he resumed, his voice sounded strained. "Pirates attacked our ship. They raided the storage area for any valuables, and then they took all the passengers they thought they could make into slaves. Mostly young women and girls. They took my sister. She screamed for help. They shot my father when he tried to rescue her from their clutches. Fortunately, he survived." He remained quiet, taking a drink of his coffee.

"I'm so sorry for you, Master Kelly."

"It's in the past now. But my hate for pirates and the rebel worlds that harbour them has never gone away. That is why I joined the Alliance forces and found my way onto the Star Hawk. I'm looking for justice."

"What is your sister's name?"

He smiled. "Ayana."

Khloe stood and took his empty mug. "Another coffee, Master Kelly?"

"No, I think I've had enough coffee today."

"Then before you go, may I offer you a small whisky? I would like to toast to our friendship and to our journey on the Star Hawk."

He nodded, and she returned with two short tumblers.

She kneeled in front of him again. "To our time together. To your lost family. To hope we can right the wrongs of the past."

"Well said." He finished his whisky in one long drink. He stood. "I best be going."

She met him at the door. "Master Kelly, we do not know what happened to Ayana after the pirates took her. But there's nothing wrong with hoping she is all right." She leaned forward, standing on her toes and kissing him on his cheek.

"Good night, Khloe. Thank you for your hospitality and those thoughts."

She watched him walk away. *A strong man with a soft heart, and with demons chasing him.*

[25]

Captain Elmwood stood as the nervous cadet, Sonya Rolison, level two, read out the report of the latest results of a local safety drill.

"Those grades are barely within acceptable parameters." He frowned. "I want the tests done again until we reach superior results. Safety is to be taken seriously, and this report tells me we have more work to do."

"Yes, sir." The cadet looked uncertain what to do next.

"Reschedule the exercise for tomorrow morning at oh eight hundred." Elmwood refrained from smiling at the discomfort the cadet was showing, not wanting her to feel worse. "Report the results to me at eleven hundred. You are dismissed."

"Yes, sir." She turned and left after pivoting on her shoe in one motion.

He sat and checked other reports on a computer monitor. He was pleased with the various tests on the Star Hawk so far. A weapons test passed, but he had reservations on the test as the weapons could not be brought fully online. They were still docked at the space station and were prohibited from bringing any weapon into firing position.

"Hi, Captain Elmwood."

He looked up at Morgan Regan, his First Officer. "Hello yourself. Captain Elmwood is rather formal." He gave her a grin.

"Yes, well, I could have used Master Julius, which is also a proper salutation from a Praxton female. There has been quite a change on the behaviour on the ship since your announcement of using Praxton values." Morgan paused and continued speaking. "If I fail to follow the etiquette of addressing a male on this ship, it would set a poor example for the other members of the crew. It could mean you could discipline me on the spot. I decided I should avoid a spanking at this time."

"The Star Hawk is due to leave port in two days." Elmwood considered her choice of words, 'at this time.' "We still need to do a few more tests regarding our capabilities."

"We have a new contractor scheduled to start today." Morgan nodded. "As you know, Diana Adoria has been given the position of Food and Beverage Manager. While she isn't of officer status since she is a civilian, I believe she should work with the executive officers."

"That makes sense. She is controlling an important position."

"I think we should invite her to have dinner with the other officers today." Morgan clasped her hands behind her back.

"Agreed. Could you extend an invitation to her? Dinner can be in my quarters at nineteen hundred. Try to ensure the other officers will be there as well."

"I will do so, Master Julius."

The entrance to the Star Hawk caused Diana to stop and stare. She felt like she had just stepped into the lobby of a large office building. Beyond where she stood, the open foyer showed where hallways stretched in several directions and the decks of several floors towered above her. Dozens of people moved past her, all focused on the task before them. Earlier that morning, she had her belongings sent to the Star Hawk. That included new clothes and accessories she purchased to fit in with the Praxton style. She decided it would be best if she showed up on the Star Hawk wearing one of her new outfits, which consisted of a lightly patterned sleeveless top, a navy-blue skirt and yellow high heels. She felt a surge of excitement when she added a collar, ankle and wrist cuffs. Thin chains joined the collar to her wrist cuffs. A voice brought her attention to a woman walking toward her.

"Hi, you must be Diana Adoria. I'm Khloe Levit. I'll show you to your room and help you get orientated on the Star Hawk."

"Thank you. I'm a little overwhelmed by its size."

"It's a huge ship," Khloe agreed. "There's a simple coding system that you can use to tell you where you are, and you'll find your way around here soon enough. If you get lost, the ship's AI is always available to help."

Khloe led the way to an elevator and down a hallway to Diana's suite. Diana noticed Khloe strolled with a gentle sway at her hips. As they passed other female crew members, she noticed all of them walked slowly, suspecting it was the expectation for women to do so. The door to her suite opened to Diana's thumb touch, having been pre-programmed for her.

"This looks nice."

The interior showed a living room, and a combined kitchen and dining room. At the edge of the living room and behind a couch, a staircase led to a second level. Diana walked inside.

"You should remove your shoes," Khloe added to Diana's surprised expression. "It's a Praxton custom. Men wear boots or shoes inside, and women are barefoot."

Diana nodded and removed her shoes. "I guess I have a few Praxton customs to learn."

"There are a number of them. I'll help you with them."

"Thank you." Diana looked around the living room, noticing several hooks on the wall. She peered at them.

"Those are for restraints. They can be attached to your cuffs to hold you in position."

Position for what? She fingered one of her wrist cuffs where a clip allowed for joining to another device. "I will be living by myself."

"I know. Perhaps that will change later. Anyway, it is a standard feature of Praxton rooms."

Diana toured the kitchen and dining room, finding them practical and with the usual features. The kitchen appliances, she discovered, offered hope she could experiment with cooking. A small washroom was located behind the kitchen.

"We gave you an upgraded kitchen since you are in charge of the Star Hawk's food."

"Now all I need is food to cook with." Diana nodded her approval of the appliances.

"You can order the food supplies you want to be delivered to your suite." Khloe agreed. "We decided that whatever we picked for you would likely be more often wrong than right."

"You're likely correct there." Diana smiled as she continued her tour, returning to the living room. Looking up, she saw the second level had a glass wall that allowed her to see into a bedroom and a shower. Diana climbed the stairs and a short walkway took her into the bedroom.

"This is a nice size bedroom." She pointed at the wall. "More hooks for restraints?"

"Standard features for a Praxton bedroom. The hooks, to conform to the ship's safety code, will come off if you apply a sufficient force to them. It wouldn't do to be held helpless during an actual emergency. The bed has restraint holds at each corner plus the sides. Of course, it includes ankle cuffs attached to chains." She lifted a cuff from the foot of the bed with a length of chain trailing from it.

"Really? Am I expected to wear that to bed?"

"Yes. All females sleep nude and wear an ankle cuff to bed."

"What if I don't?"

"You will be disciplined." Khloe gave a soft smile. "I know Praxton has a lot of quirky customs, but you will find your time on the Star Hawk will go much easier if you try to follow them and keep an open mind about them."

"Okay. I'll try. How will you know if I wear the ankle cuff or not?"

"I'll ask you. I don't believe you would lie to me."

"Trapped by my honesty." Diana laughed. She looked around the bedroom, noting the closets had her clothes already hung up. She looked at the glass wall that gave her a view of the living room below and saw hooks embedded in the clear surface. *Let me see. Restrained to the glass wall so others in the living room can see me. Now that's an interesting concept for entertaining guests.* The bedroom had a separate room containing a toilet and sink, plus a second room that had a shower. The shower, like the bedroom, had a clear wall that made anyone showering visible to the room below. "Do the walls have to stay clear?"

"The bedroom wall can be set to opaque, or various shades to clear."

"And the shower?"

"Males can set it to opaque. Females must leave it clear." Khloe continued. "Female nudity is something you need to get used to."

"I suppose I'll have to. Is there anything else I should know about Praxton customs?"

"There are few things. One important detail is when you are addressing males. If you are not using their formal title or designation, you use the term master and then their name. Always."

"Okay. I'll try to remember that."

"If you fail to address a male properly, that can lead to a very rapid disciplinary action."

Diana nodded.

"I'll show you where your workstation is and then leave you to do exploring of your own."

A short walk took them to her workstation. Rather than a simple desk, it featured a large office with a curved window that overlooked the food and beverage assembly factory a half-floor below. Her office contained several monitors, allowing her to oversee the operations below both visually and with graphs. The office had a wall made with clear glass that showed the hallway past her office.

Diana couldn't resist and sat in front of a monitors. She used both voice and a keyboard to investigate a common beverage.

"How do you find the coffee here on the ship?"

"It's okay." Khloe shrugged. "Nothing to get excited about."

"Caffeine is a purine alkaloid, and in its natural form has over a thousand chemicals in it. The coffee on the Star Hawk has two hundred and forty-seven. That makes for a rather bland cup of coffee. The formula I use has eight hundred and nineteen. I think you'll notice a distinct improvement with the coffee."

"That would be welcome. We need good coffee to make it through the day."

"I think I'm going to have fun redoing the food and beverages."

"Can you come up with a chardonnay that doesn't taste like a piece of wood soaked in butter?"

"Oh yes. I'm very good at wine." Diana didn't mention she held several patents on wine. Some of her formulas had become the standard for several varietal.

"I think we're going to be very good friends."

———

Diana walked around the ship by herself, using the electronic voice in her earpiece to guide her through the maze of hallways and different levels. She briefly stopped at a recreation area, impressed with the various areas devoted for different exercises. Besides the usual gym equipment, there were classes available for different activities. She noted the women were wearing outfits that showed off their bodies. They didn't seem to mind men were exercising in the same area. Diana continued her journey and came across two small theatres devoted to live performances. The empty seats rose at an angle and made a semi-circle around a raised stage.

Impressed with the facilities she had seen so far, Diana decided it was time for lunch. Her electronic guide directed her to the executive lounge, and she was pleased she had already been given permission to make use of it. The spacious lounge had tables set well apart from each other. One side had a large viewscreen, currently blank, and the opposite wall featured a bar with seating in front. A third wall featured a view of the outside. Because they were still docked at the space station, various spacecraft drifted by. Near the edge of the view part of Praxton could be seen, the red planet giving a perspective of the vast space beyond.

Diana sat at one of the tables. There were only a few other officers in the lounge, and she observed them. She touched the table surface and a three-dimensional menu appeared. She scanned through most of the menu, wondering how well each choice approximated the real dish. Most food items were artificial, made up with various chemicals that looked, had the texture, and hopefully the flavour of the genuine item.

She tapped on her selection and waited. She suspected the coffee would be delivered first, and she would question the server on the food and their quality.

The server wore the ship's uniform with her collar showing her rank of cadet level one, the lowest rank of the cadets. She carried a coffee mug on a small tray.

"Hi, I'm Tofina. Your order was for black coffee, but I can bring you cream and sweetener if you wish."

"No, black is what I want. I'm Diana."

"You're new here. I haven't seen you before, and you're not wearing a uniform yet."

"My first day. However, I won't be wearing a uniform. I'm a civilian under contract." She took a sip of her coffee. "How's the food here?"

"It's all right. We're using Alliance forces food processes. It's okay for the most part."

Diana took another drink of her coffee after Tofina left. *Not exactly a ringing endorsement of the food. And this coffee will be easy to improve upon.* The sandwich didn't hold any surprises. *Very edible, but without a lasting impression or a craving to have again.*

Diana left the lounge and continued her exploration of the Star Hawk. After a touring past the emergency communication centre, she returned to her workstation.

She set to work on the coffee formula, checking which chemicals were available in the ship's food supply storage. She selected a combination that she believed would provide a superior blend of coffee than the one currently used. Diana produced a test sample and headed downstairs to the food and beverage assembly area via a door in her workstation that led to a short set of stairs.

The assembly area consisted of dozens of multi-coloured tubes running near the ceiling. Various cylinder metal tanks made up most of the room with specialized equipment at the end of the room. A faint hum filled the room. *Smells like a hundred different foods.*

At the end of the tanks and taking up a corner of the room was the kitchen area, complete with cupboards, sink and an oven. A counter separated the kitchen from the rest of the room. The kitchen was used to test samples, and Diana stood behind the counter and selected her new coffee configuration from the holographic menu. A black liquid flowed from a spout located under the cupboards into a plastic mug. She first sniffed the aroma and took a small sip. *Not bad at all. This will work as the new coffee.*

"Who the devil are you, and what are you doing here?" a voice barked at her.

Diana almost dropped the coffee cup. She turned to face the uniformed man standing on the other side of the counter. He wore the insignia of a senior technician, with a tag indicating his name as Derik Holton. He stood more than a full head above her, and the loose uniform didn't hide his broad shoulders. If he didn't look so angry, she would have considered him handsome.

She regained her composure. "I'm Diana Adoria. I'm in charge of the composition of the food and beverages." She lifted the cup of coffee. "I'm testing a new formula for coffee."

"I wasn't told you would be working here today. This is my area and you better think twice before you start changing formulas and coming into this area without my consent."

Diana regained her composure and placed the cup on the counter. She put her hands on her hips. "This is the job I was hired to do. I don't understand why I would need your permission to do my work."

His jaw clenched, and he stamped around the counter. With one hand he pushed on her back, pressing her face down on the counter.

She gasped at the unexpected attack, her arms unable to lift herself. Swiftly she felt her short skirt lifted, and the corporal's big hand smacked her ass four times on each side, stinging her cheeks.

He released his hand from her back. "Consider this a warning. Your behaviour is not acceptable. I have little tolerance for Alliance females who think they don't have to conform to Praxton standards."

He marched away, leaving Diana in a state of shock. Slowly she raised herself from the counter. *What the hell just happened there?* She touched her cheeks, testing their sensitivity. *Damn him! What right does he think he has to spank me? And who should I complain about this to?* She pulled down her skirt and looked at her coffee, ignored it and looked at the electronic menu. She checked the wine list and selected a sauvignon cabernet. A moment later a red liquid filled a wine glass she took from a cupboard.

She took a drink and frowned. *Tastes like cranberries with blackberries added.*

Her mobile chirped, indicating a message. "Read it."

"Ms. Adoris, this is First Officer Morgan Regan. I understand you have just arrived on the Star Hawk, and I would like to welcome you aboard. I understand you're still settling in, but I would like to invite you to dinner with Captain Elmwood and other officers. Dinner will be served at nineteen hundred hours in the captain's quarters."

I hope this welcome is better than the one given by Holton. "Inform First Officer Morgan Regan that I would be glad to attend."

———

Morgan sipped at her glass of white wine, glancing at the entrance of the captain's quarters, just as Diana Adoris entered. She stopped just inside the doorway, looking apprehensive.

Morgan made her way toward her, smiling a greeting. She saw Diana wore a dark blue dress. It was longer than the skirt she had on earlier, but the top had a wide, scooped neck. She also wore a black collar and used the centre ring to attach chains that connected to the matching wrist cuffs. Her ankle cuffs were without chains.

"Welcome, Diana. Please come inside and I'll introduce you to everyone and get you something to drink.

"Thank you. I'll have whatever you're having."

Morgan obtained her a glass of pinot grigio and introduced her to Captain Elmwood.

She responded to his greeting, and Morgan introduced her to the other officers.

———

Khloe approached her. "Were you able to find yourself around the Star Hawk without too much of a problem?"

"Yes, thank you." She noticed food being brought in by the hospitality staff. "I would like to talk to you later about my status concerning the kitchen area."

"Of course. I'll be glad to answer any questions."

The food was good, in Diana's opinion. However, she believed it wouldn't be difficult to improve a few of the dishes in both taste and texture. She enjoyed the conversation, explaining her own background.

"This is my first military ship, so I'm out of my element here. That and the Praxton customs, which is another level to learn." She heard a few chuckles and agreement with her statement. Diana noticed that while the dinner conversation was light, the women at the table still referred to the men by using the title master in front of their names. The women's first names were used without any salutation.

She enjoyed the meal overall and felt comfortable with the officers. She was pleased when Elmwood made a point of telling her to consider herself part of the executive officer team, regardless of her civilian status, and he hoped she would join them on a regular basis.

After dinner, she had an opportunity to talk to Khloe privately as they left.

"You mentioned you wanted to ask me something concerning the kitchen."

"I thought I had control over the kitchen and processing area. However, Senior Technician Holton became upset when he saw me in the test kitchen area. I was just checking the taste of a new coffee formula when he jumped all over me for being in his area."

"Master Derik, though a civilian under contract with the military, has served in the Praxton armed forces in the past and is rather conservative on how he views things. I'll send him a message you have the right to be in the process and kitchen area."

"Thank you." She decided against complaining about the spanking. *I don't know enough about Praxton customs to know if that's normal.*

"Just be aware that these conservative men aren't used to working with women, and especially with female civilians. You may have to tread carefully how you approach him."

No kidding. I sure don't need another paddling.

[26]

DIANA WOKE up to soft music playing in her bedroom. The volume gradually increased along with the light until she woke up. She waited a few more moments and slid out of bed. She felt a slight tug on her leg and recalled the ankle cuff and chain that secured her to the foot of the bed. Diana detached the cuff, surprised it hadn't affected her sleep.

She was naked, deciding she should comply with the rule for females to sleep nude. She briefly considered disobeying the wearing of the cuff and sleeping nude, but if Khloe Levit asked her if she had, she knew she wouldn't lie. *I've already been in trouble for reasons I don't understand.*

The shower was relaxing, and she looked out to the living room below. She wondered what it was like showering with someone watching below. *Maybe I'll find out someday.* She shut off the water and turned on the warm drying air. A minute later she stepped out of the shower stall to prepare for the day, frowning at the control at the entrance. The control could make the shower outside wall to the living room opaque, but a notice indicated it was for use by males only.

She dressed in a skirt and top, adding a silver collar and four matching cuffs. She placed chains from her wrist cuffs to a belt around her waist. Diana decided to have a coffee and a pastry in her suite rather than go to a dining lounge, wanting to prepare in case of another encounter with

Holton. She headed to her workstation. *I hope Holton is in a better mood today.*

———

She studied details of the coffee she had tested the previous day, deciding her new formula was the right one. The three-dimensional display showed her various chemicals and their relative percentage of the blend. Diana knew she could add a few more subtle flavours but didn't want to tax a system that had to produce a large quantity of coffee. Some chemicals she would have liked to add did not have a large supply available. She did increase the caffeine level. The Alliance worlds, under the policy of the Charter of Conduct Office, had reduced the caffeine levels in coffee in the belief it should be avoided. The result, in Diana's opinion, was that it made for a black liquid with few redeeming qualities.

She entered the processing centre, wanting to try out the coffee again before making the final decision. This time there were other crew members in the area and, to her relief, not Senior Technician Holton.

A young woman looked up at her approach.

"Hello. Are you Diana Adoria?"

Diana confirmed her identity and was soon introduced to two other women and one male. His status of junior technician told her he and the others were likely just starting their career.

"I've just made a new formula for coffee. Would any of you like to try it and give me your opinion?"

The four readily agreed, and they moved toward the small kitchen. They stood in front of the counter while she stepped inside the serving area. She made five cups of coffee with two of the coffees requiring the addition of cream and sweetener.

The reaction to the new blend was positive with one woman commenting, "Finally, a cup of coffee I can look forward to in the morning."

Diana thanked them for their input and returned to her office. She initiated the change in the coffee process, expecting it would take a couple of days for all the older coffee formula to be used up. She began to look at the tea formulas.

"What the blazes are you doing!"

Diana gasped as she looked up from her desk at the annoyed Derik Holton.

"What do you mean?"

"The coffee, damn it." He snarled.

"Please, sit down. I don't know what I did wrong." She pointed at a chair on the other side of her desk.

Instead he walked around the desk, inserted a finger in the ring of her collar, and pulled her to a standing position. "Then I will explain."

Diana followed him, her arms hanging by her sides as he led her to one of the vacant chairs. He sat, and suddenly she was over his lap. The palms of her hands rested on the floor.

She felt a whap of her bottom over her skirt.

"One, you failed to address me by my proper title." He lifted her skirt. "You may call me Senior Technician Holton." His hand struck her ass. "Or Master Derik." The palm of his hand struck with each word. He struck her cheeks again. "Understand?"

"Yes, yes, Senior Technician Holton."

"You changed the coffee process without consulting me." He pulled down her panties to her knees, and she heard the fabric partially tear at the force. "I looked at my monitor and I see warning lights of a new process." He spanked her bare cheeks, striking each side with increasing force and in an upward motion. "From now on you must inform me of any planned changes *before* you implement them."

Diana kicked her legs from the sharp pain. "Yes, I promise. Please stop, Senior Technician Holton."

"You may think you can do as you please, but I consider this my jurisdiction. Am I clear on this?"

"Yes, Senior Technician Holton." Diana felt two more smacks on each cheek.

"Good." He lifted her by her shoulders to a standing position. "Stand up against the wall, hands behind your back."

Diana stepped out of her panties and pressed herself against the wall. She folded her arms behind her back, aware her skirt was still lifted and baring her red cheeks.

"I received a message this morning informing me you have the right to be in the processing area. I will abide by that decision. I will agree you may use the kitchen to test samples. But you better not just make changes to the processes without checking with me first."

"Yes, Senior Technician Holton." Diana felt the heat from her ass. She knew her nipples were hard. *Damn him.*

"I will expect much better behaviour from you in the future. You need to conform to the way a Praxton female would act. Tomorrow I *strongly* suggest you consider adding additional chains, such as ankle chains. You may now return to your desk."

"Thank you, Senior Technician Holton." Diana took in quick breaths of air as she returned to her desk. She saw her panties lying on the floor but ignored them. She winced as she sat.

He stared at her. "I'm sure there will be more training required in the future. I believe you can become a proper female in time." He paused at the door. "Excellent coffee, by the way. We will keep the changes permanently."

Diana stared at the door where he left. *Become a proper female? Exactly what gender does he think I am?* She looked at the image floating in front of her. The formula for tea no longer holding her interest. She stood, gently rubbing her ass. *I don't feel like sitting right now or working.*

She sent a message for Khloe Levit, asking her to meet her for lunch. Diana paced around her office, recalling the sequence of events. *Making me stand in front of the wall like a naughty child. Who the devil does he think he is?* She frowned. *Obviously, someone who thinks he's very much in control.*

Her earpiece relayed a message Khloe would be pleased to join her for lunch. Diana was glad that she had Khloe to talk to about the latest incident with Holton and hoped she would offer a solution. She picked up her panties lying on the floor and tossed them in the garbage. She looked at the clear wall separating the office to the hallway, wondering if anyone saw her rather humiliating spanking.

———

Khloe smiled as she joined her at Diana's table. "Hi, what's up?"

Diana noticed Khloe wore a leash attached to her collar with the loose end around her left wrist. "I received a spanking from Derik Holton. This one harder than the last one." She explained to her about the first spanking.

"This time I forgot to ask him if we could implement the changes in the coffee formula. He put me over his knee and spanked me, including pulling down my panties."

"Oh."

"And I forgot to address him properly."

"I told you he's conservative in his views."

"I know, but he just comes on so strong that I don't have time to think." She paused to take a bite of her salad. "He more or less ordered me to wear ankle chains. Can he do that?"

"In a word, yes. He is a male. You must defer to him socially and to his rank."

"So, he can order me around? I didn't know I signed up for that." She fumed for a moment. "May I ask why you have a leash on?"

"I'm a conservative Praxton female. I like to wear a leash occasionally. If I'm with a male officer, I hand him the end. I'm protected that way and he feels he's in control. My advice is to show him respect. When he approaches you, stand with your hands behind your back. Make sure you use his title or call him master."

"Okay, thanks. He smacked me pretty hard on my ass and ordered me to face the wall. It was rather embarrassing."

"I suspect every female on the ship has, or will, receive a spanking. Some of us will be whipped as well or placed in a cage. The males believe it ensures proper behaviour from females. I suppose it does, and I don't mind being punished occasionally. I find it stimulating."

"I'm not saying it can't be stimulating, but don't women have rights here?"

"Of course. Males can discipline us but cannot touch us sexually unless we're in a relationship with him. If the discipline is not appropriate, you can report him to a superior officer."

"Isn't a spanking, especially when he pulls down my panties, considered at least partially sexual touching?"

"Sometimes a spanking is sexual, obviously. But in this case, it was a punishment for failure to address him correctly. Look, I'll have one of the male officers discuss the situation with him. Perhaps we can later have a meeting with Master Derik and find common ground and help you avoid minor rule infractions."

"Thanks. I don't want to be scared to go to work."

Diana returned to her workstation. *I guess I'm not alone in being punished. I wish I had known this part of the deal before I signed the contract.* She forced herself to focus on the tea formulas when a member of the maintenance crew arrived.

The woman informed her she had a work order for her office.

"A work order? Okay, I guess they haven't finished with my office yet."

Diana watched her use a foot stool to insert a peg into a wall and do the same a few feet away. Then she added another peg near the floor directly below one of the higher pegs. "Are those pegs used for restraints?"

"Yes, they are."

"Well, I didn't request these."

"No, Senior Technician Holton did."

"But this is my office."

"But he is a male." The woman looked at Diana. "He can make that decision." She added another peg at the floor and finally another one at waist height. On the last peg, she hung a flogger.

Diana watched her leave and went to the flogger, touching the strands. *Let's hope this is just for show.*

[27]

KELLY WALLING CHECKED another instrument readout. He nodded his satisfaction and turned down the hallway, deciding his workday was now over. He passed an elevator when he heard a woman's voice.

"Master Kelly."

He turned and saw Khloe Levit.

"Hello, Khloe. Just getting off work?"

"Yes. Are you going for dinner now?"

"After I clean up. I was working behind control panels."

"May I join you for dinner after you wash up?" She took the end of her leash and passed it over to him.

He took the end. "Very well, if you don't mind waiting a bit."

"Not at all." She held her wrists in front of her.

He took the hint and secured her wrist cuffs together. "You do like being restrained."

"I do, especially with a male I trust."

"Thank you." He led her to his quarters. After he opened his door, she slipped off her shoes and kneeled on the floor in the living room. She looked up at him. "I'll wait right here, Master Kelly."

"All right, although you're welcome to sit in a chair."

"No, this is where I should be."

When Walling returned after washing and changing his shirt, he noticed she remained where he had left her.

He took her leash, and after she put her shoes on, escorted her to the dining lounge.

"Is there something you want to ask me?" Walling looked at her. "You look like you need to tell me something."

"You are very perceptive, Master Kelly. I was talking to another female, and she complained to me about how she had received a spanking. The female is the civilian contractor, Diana Adoria. She has an Alliance background but has made a serious effort to follow Praxton customs. However, Senior Technician Derik Holton is punishing her for every mistake she makes. It has made her nervous at being around him. Would you be willing to discuss the situation with him? I believe only another male should approach him on this."

"Of course, I will be glad to talk to him. Is there anything else?"

"Well, just that I was envious she had been spanked."

After a few steps, Walling replied, "You want to be spanked."

"Yes, I believe females need discipline. Unfortunately, there aren't many males I know on the Star Hawk who can discipline me. I don't come in contact with males outside of the executive officers."

A few more steps. "You're telling me this because you want me to spank you."

"Yes." She blushed.

"Perhaps we can examine discipline measures after dinner."

"Thank you, Master Kelly." Khloe smiled.

Walling had difficulty finding his appetite as he looked at Khloe across from him. Her wrists were cuffed together, slowing down her efforts to eat. They were joined by two other officers, neither who appeared concerned at Khloe's wrists being cuffed together.

After dinner, Walling led Khloe out of the lounge.

"Are you still wanting your spanking?"

"Yes, Master Kelly, very much so. If you take me to my suite, you can place me in the restraints on the wall to whip me. I notice you don't have Praxton style of furniture in your place."

"Whip you? I thought it was just a spanking you wanted."

"It is entirely your choice. I like the thought of you disciplining me either way."

Walling led Khloe to her suite. He paused as she removed her shoes and moved to the couch. He undid her cuffs, and without any encouragement, she slid over his lap. He rested a hand on her ass. *How did this happen that I'm about to spank a beautiful young woman?* He cautiously lifted her skirt, her cheeks exposed to him. Gently he massaged her ass and experimentally gave it a few soft smacks. He felt his erection pressing against his underwear and he shifted position to be more comfortable. Slowly he increased the pressure of the hits, watching the skin turn pink. He heard her moan, encouraging him to continue.

His own member became stiff and Khloe shifted her hips against it in a slow rhythm. He took a deep breath and reached for the waist band of her panties, tugging them down. She lifted her hips to help him remove them, sliding them down her legs until they landed on the floor.

He resumed her spanking, and her gasps excited him even more. He stopped and slid a hand under her top, feeling her back. He undid the top and bottom buttons, baring her back. Next, he undid her skirt, and he admired the naked form lying on his lap. He continued the spanking, and her cheeks turned red. She groaned.

"Your ass is getting very red."

"I think it must be." She rolled off his lap, shedding her top on the floor as she stood in front of him. "I need to please you."

Walling watched as she dropped to her knees and undid his fly. Slowly she eased his swollen member into her mouth, dropping lower until the thick, long shaft almost disappeared. She lifted her head and plunged down again. He rested a hand on her head. "Very nice, but perhaps I can put it inside that warm pussy of yours."

She lifted her head. "It is the Praxton way that the first time the male must be given pleasure. Plus, I enjoy having you in my mouth."

The penis disappeared into her mouth again. Walling was too excited to argue. She worked her mouth around his penis, her tongue playing with the head. She paused to gasp for air and pressed down on his erection, making the length disappear inside her mouth once more. After several more repetitions, he felt a surge of heat and closed his eyes as Khloe desperately tried to swallow all the warm fluid. She didn't quite succeed but looked up at him, smiling with her face glistening.

After he regained his composure. "Well, Khloe, that was wonderful. Perhaps after a drink you will allow me to please you."

"Of course, Master Kelly. I will get us a drink."

Walling sipped his whisky, staring at the naked woman sitting on the floor in front of him. Not quite naked, he noted. She had shed her uniform save for the phantom sleeves. He thought it gave her an exotic look. He became aroused again, a gentle pressure in his pants. "I don't know what to do with you."

"You have complete control, Master Kelly. You may do anything you want with me." She looked over into the corner where a cage sat. "Did you want to punish me?"

"No. Not punish. I enjoyed spanking you, but I didn't consider that a punishment."

Khloe smiled. "I believe we understand each other."

Walling stood. He took off his shirt and took off the rest of his clothes. He noticed her watching him intently, but his excitement took away any thoughts of shyness. He bent down and helped her stand. "Now it's my turn to please you."

"Yes, Master Kelly. Whatever you think is best."

He took her hand and led her upstairs to the bedroom. He gently pushed her on the bed and lay a series of kisses on her body. He listened to her moans and small cries. Her legs spread as he moved down past her stomach. Walling licked her wetness, squeezing her ass with his hands. Her hips lifted to his mouth. She gave out a long and slow moan.

Walling gripped her hips and turned her over onto her stomach. With her knees around his waist, he began to spank her ass.

"Oh, oh, oh!"

He stopped to massage her cheeks and ran his hands up her ribcage. His erection pressed against her stomach. He saw her clutch the bed sheet tightly in her hands above her head.

"Please, Master Kelly, now. Please!"

"No, not yet." He shifted his position, climbing on top of her. He held back his full weight on her, using his legs to support himself. His hands reached under her, squeezing her breasts and pinching her nipples. "Turn over."

Khloe twisted around, her chest heaving.

Walling pushed forward, holding her wrists in one hand and pinning them above her head. His other hand cupped a breast as he slid his cock across her stomach.

Khloe cried out, lifting her chest.

He straddled her and released her wrists. She left her hands locked together above her as his member brushed over her nipples, leaving a trail of wetness over her skin. Her mouth opened as she gulped for air.

Walling moved down, using his hands to fondle her breasts.

Girl, you're going to come now. Walling worked a hand at her swollen clitoris. He moved his body on hers, filling her with as much as she could take.

Khloe wrapped her legs around his waist, wanting to tighten her grip on him. She shifted her hips to ride with his exertions.

He pounded into her as she cried out. He continued his thrusts, his hands under her ass. He let out a groan and collapsed on her, gasping for air.

Slowly he rolled off her. "Damn, that was good."

She reached for his hand, breathing through her open mouth. Gradually she stirred. "I need some water." Khloe went to the kitchen, returning with two glasses.

"Just what I need. A drink and you."

Walling sat in bed with her, sharing a drink. She rested her head against his shoulder.

"Master Kelly, I would like you to be my guardian. If you don't wish that responsibility, I understand. I would still like to obey you and please you."

"I do like you very much, but this all rather sudden for me. I've never been married or even been in a serious relationship before."

"A guardian is a serious responsibility." She paused. "You can still control me, even if you don't wish to be my guardian. I will accept it if you decide to have another female under your control. It is the Praxton way for a male to have two or more females to care for. If you decide to look after me, that does not exclude you from other females."

"I see."

"Why don't you make that decision when you are ready to do so. Tonight, I just want your company." She reached toward the end of the bed and attached an ankle cuff. "It is a Praxton custom. All females must sleep nude with an ankle cuff attached."

"Oh."

"You can establish other rules for me as well."

"Really. Like if I ordered you to be nude at all times in your suite you would do so?"

"Yes."

"Interesting. I have options to consider."

"Can we go to sleep now, Master Kelly?" She yawned. "I am exhausted."

"Of course." He put his arm around her and slid down in the bed. *Tomorrow is another day.*

[28]

As DIANA DRESSED for work in the morning, she considered Senior Technician Holton's suggestion to wear ankle cuffs more of an order than a recommendation. She thought of defying him briefly and rejected that option, not sure if that would lead to immediate discipline. She looked at her clothes hanging in the closet.

She picked out a short, yellow pleated skirt. Diana added a dark green sleeveless top, the lacy fabric hinting what she had underneath. She attached two nipple jewellery rings, feeling they would be appropriate considering how thin her blouse was.

Diana finally attached a chain between her ankle cuffs, inspected herself in front of a viewscreen, and headed to her office.

She wondered why she wasn't angrier with Holton, but kept thinking about the compliment he had given her about the new coffee formula. She left her suite, remembering to take careful steps with the chain between her ankle cuffs. She surprised herself by how soon she adapted to the smaller steps.

Diana arrived at her office and inspected changes to the tea formula. She looked at the three-dimensional graphs, looking for potential areas to work on. *The amino acids look normal. Hmm, the manganese looks low. I should check on that.*

"Ms. Diana."

She looked up at Holton approaching her desk. Diana quickly stood. "Master Holton. I mean Senior Technician Holton. Sir."

His eyes, a light brown, narrowed. A smile creased his lips for a moment. "I'm checking to see if you complied with my instructions yesterday."

"Yes, Master Derik." She stepped around from the desk, her hands held behind her back. She watched his eyes check the ankle chain between her ankle cuffs.

"Very good. What are you working on today?"

"Tea. It's the second most common beverage, so I thought I should examine its properties and see if I can improve its flavour."

"You did well with the coffee, so I expect you will do the same with tea. Carry on but inform me before you implement changes in our process."

"Yes, sir."

He glanced at the wall hooks. "Otherwise there will be consequences."

She watched him leave the room and stared at the wall restraints. *Can I avoid that punishment?*

━━

Diana finished with a new formula for the tea and initiated the sequence of the combination of chemicals for a test sample. She stepped away from her desk and headed to the test kitchen, moving carefully with the ankle chain inhibiting her steps. She passed two workers, each one giving her a smile of acknowledgement.

Do they know he spanked me yesterday? I hope not, but there's nothing I can do about it now. She poured herself a mug of tea, breathing in the vapours. Satisfied with the aroma, she took a small sip and rolled the liquid around in her mouth. Diana sat on a bar stool to finish her tea, trying to determine if it lacked any flavours or had any undesirable ones.

"Would you like to try this new batch of tea and tell me your opinion of it?" She called out to the two technicians.

They stopped their inspection of the tanks and the monitors, quickly agreeing to a change of their routine. They each sat at a barstool and each accepted a cup of tea. She passed a cup to each one, introducing herself.

The man, slim and tall, responded first. "Keith Rolland."

"Chiela Bently." The redhead had blonde streaks in her hair. She was of medium height with a well-rounded figure.

Diana saw Holton approach and stood.

"How is the tea? I understand you are running a sample test."

"It's good, Master Derik. Would you like to try it, sir?"

"I'm not much of a tea drinker." He shrugged. "But I'll give it a try." Holton took a barstool and slid it near where Diana stood. He sat and waited for Diana to pour him a cup.

Diana poured another cup of tea. She looked at the technicians, who looked unconcerned that the senior technician joined them. *Am I the only one scared of doing something wrong?* She carried a cup of tea to Holton, unable to avert her eyes where his member pressed against the semi-transparent weave of the pant's fly.

Holton acted relaxed and took the cup from her.

"Not bad for tea."

"Thank you."

"I'm pleased to see you're now acting closer to how a female should behave and dress. That being said, I still look forward to administrating discipline measures on you. Strong ones, I will add." He placed his cup on the counter and strolled away.

Diana was shocked at his intention to punish her further. *Why does he hate me?*

Chiela smiled at Diana with a look of surprise. "Wow, Master Derik must really like you."

Diana returned to her office. *I really don't understand this Praxton culture. Holton wants to punish me, and Chiela says that means he likes me?* She looked at the pegs on her office wall designed to hold her in a spread-eagle position. A flogger was held next to the set of hooks. She picked up the whip and brushed the strands across her arm. She tried harder strokes and determined the whip wasn't designed to inflict much pain.

"Okay, so this isn't much to worry about." She sighed. "Other than that, what do I do about Derik. He scares me, yet he excites me too."

MORGAN SAT to the right of Elmwood, who sat at the head of the boardroom table. She watched him study the tablet with the meeting agenda.

"Okay, just a few more agenda items," he said. "Morgan, you have information on crew changes."

"Yes, four females have left the Star Hawk. Three females were from Praxton, and to generalize, they were not comfortable working without a guardian. Homesick is another way to say it, I suppose. The fourth female came from an Alliance world and didn't adjust well to the Praxton culture. The females have been replaced, and I believe that will be all the female crew changes we will have prior to ship departure.

"A few males have also left the ship. Two stated they preferred to continue their career on an Alliance culture ship. Three others were strongly encouraged to seek employment elsewhere, and they have done so. There won't be any negative reference on their personnel file that way. We have replaced all five males."

"Can we assume there were problems with the males because of the Praxton culture?"

"Yes, the males had trouble with the female nudity. There were not any serious indiscretions, but I didn't want to risk a repeat problem when we were in deep space."

"Well done."

Morgan glanced at her own tablet, seeing the weapons officer was next to address the officers. She heard Elmwood ask, "Kelly? How is the armament situation?"

"The latest tests are positive. We will do another test after a jump to deep space."

"Excellent. Khloe, what is the situation with the females and their behaviours?"

"Much better, sir. Since we have introduced discipline measures, the females are acting much better. The females from Praxton rapidly adjusted, and now the females from the Alliance worlds are adjusting.

"On a side note, the males have adjusted after the initial period. The biggest problem was long stares at the females in uniforms, but that has subsided."

Elmwood looked at the last member of the meeting. "Diana. You have done a fine job of upgrading many of our foods. In my opinion, the coffee was the most significant improvement." He gave a grin. "How are you finding your situation? Being an Alliance female and a contractor, you have likely faced a few challenges."

"Yes, I have. There are a few nuances I have had to learn and adjust to and have received help there. I am working through food and beverages, starting with the most common and easiest items to change. Foods can be very complex, and I have to make sure I don't overtax our production facilities by introducing too many changes at once."

"Do you require any help from myself? I can assign you a personal assistant, for example."

"Thank you, sir. But I believe I have things under control for integrating the new food and beverages."

"Good to hear." Elmwood made a note on his tablet. "That concludes our meeting. Just in time for dinner, I will add."

"I don't need any more encouragement." Kelly stood. "My stomach has been rumbling for an hour."

Khloe walked with Diana to the executive dining lounge. "May I ask how are things with Master Derik?"

"I'm treading carefully around him. I make sure I call him Senior Technician Holton or Master Derik and stand with my hands behind my back when addressing him. Still, he acts really aggressive toward me. He even had restraints placed on *my* office wall. What really confuses me is he told me he's waiting for an opportunity to punish me. After he told me that, one of the junior technician cadets told me he must really like me. That sounds bizarre to me."

"I understand how it must be difficult for a civilian to be on a military vessel and to be on one adopting Praxton social norms. From what you've told me, it seems to me he likes you. It is a Praxton custom for males to use mild discipline to seduce females."

"One of those spankings I wouldn't exactly call mild discipline."

"Believe me, there can be much harsher punishments." Khloe smiled. "Many females receive a spanking regularly. It is accepted as a normal control measure by their guardian. My suggestion is to refer to him as Master Derik. It's a more personal address. You can also inform him whether or not you see him as a guardian. If you tell him you don't want him as your guardian, he may curtail his attention to you. I have asked one of our male officers to speak with him."

"Thank you. I'm not sure how I feel about Master Derik. Can't he just stop trying to dominate me so I can know him better?"

"That's not the Praxton way. By disciplining you, he is showing his desire to be your guardian."

"Okay, thanks. At least I have a better understanding of why he's punishing me."

"Are you going to accept him as your guardian or tell him you're not interested?"

"I don't know. I would like to know him better first."

"There are ways to know him better, if you know what I mean."

"I do." Diana laughed. "But I want to know him without the threat of a spanking."

[30]

DIANA COMPLETED another test of apple filling, often used for desserts. She hoped this one retained the flavour of the previous sample plus an improved texture. She headed to the test kitchen, uncertain if she wanted to avoid or see Holton.

At the kitchen, she directed the equipment to prepare the sample of apple filling. A minute later she examined the heated texture with a fork and nodded her approval. *That looks better.* Diana carried the plate around the other side of the kitchen and sat on a barstool, crossing her legs and used a fork to taste the filling. She smiled. *Nailed it.*

She heard a man's footsteps and turned to see Holton. Diana gave a hesitant smile. "Master Derik, sir. I was just testing a new apple filling. Would you care to try it?"

He crossed his arms, staring at her. "I knew eventually you would make another serious error."

"I don't understand." She looked at the filling and back at him.

"No, not the filling. You have your legs crossed. A Praxton female must never cross their legs. That is considered an insult to any male present."

"Oh." Diana quickly uncrossed her legs. "I'm sorry, sir. I didn't know."

"You should have." He frowned. "I'll try a sample of the filling."

"Yes, Master Derik." She obtained a sample for him, passing him a plate across the counter.

He tried it, nodding his approval. "Very good. You have a talent, there's no doubt about that."

"Thank you, sir."

"Concerning your indiscretion. I believe you would agree that a discipline measure is required."

Do I have a choice? Will it be another spanking? "If you think so, sir."

"I do. I will meet you in your office at the end of the shift."

Diana watched him leave. *So, what happens at the end of my shift? What kind of punishment is he going to administer? Will he use the restraints on the wall on me?* She strolled back to her office, unsure of her emotions about him, and not happy about the prospect of being disciplined.

"Senior Technician Holton."

Holton looked up, seeing the weapons officer standing at the doorway of his office. "Yes, Lieutenant Walling?"

"I would like to have a discussion with you. It's of a personal nature." Walling stepped inside the small office and closed the door. "May I sit down?"

"Of course, sir."

"Mr. Holton, we have both served in the military. As such, we are very cognisant of rules and procedures. However, not everyone working on the Star Hawk has our experience. Some personnel are new to the military and the Praxton culture."

"I believe you would be referring to Diana Adoris."

"I am. May I inquire if you like her?"

"I do."

"I have met her." Walling nodded. "She is attractive, smart and considerate of others. Unfortunately, she is scared of you."

"I am strict with her, but I don't mean to frighten her."

"But you have. Perhaps because you're treating her as a Praxton female, while in reality she is new to the ship and is from an Alliance background. She is trying to learn the way of doing things on a new military ship that endorses Praxton social customs. Ms. Adoris is on a steep learning curve. You may believe you are helping her learn, but she sees it differently. Mr. Holton, she is scared of you and believes you dislike her."

Holton's jaw dropped. "I assure you I do not dislike her."

"Would it be fair to say that you believe a Praxton female would view your discipline methods as a sign you care about her?"

"Yes, I believe so."

"I would suggest that the discipline method is having the opposite effect on her."

"Duly noted. Perhaps I have been too aggressive in promoting Praxton values. I will change my dealings with her."

"That is excellent to hear."

Diana spent the rest of the afternoon compiling reports. The apple filling was a success, and she decided to use similar formulas for other fruit fillings. A half hour passed after her shift ended when Holton arrived. She stood with her hands behind her back and clutched her fingers together.

"Master Derik."

"My intention coming here was to discipline you. However, I had a conversation with an officer who told to me that I have been too harsh with you. He said I gave you the impression that I didn't like you." He took a deep breath. "Diana, I want to stress that I respect your abilities, and you are a most welcome addition to our crew on the Star Hawk. I do like you, and I'm sorry my actions seem to be contrary to that."

"Oh."

"I suggest that instead of my planned disciplinary session, we have dinner and get to know each other."

"I would like that very much." Diana felt relieved.

"Very good. I am sorry if I made you uncomfortable around me. That was not my intention. May I escort you to dinner in an hour's time?"

"That would be nice."

Diana hurried to her room, and a changed to a green and blue-grey banded dress. The fabric dress was lighter and more transparent above the waist than the bottom. The clinging cloth only partially obscured her breasts and the nipple jewellery underneath. She avoided the sight of panty lines by not wearing any. She placed a pair of blue stilettos by the door and was ready well before Derik's time of arrival. *I guess the fewer clothes you wear, the faster you can get dressed.* She checked her hair one more time and waited downstairs for Derik.

At exactly the appointed time, Holton arrived at her room. She opened her door and invited him in, offering him a drink before going for dinner.

"That would nice. Scotch, please."

Diana disappeared to the kitchen, returning with two tumblers. "I chilled your scotch. I hope that's the way you like it."

"It'll be fine. You drink scotch as well?"

"I have a pretty wide palate when it comes to drinks." She smiled as she handed him a tumbler.

Derik sat in an armchair with Diana picking the loveseat. He took a drink of the whisky and sighed. "Ah, I was looking forward to a drink. It wasn't a good day for me when it was pointed out to me I had been unfair to you. I was in the wrong."

"Thank you for saying that, and I'm sorry I haven't followed all the Praxton customs. I will try to do better."

"Not to worry. We will be on the Star Hawk a long time and there will lots of time to adjust. So, no more discipline. Or rather, at least less of it."

"Just less of it?" Diana laughed. "Does that mean I could still be in trouble occasionally?"

"I have to admit I would enjoy having you over my lap while giving you a spanking." Holden grinned. "Or stripped and whipped. Nothing too painful, mind you. It's more of a case of my wanting you helpless and undressed."

"I suppose anything could happen." Diana felt her nipples stiffen, and she quickly took a drink. "I would rather know you better before you put me over your knee. Your previous spankings didn't give me much of a chance to be prepared, and I certainly didn't enjoy them."

"I'm sorry I did that. In hindsight, I realize I overreacted."

"You're forgiven."

He finished his scotch. "Shall we go for dinner now?"

The restaurant was typical of each of the dining rooms on the various floors and locations. The rectangular shaped rooms featured different sized tables for groups of four to eight. One wall had a large viewscreen that showed various images of scenery. Opposite to the entrance a wall separated where the kitchen was located, and on the other side of the kitchen a lounge was located that catered more for those interested in drinks and lighter foods.

Holton requested a table away from most other diners and they continued their conversation. "So, you moved from working for restaurants to being the head of food and beverage on various ships. You must have seen a few worlds."

"I did. I really enjoyed seeing the different planets, people and culture."

"And the Star Hawk offers you few more planets to visit."

"It does." She grinned. "I just didn't expect to see such a difference in culture right here on the ship."

Holton chuckled. "I hope all aspects of the Star Hawk culture aren't negative."

Diana sipped at her wine and took a bite of her food. "I do like some aspects of it."

"Which parts are that?"

She took another drink of wine and tilted her head. "Well, before I tell you that, how about I learn a little bit about you? You were once in the military?"

"I joined the Praxton forces as soon as I could. I don't have much to tell. I'm a believer in the Praxton way of life and joined the Star Hawk because I thought this was a ship that will help preserve the Praxton way of life. I, like many on Praxton, are still angry the Alliance worlds invaded Praxton and tried to make it like one of their bland worlds where everyone is supposed to be the same."

"Master Derik, Praxton came out of that invasion an independent world and has done very well. The Praxton way of life is still very strong."

"I know. I want to ensure it stays that way."

"I'm sure it will be, judging the support for Praxton social customs on other worlds." She touched her collar. "These are becoming more popular on Alliance worlds."

"That's good to hear." He smiled. "Is that one of the things you like about Praxton?"

"It is. I like my men with strong personalities. Praxton men are certainly that."

"And the discipline?"

"It intrigues me, I must admit. However, I'm not much for being taken by surprise, and given a spanking for something I didn't know I was doing wrong."

"Yes. I'm sorry how I acted then. I won't offer an excuse. I don't want you to think of me as a tyrant."

"I don't now."

"That being said, I still would like to spank you and use the flogger on you. I want you to understand it is not merely to punish you."

"I see. Well, I don't reject that could happen in the future or even mind that it would happen." She took a drink of her wine. *Perhaps even in the near future.*

"Good. I believe we are moving to a common ground." He smiled. "I believe giving you a spanking could be enjoyable to both of us."

"It just might be." Diana took a drink of her wine, trying to hide she had started to blush.

"What you're wearing right now is very flattering to your figure."

"Thank you."

"Would I be incorrect to think if you were to remove your dress you would be naked?"

"And if that was true?" She gave him a smile.

"Then I would like to take you to my place for a nightcap."

"Master Derik, while that is very tempting, I'm not ready for that step in our relationship."

"I suspected as much." Holton nodded. "Just so you know that eventually I want to have you naked, collared and in my control. Fair warning?"

"Fair warning, but I won't give in easily."

He laughed. "Game on."

[31]

TEELA CHECKED her appearance once more in the viewscreen in her room, pushing her hair into position with her fingertips. When she left her room, Narcel was waiting for her.

"Remember, you are to be on a leash at all times. I expect you back here by twenty-two hundred. Is that understood?" She clipped a leash on Teela's wrist and held the loose end.

"Yes, Ms. Narcel." Teela looked and saw Mitch Gallow standing at the entrance to the common room. "Master Mitch, I am ready."

Narcel held Teela's leash and passed it over to him. "Master Mitch, I have instructed Teela she needs to be on a leash at all times and she is to be back here at twenty-two hundred."

Mitch took the leash. "I will escort Teela with a leash past the women's quarters and will return her here with a leash as a courtesy to your authority. However, it is my prerogative if she stays on a leash during our entire time together and what time I bring her back. Do we have an understanding, Narcel?"

"Yes, of course. I didn't mean to imply that I was giving you an order, Master Mitch. My apologies."

"Apology accepted." He looked at Teela. "Shall we go?"

As soon as they were out of hearing range of the common area, Teela let out a laugh. "Oh, thank you so much for putting her in her place. That was great."

"I'm glad that helps you, although she may make your life difficult later."

"Let her. I'll take this victory."

They reached a lounge that served both men and women. The bar was more than half full with the sound of people enjoying music and conversation. Mitch unlatched the leash from her wrist, folded it, and placed it on the table.

"To prevent any problems for you later, I will attach the leash when I return you the common room."

"All right. I never thought I would wear a leash when I applied for service on the Star Hawk."

"And yet you decided to stick it out on the Star Hawk. Some females have left the ship because they didn't want to adapt to the Praxton customs."

"It crossed my mind, but I chose the Star Hawk to further my career. I decided I will survive Narcel's training."

"Good for you. I imagine it's an adjustment for you."

"No kidding. I have to say, though, I have learned a few things."

"Such as?"

Teela laughed. "Like how to apply makeup at places I thought no one would ever see. I learned my smart mouth can get me into serious trouble. And I learned if a man you like is holding your leash, you feel protected." She looked down at the table momentarily and took a drink from her wine glass.

"Just so you know, when a male holds a female's leash, he is not only her protector but also is in control of her."

"Should I be worried?" She smiled. "Does that mean you may order me to do something or discipline me?"

"You never know. Maybe I'll make you walk topless back to the common room."

"Oh, Narcel would like that. A bit of humiliation for the Alliance female."

"She would. Now, would you enjoy that experience?"

Tella covered part of her face with her hands. "If I must tell the truth, part of me does."

"Good, then we'll have you topless at the end of the night when we reach the women's quarters."

"I may need to be a bit drunk for that."

"That can be arranged. We may find out what else we can do with you when you've been drinking."

"You would be in control so I would be at your mercy." Teela grinned.

"Shall we go to another place and have dinner?" He finished his drink.

"Sure." Teela stood and watched as he picked up the leash. She wondered when, and not if, he was going to attach it to her again. *I suppose that's when he'll make me go without my top. And what does he mean, what else he can do with me?*

They strolled a short distance down the hallway to a lounge that focused on food, with low tables and a more formal atmosphere. The dining area was half-filled, and orders were done via a menu tablet on the table.

Mitch looked around and saw a woman sitting topless at a table she shared with a man. "A topless woman is over there." He indicated with a nod of his head. "Perhaps you should go topless for dinner as well." He gave her a smile.

"I'd rather see men without their shirts on." She laughed. "You, for example."

"That's not allowed on this ship. Women can be naked off duty. Men have to be dressed, on and off duty."

"That's unfortunate. I do like looking at male bodies. Oh well, I'll just have to use my imagination."

They ordered their food, plus wine to drink. A server brought their wine first, and Mitch noticed she wore chains between her wrist cuffs and between her ankle cuffs.

"Do you have trouble walking with chains between your ankle cuffs?" Mitch asked.

"Not at all. Small steps, that's all. The head of the hospitality department has ordered all servers to adhere to the Praxton style of dress. I don't have to wear ankle cuffs, but it's better for my performance review if I do. I find the chains add a bit of elegance."

After she left, Mitch advised Teela, "You see, there are other women who like Praxton fashions."

"I know. I do like them. It just takes a while to get used to those chains." *Such as wearing nipple jewellery.*

They ordered dessert, and finally a liqueur to finish the evening.

"I think it's time to return you to your room. It's a half hour past your curfew." Mitch gave a smile.

"Yes, I guess so. It will be an early morning as usual, and I'm sure Narcel will try to make my life difficult."

When they were near the entrance to the women's quarters, Mitch instructed her to take off her top.

"I wondered if you were serious about that earlier." She undid the two buttons holding her top together and removed it. Her erect nipples were joined by a chain attached to a pair of nipple clips. She saw him take a long glance at them.

"Wrists together." He took her top from her.

"Yes, Master Mitch." She waited as he secured the wrist cuffs together at her front and attach the leash to her right wrist.

She looked at his face as he led her down the hallway. "This will cause a stir at the common room." Teela received a few friendly looks as they made their back to her common area, making her feel better about her nudity.

"It will make you even more popular."

"The wrong kind of popularity." Teela touched her leash. "You have me topless, wrists cuffed together and on a leash. Everyone will wonder what else you did to me."

"I haven't spanked you. Yet."

"Oh, does that mean you're planning to do that to me as well?"

"Not here and now, but we can work toward that. I promise you that eventually you'll be spanked." He chuckled.

"Which means I have a spanking from you to receive later. I suppose better from you than Narcel."

"She spanks harder?"

"No, not that. I'd rather be spanked by a male than a female."

"Fair enough. We can discuss your spanking at work."

She played with the chain of her leash nervously. "Yeah, that's something to look forward to."

Mitch gave her a kiss on the lips, keeping his hand at her waist. The kiss was the extent he could do in a public area of the ship.

Teela entered the common area carrying her top and several heads turned in her direction. She heard one female call out to her, asking what she did to deserve to be cuffed and stripped. Teela grinned. "Just lucky, I guess."

Narcel didn't look displeased. "I see you're acting like a proper female. I approve." She undid Teela's wrist cuffs. "I shall assume you had a good time."

"I most certainly did, Ms. Narcel." She took off her shoes and carried them to her room, where she left them and her top before returning to the common area. She felt too excited to sleep and watched a video on the large viewscreen. She glanced at Tess and Julia sitting by themselves on a loveseat. Julia sat topless while Tess used a hand to touch her thigh, sliding it up to the hem of her skirt and down again. Julia pushed her hand away, and Tess wrestled with Julia's arm.

Teela observed the short argument between the two women. *This is more interesting than the show.* She didn't think Julia put up much of a fight. Tess moved to her knees on the loveseat and pushed Julia facedown. She pulled her arms behind her back and soon had Julia's wrists cuffed behind her back.

Julia resumed sitting on the loveseat with Tess next to her. With her wrists cuffed behind her back, she couldn't stop Tess running her fingertips up and down her thigh, although now she pushed up past the hemline. The hand glided up past the skirt and lightly touched her breast, squeezing the nipple.

Julia moaned.

Narcel spoke. "Perhaps you should take this to a room."

Tess helped Julia up by the arm. "I'll take her to my room."

Teela watched Tess pulled Julia by her arm into her room. *I guess those two are now partners. Julia doesn't appear enthusiastic about it, but doesn't show much resistance either. Time for me to go to bed.* She stood, heading to her own room. *I'm looking forward to seeing Mitch tomorrow and perhaps discuss my spanking.* She smiled.

[32]

ELMWOOD SNAPPED OUT A COMMAND. "Inform port authority that we are ready to depart."

Communication Officer Janice Madison relayed his command.

"We are free to navigate to inner space," she replied.

"Then let's go there. You have navigation control, Steermaster Redding."

Steermaster Nicole Redding made several finger touches on the control console. "We have disengaged from the port hold, sir."

Elmwood watched on the viewscreens as the Star Hawk left port and navigated through inner space, the region up to the outermost planet. Once the monstrous ship reached the outer boundary, Elmwood asked the steermaster if she was ready to initiate their first jump.

"Yes, sir. Very much, sir."

"Let's make it a good one. Quadrant one seventeen, zone three point two."

"Yes, sir. At your order."

"Now, Steermaster Redding."

The view of the starfield changed suddenly, and Elmwood looked at their new position. A blue-white star dominated the viewscreen among the scattering of white dots. Elmwood stared a few moments at the screen. "It's good to be out in space again." He spoke to the steermaster. "Let's run those engines and make sure everything holds together."

"Aye, sir. I'll let you know if a bolt comes loose." She grinned.

The Star Hawk cruised through space, not coming across anything unusual. The blue giant star in their area didn't have any planets with life beyond simple plants, and there was little to investigate in the area. Because everything was new on the Star Hawk, Elmwood wanted to make sure the engines had a good test before they travelled too far from Praxton. He contacted Walling at weapon control. "Kelly, there's an asteroid about three kilometres away on our starboard side. I've highlighted it on your enemy craft monitor."

"I see it."

"I suggest we use it as a weapons test."

"I can agree with that. I'll have the weapons team give it a blast with our medium guns."

Elmwood instructed the steermaster to hold position while the weapons test was being conducted. Fifteen minutes later, Walling informed him they completed the weapons test.

"There's nothing left of that rock but dust. The crew did a perfect job."

"Great to hear. Send me a full report later." He walked up to the steermaster. "Let's do two jumps, one following the first as quickly as possible. Let's see if our jump crew can respond well under pressure, and when they don't expect a second jump."

He watched Nicole work at her console. The holographic graphs and lines looked like chaos to him, but she moved her fingers deftly through them. The display changed. Satisfied with what she saw, Nicole touched a button that would signal the jump crew to power on the generators required for the jump.

The starfield in the viewscreen suddenly changed and, seconds later, was replaced again. A yellow dwarf sun dominated the pinpoints of white stars around it. He commented to the steermaster, "Looks like we hit in the middle of the Margus system."

"We have. Three-point-two AU from the star."

Elmwood calculated that was just over three times the distance of the Earth to the sun. "How were the jumps? Within parameters?"

"Close to specifications. I believe the crew are still getting familiar with the controls. The command for the second jump right after the first likely caught them off guard."

"Understood. Let's move to Margus six. The gas giant has several moons and let's see how well we can establish orbit around it."

"Course is set."

"Morgan, you have command. I'll be in my office." Elmwood left the command centre and headed to the captain's quarters a short distance away. In his office he opened a link to General Noreen Howler of the Alliance forces. The video link was clear, although there were a few seconds of time delay. After he spoke, he had to wait for her to respond.

"General, I wanted to report that we have successfully tested the engines, weapons and completed two jumps. All indications the equipment operated correctly."

"That's good to hear. You said the equipment operated correctly. Are there any concerns?"

"As we discussed earlier, we have made minor personnel changes. It is still a work in progress of everyone adhering to the Praxton standard on board of the ship, but it is trending in the right direction. We initiated two rapid jumps and there was a delay in the second jump by the crew. I believe that is due to the lack of familiarity of the equipment and procedure."

"Very good. Please continue to test rapid jumping until you are satisfied with the crew's expertise."

"I will."

"One reason the Margus system was picked for your destination was due to its isolation. It's not likely any rebel craft will be there to see our newest ship. As a second test of the Star Hawk's capability, orbit Margus four. The planet has primitive life but has not been fully investigated. After establishing orbit, send down a landing party to inspect the terrain and report any new findings."

"Understood. An exploratory mission."

"Yes." She gave a tight smile. "Don't get into any trouble. Everyone is keeping close tabs on the Star Hawk."

———

The orbit around the gas giant was routine, situated among the sixteen moons. Elmwood had the scientific team take measurements and record all pertinent data, including the magnetic field, temperatures, and composition of the coloured bands that circled the globe. A little later, the Star Hawk moved away from the gravity field of the gas giant.

Elmwood ordered another test of the ship's jumping capability. First, the Star Hawk left the vicinity of the Margus system and then immediately returned, stopping near Margus two.

He spoke to the steermaster. "Well, how was that effort?"

"I'm not too impressed. The purpose in having a second jump equipment is if we jump into a difficult situation, we could leave immediately. The second jump is too slow."

Elmwood frowned. The Star Hawk was the first ship to operate with two hyper-jump pieces of equipment. Normally when a ship made a hyperspace jump, it took from half an hour to a full hour before they could make another jump. The equipment could only be charged up for another jump at a defined rate. Rather than trying to charge the jump equipment faster, the Star Hawk was given two identical jump mechanisms. If the ship were to jump into a hostile situation, seconds might mean the difference between escape and being fired upon.

"When does the next jump crew come on duty?"

"Three hours, but I can order the new crew to take over now if you wish. They are on standby."

"Let's do so. When the new crew is ready, let's repeat the two-jump sequence."

An hour later the Star Hawk made a series of two jumps, this time stopping near Margus four. Elmwood approached Redding. "Any better?"

"Yes. Very close to what we expect."

"Good. Establish orbit around Margus four. We will take a shuttle to the planet's surface."

"Yes, sir."

"I'll be in my quarters. I want to speak to the jump crews and find out what was going on from their perspective."

Jump Engineer, Hailis Moreau, stood in front of Captain Elmwood's desk. She waited patiently as he studied a tablet. He finally looked up, frowning.

"Lieutenant Moreau, you are in charge of Team A, which is the unit responsible for the majority of our jumps." He tapped the tablet. "Your team not only failed to meet the target of the second jump, but your team didn't even have the best time. Do you have an explanation for this?" He studied her posture and appearance. Tall, slim with dark shoulder-length hair, Moreau kept her hands by her sides. While she wore the collar and cuffs of the Star Hawk women's uniform, she didn't add any chains.

"I'm sorry, sir. I believed my team to be ready and able to perform the initial jump, plus the following jump within accepted parameters. I have reviewed our process and will make the necessary changes in personnel and procedure."

"Does that mean you have identified the problem?"

"Yes, sir. Corporal Alicia Tulet has not proven capable of determining the null points quick enough. I will see who can replace her."

"Isn't Ms. Tulet a Praxton military recruit?"

"Yes, sir."

"Then replacing her is not a simple matter. It is the mandate of the Star Hawk to prepare Praxton females for advanced training in skills pertinent to those required in Alliance worlds. Ms. Tulet is a promising candidate in this area."

"Can't we just replace her with another Praxton female?"

"Negative. Even if we were to replace her with a successful candidate, then our recruitment process would be at fifty percent for her position, which is well below our target of seventy-five percent."

"Understood, sir."

"You need to do two things. One, you need to train Tulet to be an effective null jump engineer."

"Very well, sir. I will work with her. What is the other suggestion?"

"That you do not blame your subordinates for your failure to accomplish your assignments. Your crew is your responsibility. If they fail to succeed in a task, then you must accept full responsibility. Please inform me if I'm not being clear on this." He stood.

"Sir, I am certain there will not be any misunderstanding of the priorities in the future."

Elmwood nodded. "You have spent your career with the Alliance Forces. It is important for you to allow yourself to understand the Praxton point of view. In particular, study their history and culture. This will help you integrate them into the Star Hawk operations."

"I see, sir. I recognize I need to make more of an effort to help the Praxton women work on my team."

"Excellent. How will you do that?"

Moreau looked surprised by the question. "I, I will try to understand their social attitudes. If you have any suggestions, sir, it will be appreciated."

"Good. You can start by showing more empathy with the Praxton females. You may wish to consider wearing chains and exhibiting more Praxton customs."

"Understood, sir."

Moreau looked relieved to be exiting his office. Elmwood considered he had successfully stressed the importance of producing satisfactory results from her team.

His next visitor, Lieutenant Jex O'Doul, the leader of Jump Team B entered Elmwood's office looking confident. "You wanted to see me, captain."

"Yes, I did. What is your perception of the recent tests concerning the double jumps?" He watched the heavy-set, medium height man think before replying.

"The results were unacceptable. My team, while having the best times, produced inadequate grades."

Elmwood raised his eyebrows. "And what would you contribute that to?"

"I failed to prepare my team for the possibility of a second jump. It was my fault, sir."

"I'm glad you recognize that." Elmwood nodded. "What are your plans to rectify the next series of jumps?"

"Review our performances and practice. Sir, my crew is new to the jump process in this ship. I ask for consideration that they were at a disadvantage in performing their tasks."

"Well put, Mr. O'Doul. Yes, I will give your team a small leeway.

However, lets be certain I expect better results at the next jump or there will be consequences. You are dismissed."

Elmwood relaxed with a cup of coffee. As the coffee disappeared, the last of the jump leaders asked permission to enter his office.

Elmwood appraised the blonde woman, who had added chains from her wrist cuffs to her collar. Torleen Watson stood, looking apprehensive.

"Lieutenant Watson, your team has registered rather poor results on the dual jumps. The first jump went very well, well within expectations. The second jump is what I have serious concerns with. The time for the execution of the second jump failed to meet requirements."

"Yes sir, I have read the reports, and I know my team failed on the second jump. That was entirely on me, sir."

"I have reviewed your personnel file. You were fast tracked to the position of leader of Jump Team C because of your excellent marks in studies and showing an above average ability in understanding jump technology. So, what makes you believe that you were at fault?"

"Sir, after the first jump I congratulated my team on the successful job. I was excited about the jump and immediately analysed the reports. I'm sorry, but I became distracted and didn't notice the call for a second jump. I know that's inexcusable, sir."

"Very well, I can appreciate the excitement you must have felt with your team's first successful jump. In the future, you need to be more diligent. Having said that, I believe your team has had a good first start and I expect they will do better in the future."

"Thank you, sir."

Elmwood dismissed Watson and returned to his work. A few minutes later, he returned to the command centre. "Ms. Redding, I see we have established orbit."

"Yes, sir." She pivoted in her chair to look at the large viewscreen. A globe of white clouds, green terrain, blue oceans filled the screen. Large polar caps of white, especially on the northern pole, suggested the planet was not a warm paradise. "Pretty looking planet."

"It is. What is the climate and environment at latitude thirty on the northern hemisphere?"

"On land, the temperature is around fifteen degrees. The air is dry. Nitrogen is seventy-five percent, and the oxygen is at twenty-two percent."

"Okay, quite tolerable for a short visit." He turned to Morgan Regan. "Organize a shuttle team to go to the planet's surface. Make it a scientific team and collect plant samples. This is strictly a test run on how well a shuttle can be used for exploratory work."

"Do you want me to lead the team?" asked Morgan.

"Yes. I don't expect any problems. Let me know if you observe anything unusual with the shuttle's performance."

The shuttle Falcon One left the Star Hawk without incident. The oversized bay doors and a force field prevented the air in the hanger from escaping to the vacuum of space. Morgan piloted the spacecraft, circling the Star Hawk first before heading toward the planet. She wanted to have a look at the massive, blimp shaped ship with various bulges and antenna. Morgan glided the shuttle to the planet's surface, pleased with how the small ship handled as it sliced through the atmosphere before it landed on a grassy area with a scattering of rocks.

"Okay, we know what we need to do. We have just under two hours to accomplish the task of taking readings and obtaining plant samples." Morgan did one final check of the climate and atmosphere readings and opened the shuttle door.

The five-person crew stepped out into the cool air. Each of them wore an earpiece to for communication that included a microphone. Most of the crew wore light jackets, although Amis Carter decided he didn't need a coat. The big man told Morgan he was used to much colder weather on his home world. "This is nice, and the clouds aren't blocking the sun."

She watched him carry a trowel and a bag, reaching a clump of green plants. He dug in around at the roots. Morgan looked at the other crew members carrying out their tasks, which include pounding spikes with instruments into the ground. The men wore their normal ship's uniform, but the women wore outdoor clothing, consisting of coats and pants. One woman, Millan Reaves, confessed it was the first time she had ever worn pants. "I was born and raised on Praxton. Females never wear anything but skirts and dresses. This feels odd."

Morgan watched her briefly before turning her attention to Terric

Strom, a geologist from one of the Alliance worlds. The man was average height but built slimly. He struggled to carry the bulky equipment near a rocky area and began to set up the devices.

Millan, a petite woman with brown skin, spoke to Strom briefly before continuing on to do her own work. The friendly woman, a biologist, specialized in insects. She began collecting specimens near the plants.

Gar Parson, an older man and head of the military scientific team, exited last. He was in charge to set up climate and atmosphere testing equipment. They would leave the equipment on the surface and record changes. When the next visit from an exploration team came to the planet, they could download the recordings to study the planetary changes.

Suddenly Amis Carter screamed, holding up a bloody wrist.

[33]

CARTER RAN TOWARD THE SHUTTLE. After a few steps he stopped and looked around bewildered. He gave out a howl, turned and ran off into the green foliage.

"Amis, where are you going?" Morgan watched him disappear past a small tree. The other shuttle members looked at where he had vanished and at her. She waved them to huddle with her.

"Something bit him, and it appears maybe a toxin from that bite is causing him to be confused." She pointed at Terric Strom. "Terric, see if you can find the creature that bit him. Use extreme caution and use a weapon to stun or kill it. We need to find what toxin this creature uses. The rest of us will try to find Amis."

Morgan took the lead position, Millan Reaves and Gary Parson moved behind her, forming a triangle as they moved. She contacted the Star Hawk and gave Elmwood a report that a crew member was injured from a bite of an unknown creature.

A scattering of birds was the only sign of movement in the bushes. They heard the rustle of creatures in the brush and readied their weapons in case of a second attack. Morgan spotted a shirt lying on the ground. She picked it up. "The buttons are missing. He must have ripped it off."

Shortly later, they came across a boot and later a pair of pants. Like the shirt, it appeared damaged from being torn off in haste.

"This can't be good," Millan commented. "It's cold, and he has taken off his clothes."

"I think he can handle the cold. It's if he gets attacked by another creature is what worries me," Morgan replied.

They continued their search when Elmwood contacted her. "Morgan, our infrared sensors show he's about ten o'clock and fifty to sixty metres away."

"Thanks. We'll move toward there."

As they approached the area, they spotted him run across their path, and disappear into the brush again. Morgan saw he was naked and with an erection. *What the hell did that toxin do to him?* A minute later they saw him again, this time closer but behind where they were standing.

"We've found him, but how do we catch him?" Parson asked. "He isn't running away from us. I'd say he seems to be circling us."

"If he gets close enough, maybe we can catch him. But how do we bring him back to the shuttle?"

"I can run back to the shuttle and get the straps we use to hold down cargo."

"Good idea. You get the straps, and Millan and I will try to see how we can catch him."

After Parson hurried off, Morgan looked at Millan. "Any thoughts?"

"I do. Amis is still moving around us, and I think I know why." She paused. "He has an erection, and if he's that aroused, I suspect he has eyes on us for one reason."

"It seems he has gone to very primal responses." Morgan agreed. "When he became injured, he fled away from what he perceived as a danger. His erection tells me he wants one of us. I hope Gary hurries back. We're going to need him if Amis attacks us."

"I have a plan. If Amis is attracted to us, I can act like bait."

"Bait?"

"Yeah, I can set myself up so he'll approach me, and then Gary and you can grab him."

"Maybe. I don't want to risk you getting hurt." She heard footsteps and saw Parson and Strom run toward her.

"Good news." Strom announced. "I caught one of creatures. It looks like a lizard with fur. I stunned it and put it in a cage." He held up several cloth straps. "We brought a bunch of these."

"Excellent. Millan has come up with a plan."

Morgan walked at a constant pace, following Millan. The other two crew members were ahead of Millan, and they waited for her to travel to a designated spot that had a high rock elevation along one side. Occasionally she had a glimpse of Amis and it appeared the plan was working. Millan had taken off her coat and top, and Morgan hoped she wasn't too chilled. Millan had the opinion Amis needed more of an enticement to go after her.

Morgan saw Millan make her way to the position just in front of the rocks and wait. She crotched down and whispered, "Is everyone in position?"

One by one, she heard their affirmative response in her earpiece. Morgan watched and saw Amis slowly approach Millan, taking one hesitant step after another. His body had a sheen to his bronzed skin, and it appeared the cool air wasn't having any affect on him. He leaned forward and Morgan wondered how he maintained his erection despite his earlier exertions. She noticed he had hair on his chest but was clean shaven at his pubic area. Morgan watched Millan sit quietly and give him a reassuring smile.

Amis moved within a few feet of Millan when Morgan gave the signal to attack. At first Amis's attention stayed on Millan. By the time he turned around, Morgan and the others were able to subdue him. They used the cloth straps to secure his arms behind his back. Despite his arms behind his back and his knees tied together, he continued to struggle, and cried out in a gargle of words. He bucked and tried to roll away.

Morgan saw Millan kneel by Amis, talking to him in a quiet voice. She rested a hand on his chest. Slowly he settled down.

"So how do we get him to the shuttle?" Strom whispered to Morgan.

Morgan understood the problem. Trying to carry a struggling man as big as Amis would be difficult. "How about if we untie his legs and see if

Millan can convince him to follow her back to the shuttle. If he tries to escape, I'm sure we can recapture him with his arms secured."

Millan reduced Amis's anxiety by talking and stroking his arm and chest. Slowly she untied the strap tying his knees together. He remained lying down, watching her as she continued to talk to him, repeating his name among words to stay calm. She stood and encouraged him to do the same. Gradually he rose, looking uncertain.

Millan tugged on his arm. "Come with me." She smiled and looked up at him.

Morgan had the two men walk behind Amis, while Millan and herself walked on either side of him. Millan kept talking quietly to him with one hand on his arm to help guide him. Morgan touched his back, noticing the skin was hot and slightly damp. *He's running a fever.*

When they reached the shuttle, Amis hesitated, but finally allowed Millan to lead him inside. She sat with him on a pair of seats, talking to him in a quiet voice.

Morgan contacted the medical facilities on the Star Hawk, describing the symptoms. After a brief conversation, she opened the shuttle's medical kit and prepared an injection. After carefully approaching him, she pressed the injector on his arm. A small puffing noise, and the drugs were administered into him.

"It's a sedative and an anti-histamine. It might help him relax and counter the toxin." She glanced down, noting his erection still hadn't disappeared. "I'll get him a blanket."

The shuttle returned to the Star Hawk, and medics quickly entered it to assess Amis. He now acted less anxious and could utter a few monosyllable words.

Morgan left the medics to take care of him and noticed Millan went with them to the medical room. She found Captain Elmwood at the command centre, looking at a tablet in his hands.

"That was supposed to be a quiet mission." He raised his eyebrows at her.

"We had an unexpected situation. That lizard, or whatever it was, sure caused a problem with Amis Carter." She stood with her hands behind her back. She wondered if he was going to chide her for her role in the less than perfect mission. *Will he tell me I need discipline? I wish he would give me sign he wants alone time with me.*

"I heard. I just had an update, and it looks he'll be fine. They'll release him in a few hours." Elmwood lowered the tablet.

"Poor guy. Whatever made up that toxin sure caused him grief. Now that the shuttle mission is over, what comes next?"

"As it happens, General Howling has given us our first mission."

"That's exciting. What is it?"

"It looks interesting. Let's go to my quarters and I'll fill you in."

Okay, so maybe this will be the place he'll show more on how he feels about me.

[34]

TEELA MEZCAL CONTINUED her work monitoring incoming signals. Her work was noted as being first rate, and she was given a promotion as the lead in her group. She increased her attention to the minor disturbances of the incoming signals.

Narcel Cannith, her common room senior female, had removed restrictions on her. Her excellent work reports and her compliance with accepting the role of being a Praxton female had made discipline unnecessary for the time being. Mitch Gallow had a positive influence on her behaviour. He had become her unofficial guardian. He occasionally used a leash on her wrist to show he was in control, and she hoped he would soon take her to his quarters. The problem with the Star Hawk leaving port, and executing a series of jumps, meant the crew was expected to curtail personal activities until the Yellow Standby Alert was removed.

Lunch time arrived and Mitch escorted her to the dining area. He didn't use a leash on her during working hours, but it was as if an invisible one was still there. He took her to a table where she sat and waited while he decided what they would have to eat.

Mitch returned with a tray of soup and sandwiches.

"Thank you, Master Mitch." She waited until he took a bite of his sandwich before starting to eat.

"I trust you remembered not to wear any panties today."

"Yes, I did as you ordered. I also wore the flowered nipple clips that you liked."

"That's good to hear. I hope this alert ends soon so I can make up for lost time with you alone. I believe you deserve a small spanking for past indiscretions."

She grinned. "Did you hear about the shuttle mission?"

"Yeah, one of the crew was bitten, and they had to take him to the medical room."

"I heard there's more to it than that. I guess whatever bit him acted like a drug. He became like a wild man and tore off all of his clothes. Apparently, he ran around naked with this big hard-on. Even after they brought him back to the Star Hawk, he still had an erection. One of the women on the shuttle who helped him has been in his company ever since."

"So, to catch a woman all one has to do is to run around naked?"

"Don't you dare. I want you all for myself." She smiled. "Master Mitch."

He laughed. "I want you for myself too."

"Speaking of wanting someone, I told you how Tess tried to seduce Julia."

"Yeah, you said Tess had finally got her to sleep with her."

"Well, Tess now usually keeps Julia wearing only her panties in the common room. She kneels where Tess is sitting and is very obedient. Tess has her under her complete control."

"Interesting. Maybe that's what I could do to you, keep you naked and by my side."

"Well, being naked, and under your control, has its advantages. Maybe after this alert is over, we can spend a few evenings together that way."

———

Diana finished with her adjustments to a green tea at her workstation. It wasn't difficult changing the formula once she had the basic tea formula set. She walked to the kitchen to taste her newest beverage. Unlike earlier times, she hoped to see Derik. She was confident Corporal Holton had learned that she required a different approach than Praxton born females, and his discipline for minor transgressions had not drawn her closer to him.

The green tea didn't meet her expectations, and she tried to detect the subtle flavours it was missing. She sat on a barstool, refreshing her palate with a cracker and a cup of water. She tried the tea again. *I think it needs less acidity. It needs a better balance.* Rather than going back to her office, she made her way to Holton's office, and was pleased to see him working at his desk.

"Hi there, Master Derik." She stood at his office door with her hands behind her back.

"Diana." He looked up. "Testing another product?"

"I am. Green tea."

"Good luck on that. I don't drink the stuff myself. Let me know when you get to the spirits."

"I think whisky is after the wine." She laughed. "How are food processes going?"

"It's on the quieter side. Whenever we do the hyperspace jumps, food consumption goes down. Scientists and doctors claim the human body isn't affected by the jumps, but after a jump, and in this case a series of them, people don't eat as much. They drink less coffee and alcohol. The main food item is usually soup and lighter styles of food. Yet, there's nothing wrong with them according to medical tests. But as far as I'm concerned, there is something to hyperspace jump syndrome, even if doctors don't want to recognize it."

"So is your appetite down as well?"

"No, I'm one of those immune to jumps. I can eat just about anytime."

"You know I'm a pretty good cook, if I do say so myself. How about if you come to my suite and I cook you dinner?"

"I'd love that, except with this slow period I'm recalibrating the processing tanks." He gave a smile. "Someone has upped the quality of the food and beverages, and now I need to make sure the equipment is operating at peak efficiency. Otherwise, your fine efforts may go to unnoticed. It means I'm having dinner in the office to save time."

"Sorry." She gave a short laugh. "How about breakfast? You should start your day with a good breakfast."

"Now that I can do."

"Great. Seven-thirty tomorrow morning?"

"All right." He rubbed his chin. "Now what would happen if I were to show up at seven hundred instead?"

She tilted her head. "Sir, you may catch me in a state of undress if you were to do that. I may be in the shower."

"That would be a bonus. Breakfast and a beauty."

"Don't get your hopes up. I'll see you tomorrow morning." She waved goodbye, her thoughts already on what she would she make for him, and if she should let him see her in the shower. *That view from the living room to the shower is there for a reason.*

Diana studied the composition of the green tea once more and corrected a minor error. She tested the new sample, and a smile crossed her face. "There, much better." She let out a sigh as she finished her tea.

"Now, Master Derik, what do I do about tomorrow morning?" She considered that he already indicated that he would be at her door a half hour early, with the main reason to see her still undressed. She sat in her office and decided she had done enough for one day. She sent a message to Khloe Levit, asking her to meet her for dinner.

Khloe rested on her arms at the table across from Diana after they had put in their order for food. "Okay, what's up? Is it about Master Derik?"

"It is. I invited him to my place for dinner, but he was too busy with equipment setup. So, I suggested breakfast instead, which he accepted. Then he said he might show up a half hour early just to catch me in a state of undress. What should I do?"

"If you're inviting him for breakfast, then I assume you're very interested in him. Give him permission to enter your suite. That way you can be upstairs when he enters. I suggest you use the shower while he's waiting downstairs."

"I'm nervous about that."

"Don't be. Female bodies are meant to be admired. You can look up how to do showering the Praxton female way."

"How many ways are there to shower?" Diana laughed. "Okay, I'll look it up."

"After you finish showering, stay naked or put on a top and nothing else. Cook him breakfast that way. He'll appreciate it."

"I'm not sure about that."

"Come on. He's already spanked you. You're past the point of being shy in front of him."

"I guess that's true."

"Remember to show respect at all times during breakfast or you'll end up with another spanking. Of course, that may be something you want."

Diana laughed. "When it comes to Praxton men, I'm not sure what I want."

―

Diana rolled out of bed at six o'clock. She yawned as she undid her ankle cuff and made her way to the makeup table. She carefully applied makeup, using a waterproof type. *It wouldn't do much good if this washed off in the shower.*

She carefully picked out the top she wanted to wear while cooking breakfast, choosing the cream coloured top partly because of its length. The long-sleeved top reached just past her cheeks, exposing them if she lifted her arms. The next item Diana selected was star shaped nipple clips attached by a gold chain. Those were the only items she planned to wear while she made breakfast for Derik, other than a collar.

Diana went downstairs and checked the view from the living room to the shower again. She made sure the room was clean but still had a lived-in look. Satisfied, she made herself a cup of coffee and carried it upstairs to her bedroom. She set the wall visibility to the living room to half, which she thought would allow him to see her with a bit of mystery. She sipped at her coffee and checked the time, suspecting he would arrive at exactly seven o'clock. He did.

She heard Derik Holton first use the door chime and then enter the suite. She watched him look around and proceed to the armchair that faced the wall of the bedroom and shower. After sitting, he looked up, and Diana suspected he saw her move across the bedroom as a shadow. She pretended to check her clothing in the closet and examine her jewellery on a table. Diana finally made her way to the well-lit shower that would give him a full view of her. She adjusted the water spray temperature and the height to avoid getting her hair and face wet.

Diana stepped into the water, hoping it would obscure her from his eyes below. She used a sponge-like pad to soap her skin, using more soap than necessary. Turning around in a circle, Diana tried to keep one heel raised as the instructions for Praxton females indicated was the preferred method for sensuous showering. As she pivoted around in a circle, she had a glimpse of Derik watching her. She rinsed off and turned on the warm drying air. A minute later she exited the shower and put on her nipple jewellery, collar and top. Diana ventured downstairs, giving Derik a smile.

"I see you are right on time, Master Derik."

"I didn't want to be late for your shower. I enjoyed watching you very much."

"Thank you." She made her way to the kitchen, suddenly feeling too warm. Diana prepared the breakfast, adding ingredients to different bowls. As the food cooked, she brought Derik a cup of coffee.

"Breakfast will be ready in a few minutes."

"I better wait at the table. It smells good from here."

She added the various items on plates, which included French toast, scrambled eggs with peppers, sausages, and fruit slices. A bowl held whipped cream, and a pitcher held warm syrup. It took two trips, but Diana placed everything on the table. After she sat, she waited for Derik to fill his plate before taking any for herself, understanding the Praxton etiquette.

"This is very good. You really know how to cook besides the chemical aspect of food."

"Thank you, Master Derik."

"I would like to say I appreciate that you gave me entrance to your suite. I really enjoyed watching you shower."

"Thanks." Diana blushed. "I do like the shower. I have a touch of claustrophobia, so the transparent wall makes me feel less confined. For the same reason, I don't like my arms and legs being tied up. Loose chains to cuffs are okay, but I don't like being restricted."

"That's good to know. If you live as a Praxton female, there would be restraints placed on you."

"I know. I don't mind the collar and cuffs, but I prefer to keep the chains loose. I need freedom of movement."

"So, no gag or blindfold?" He smiled.

"Definitely no gag. Maybe a blindfold under the right circumstances." She grinned at him. "I guess I need to have a lot of trust first."

He finished his breakfast and after another coffee, stood to go to over to the couch. "I want to inform you of a Praxton custom."

"Oh?"

"When a male finds a female interesting, he will often spank her."

"You've already spanked me."

"Yes, but that was more for discipline. What I want to do is to spank you as a sign of affection."

"Affection?" Diana took a hesitant step toward him. "Really?"

"Really." He held out his hand. "I know you want this too." He sat on the couch.

Diana took more slow steps and touched his hand with her own. "Are you certain this is a normal Praxton custom?"

"It is." He gently pulled her over his lap and paused as she settled into a comfortable position with her head and arms resting on the cushions of the couch. He lifted up her shirt and rested a hand on her ass. "I think you'll enjoy this."

He lightly smacked her ass, paused to squeeze her cheeks, and then continued with her spanking.

Diana sighed, enjoying the mild spanking.

Derik increased the intensity of the spanking, striking harder as he alternated between sides. He heard a small moan escape from Diana as she kicked her leg up once and shifted her hips. Derik pulled her tighter against him and resume the spanking, turning her cheeks a hot pink. "Don't try to pull away or I will secure you."

"Yes, Master Derik." Diana breathed out. She felt his erection press against her.

Derik changed the pattern of his hits, striking her ass in an upward motion, and worked on one cheek before switching to the other. "I very much enjoyed your preparation of breakfast, but the next time I come over for a meal, I want you to be nude. Whether it is for a meal or drinks, I prefer you to be nude. Understood?"

"Yes, Master Derik. I understand I must be naked when you arrive and will stay that way until you tell me I may get dressed." Diana gasped out the words. A rush of warmth rose from between her legs.

"Good." He massaged her ass and pushed up her shirt to rub her back. "Spread your legs."

Diana spread her legs, and the spanking resumed. She groaned. *Will I be able to sit after this? My ass must be so red.* She released a second, louder moan.

His big hand gave each cheek four more hard strikes, and Diana kicked her feet with each hit. "Unfortunately, Praxton custom means I cannot do much more than spank you until you have accepted my collar or my being your guardian." He pushed his hand between her legs, cupping her swollen vagina. "I do hope we can proceed with our relationship."

Diana realized she was rotating her hips, trying to use his hand to bring more pleasure to her clitoris. She stopped, knowing she wasn't likely able to climax and would end up being frustrated.

"I would like to get to know you better as well, Master Derik." She waited, wondering if her spanking was over, or if he planned to do more. She was content to let him do what he wanted with her.

"You have nice legs, but most of your skirts are on the long side. From now on they must be noticeably shorter that the ship's uniform skirt."

"Understood, Master Derik. I will wear shorter skirts and dresses."

The palm of his hand pressed against her wetness. "You may now get ready for work. Bring a leash with you, as I will escort you to your office. I also forbid you to come or pleasure yourself until I give you permission to do so." He smacked her ass hard. "Understood?"

"Yes, Master Derik." Diana felt weak as she made her way to her bedroom. She retouched her makeup and added cuffs. She picked out one of her shortest skirts and changed her shirt to a see-through black lace sleeveless top. She was aware he could see her dress through the semi-dark wall in her bedroom.

After adding a chain between her wrist cuffs, she carried a leather-like leash downstairs to Derik.

"You look very nice." He first attached the leash to her wrist and then dropped to his knees in front of her. He slid up his hands and pulled down her panties to her ankles, where she stepped out of them. "I like the thought you're not wearing any."

I like the feeling of when you take them off. "I'll try to remember that."

She saw him toss her panties toward the stairs that led to her bedroom. "If I do find you're wearing panties, I may just remove them wherever we are." He gave her a grin.

"That may make it interesting, depending where we are." She laughed, put on her shoes, and walked with him to her office. "Will you be working late tonight?"

"Yes, and for the rest of the week. It's just calibrations, but it takes a long time to do. A lot of waiting for results to show up on the monitors."

"Well, when you get a free evening, I hope we can get together."

"We shall."

They reached her office, and he removed the leash, folding it and placing it in his pocket. "In the future when we travel together, I will probably add the leash to you."

"Of course, Master Derik." She hoped he would kiss her, but it seemed some Praxton, or military custom, prevented him from doing so. She carefully sat, wincing as her cheeks touched the chair. After office work, she contacted Khloe Levit, getting an agreement to meet her for lunch.

———

"Okay, now what's up? You look excited."

Diana described her breakfast date. "That was one long, serious spanking. I can barely sit."

"That's the best kind." Khloe laughed. "Master Derik must really like you."

"I think he does. He took me by a leash to my office but ordered me not to pleasure myself until he gave me permission. If he hadn't, I would've used a vibrator after work."

"I don't know in your case, since you're a civilian contractor, but females are not allowed a vibrator under Praxton rules." Khloe shook her head. "The only exception is a vibrator remotely controlled by her guardian."

"You're kidding me."

"Sorry. Females are supposed to depend on others for their sexual needs. Vibrators would make it too easy to go it alone."

"Men have too much control over women." Diana let out a long sigh. "Okay, so no vibrator then. Can he really order me not to pleasure myself?"

"He can if you accept his control of you." Khloe grinned. "I like the men being in control and a guardian taking care of me. I enjoy being on a leash, so I think you're lucky. As for not being allowed to come, I guess that's part of his control over you. I suggest you better obey, or you'll find out what other types of discipline can be used on you."

"I guess I don't want to find out. I now have to order skirts and dresses with a higher hemline. Master Derik wants me to show more leg."

"That's good. I love wearing short skirts and find this uniform too long. Remember when a female sits, she does not pull down her skirt. She lets it rise normally. If the skirt is loose, flare it behind you so you don't sit on it. And never cross your legs."

"That last part I know." She grinned. "I got in a lot of trouble for that one."

"Seeing that you're still learning Praxton customs, I suspect you'll get into more trouble. I'm looking forward to watching your first flogging. Naked, of course, while secured."

A public flogging while I'm naked? I guess I better assume that's going to happen with Master Derik eventually.

35

TEELA STOOD NAKED, grouped with six other naked women as they faced their instructor, Della Knack. She now had several lessons on fille d'affichage and was pleased with how well she had accomplished the routines. Teela had fallen a few times on the padded mat below the horizontal rectangular frame holding the coloured cloths, but gradually learned the technique of wrapping and unwrapping one limb at a time.

Della, a slim blonde with long hair, spoke in a friendly voice. "We're all doing very well on a difficult art to perform. Yesterday, we tried the Flamingo manoeuvre and did very well at it. Remember that the Flamingo requires one leg to freeze in position for several seconds. Some of us hurried lowering the leg, and the lesson here is to make sure we are balanced before bending our knee." She smiled and continued, "Today we shall do the Ocean Wave." She pointed at a large video screen that showed a demonstration of the segment. "Let's give it a try and try to master it."

Teela approached her bed, a metal frame with the various strips of cloths strung across. Most were loose and required her to wrap her limbs around to supply enough tension to hold her in place. She easily started the process of securing her body horizontally. When she was comfortable, she tried repeating the Flamingo manoeuvre again, stretching out her limbs save for one leg that she bent at the knee. She held it in position for several seconds, pleased at her balance. She knew the Flamingo was important to learn because by rotating the leg across the other, it forced the body to rotate and allowed for a new position to begin. Now she tried the new segment. She twisted along the cloths until her back arched and her head hung down. She used one hand to pull a loose cloth across her breasts. The cloth imitated a wave as it crested over her one way and gently slid back before repeating the procedure.

"Very good, Teela. You seem to have a natural ability for fille d'affichage."

"Thank you. I find it fun, too."

"At the rate you're learning, I believe you'll be an expert at it. That brings me to something I want you to consider. Next month, we will do a live performance in one of theatres. I would like you to do one of the acts."

"Really? On stage?"

"Yes, in a month you'll be easily good enough to do a performance."

"Thank you. I'd like to do that."

"Good. I would like you to spend extra time here on the double bed."

Teela had seen the double bed, but not used it. It was for two women to perform together, and rather than just artistic moves, the double bed usually told a story. The performance normally consisted of one of two women battling for supremacy, with one eventually seducing the other. "I've never been on it."

"It has a few peculiarities because of more cloths and being longer. But I believe you will master it quickly."

Teela untangled herself from the cloths on her bed and stood. "Okay, I guess I could try it. Who would my partner be?"

"Me. I thought we could pick out a play and see how it goes."

"Okay. When do we start?"

"After this class is over, let's go over a schedule that works for you."

———

"Master Mitch, guess what?" Teela hurried to meet him outside the exercise area, pleased he had decided to walk her back to the women's common area after her lessons. She walked topless with her shirt in her gym bag, knowing he liked her bare breasted with nipple clips. She handed him the handle of her leash with the other end secured to her collar.

"What? You got a gold star for dropping your ass on the mat?"

She laughed at his joke and explained she had been picked for a live performance.

"That's great. I'm looking forward to seeing that."

"Good. If you didn't want me to do that, I wouldn't."

"Why would I want you not to do that?"

"Because I'll be naked in front of everyone. It's your prerogative, as kind of my guardian, to decide if I can do it or not."

"I like it when you're naked. Others should get to see you that way too."

"I'm almost naked right now."

"No panties?"

"Of course not. You told me not to wear any and I listen to your orders."

"I sure wish I could take you to my room right now."

"I do too. Soon that Yellow Standby will be over, and then I will get to please you."

He laughed. "Not if I please you first."

36

CAPTAIN JULIUS ELMWOOD stood in front of his executive officers as they gathered around in the captain's meeting room. "Great news, we have our first assignment in rebel territory. We are going to the star system Bellator and the lone habitable planet they call Proelium. We are to offer diplomatic ties with the rulers of the planet."

"Proelium has not posed much of a danger to Alliance vessels," Morgan Regan added. "They don't appear to do any pirating. In fact, my understanding is their civilization has gone backward and they live almost as a medieval world."

"That is correct. There likely won't be any danger to the Star Hawk, and this mission is meant to extend formal ties with Proelium. We hope we can improve their technology level, establish trading, and eventually have them be part of the Alliance group of planets."

———

The Star Hawk entered the Bellator system. It was safest to establish jumps beginning and ending outside of strong gravity fields. The Bellator system was far enough away from the Margus system that the Star Hawk needed to use two jumps to arrive at the Bellator sun, a medium-sized yellow star.

They did the rest of the journey to the planet by normal propulsion, which could approach ninety percent of the speed of light.

After the Star Hawk passed the orbits of two gas giants, they arrived at Proelium, the fourth planet from the star. Elmwood expected a challenge as their ship drew closer to the planet. The response was only a single, older style shuttle that moved between the Star Hawk and Bellator four.

Elmwood studied the image on the viewscreen. The Earth sized world had three small moons, numerous artificial satellites and two space stations. One space station appeared to be in disuse, with only one spacecraft attached to the cylinder structure. The other space station was shaped like an hourglass with a rod going through the narrowest part. A dozen ships clung to the oddly shaped space station.

"What do you make of the spacecraft and space stations?" He asked Khloe.

"According to the sensor information, one of the space stations is barely being used. Very little power is being consumed. The second space station is more active. However, all the space craft are old. Some may be several decades old. There isn't any threat from any of them. It appears there may be only four of them capable of a hyperspace jump."

Janice Madison, the communication officer, announced, "We're being hailed by the approaching shuttle craft."

"Send it to my station." Elmwood sat and looked at his viewscreen. Moments later, a bearded man appeared wearing a pale blue uniform.

"Hail, strange vessel. We ask you to respect our independence, and we seek no quarrel with thee. I am Captain John Geroa."

"I'm Captain Julius Elmwood of the spaceship Star Hawk. We represent the Alliance worlds and wish to open a dialogue with the leader of Proelium."

"I see. Please give me a few minutes while I converse with my superior about your request."

The viewscreen image went blank, and Elmwood spoke to Madison. "Can you listen in on their conversation?"

"Of course. Their encoding is simple. I'll patch it through to your console."

Elmwood watched Geora on the viewscreen speak to someone, and they listened to the second voice that sounded like a woman.

"They are asking for a meeting with our planet leader. They claim to be from the Alliance worlds and want to open a dialogue."

"Well, it doesn't matter if they are from Alliance worlds, or one of the demon worlds. By the size of their ship, we can hardly refuse. Tell them they can meet with me. You may have to transport them to the station as there ain't no way that beast is going to be able to dock with us."

"I'll inform them of your decision."

Shortly later, Geora resumed speaking to Elmwood, unaware he had listened to his conversation. "Captain Elmwood, we would be most honoured to converse with you at our space station. As your spaceship is too large to dock with us, I would be pleased to provide transportation with my shuttle."

"Thank you, but we will use our own shuttle. Please standby."

———

The Falcon Two departed from the Star Hawk carrying Elmwood, pilot Cerrie Vox, diplomat Tiffany Harris, and weapons officers Rickey Spelling and Thomas Vice.

The Falcon Two followed the older shuttle piloted by Geora to the space station with other shuttle crafts attached to the long rod that pierced the centre of the hourglass shape. Elmwood saw only two of the ships looked capable of carrying more than a dozen people. Everything he saw looked old and in need of repair.

"I hope it's safe to enter that space station," Spelling commented. "I doubt it would pass any modern safety inspection."

"It likely won't fall apart the moment we enter it." Elmwood could understand her concern, spotting damage to part of the rod that had been repaired with different material than the rest of the station.

They requested the Falcon Two to dock at Port Seven, and the pilot carefully aligned the ship's exit door with the port doors.

"Sensors show normal air concentration, although there are additional organic components." Vox read out the sensor readings.

"What does that mean?" Spelling asked.

"It means we can breathe the air, but it probably has an unpleasant odour to it." Elmwood smiled. "Likely the result of poor air filtration. Open the doors and let's see who wants to talk to us."

The same man who greeted them in the shuttle appeared to meet them when the door opened.

"Captain John Geora. How nice to meet you in person." Geora was on the short side, although heavily built. His dark skin showed blemishes, looking like scars that healed poorly.

"To be precise, it is Sir John when I'm not on a shuttle craft." He didn't introduce the two men standing behind him. Both wore the same blue uniform Geora wore, although they were ill fitting and of need of a cleaning. Both men wore a beard and appeared to be younger than Geora.

"Thank you for the clarification." Elmwood introduced the rest of the crew and they followed Sir John down the narrow walkway. The two other men with Geora remained where they were.

"The air smells like we're passing through a food recycling centre. It stinks." Spelling whispered.

At the end of the walkway they reached an elevator. The elevator easily held everyone and appeared to be designed to hold cargo as well as people. It rumbled upward and stopped. Sir John had to hit the 'Open Door' button twice before the door slid open in a jerking motion.

They were ushered into a large, and according to the space station standards, a well-appointed circular room. It included an office and several pieces of furniture used for conferences. They met a tall woman who appeared to be middle age. She had a medium frame and walked with a limp as she approached them. Her clothing consisted of a long lightly coloured pattern skirt and a dark blue shirt.

"Welcome to Proelium. I am Gatekeeper Marsia."

Elmwood again did introductions. "We present the Alliance worlds and have come here to open a dialogue with you in hopes of ensuring peace, good will and perhaps someday asking your world to join us."

"Thank you for those words." Marisa smiled. "As you have no doubt noticed, Proelium is in no position for battle. I am not certain Proelium can offer the Alliance worlds much in the way of benefits for trade."

"Why do you say that?" Tiffany Harris asked.

"Please, let us sit down, and I will give you a brief history of Proelium."

Elmwood choose one of the armchairs, surprised to see it was covered with leather. Another chair had wood for arms, another material uncommon in the Alliance worlds. *Our Charter of Conduct officer would have a fit seeing these being used. Wood and leather are restricted items.*

A servant, wearing a long dark skirt and top, brought tea in clay mugs as Marisa spoke.

"Proelium was one planet established after the Wave by men and women who wanted to leave our dependence on modern devices behind. Initially the goal was for technology to be used only for electricity and simple mechanical devices. For over a century Proelium kept its promise to use technology to help make life easier while not depending on it for life itself. We did a modest trade with other worlds and we were content. Then a new political force on Proelium came into being, claiming God inspired them to remove all modern technology from the world because it was the work of demons. The New Guards of Tower, as they identified themselves, soon rose to power. The methods they used to control others were violent and opposition to their beliefs was not tolerated."

Elmwood reflected on the Wave, the name of a strange phenomenon that originated from the centre of the galaxy. The Wave obliterated anything electrical, almost wiping out the civilization on Earth and other human worlds. For decades the various planets humans had established a presence on were left isolated and on their own. It would take another decade for the Alliance worlds to reform a partnership, with many other worlds choosing not to join.

"You are telling me this because you must be part of an organization that does not subscribe to the New Guards of Tower beliefs."

"That's true. We are small in number but are determined to bring Proelium back to a reasonable level of technology. We call ourselves the Reformers. I don't know if you and the Alliance worlds can help us, but we see you as our only hope."

"How exactly can we help you?" Harris asked.

"It involves your party discreetly approaching one of our kings."

"One of your kings?"

"Yes, we have eight kingdoms. However, King Bennett Whitehall is the most powerful king and commands a lot of respect. If you can convince him to begin negotiations with the Alliance worlds, then the other kingdoms will fall in line and the end of the New Guard will follow. King Bennett is sympathetic to the Reformers cause."

"We will do our best." Harris looked at Elmwood. "We can meet King Bennett, can't we?"

Elmwood nodded. "However, just how do we meet him? Is there a place to land our shuttle?"

"No, you cannot land your shuttle on Proelium. The people think of shuttles as devil birds and will want to kill anyone inside. You can arrive only in one of our special shuttles. It is disguised and we can take you to the planet surface at night. From there you must travel on foot to see the King."

"Anything else we should know?"

"Yes, you cannot wear what you're wearing. I will arrange for proper attire for you to wear. You must be very careful that no one but the king knows you're from another world. Many of the peasants are superstitious and believe all outsiders are demons in disguise."

⬭

Elmwood peered around the small, circular shaped shuttle. He had already seen the craft from a window in the space station, noting the bottom half of the saucer shaped vessel was painted with a light-absorbing black substance. He determined that allowed for a secretive landing at night. The inside of the shuttle contained the power unit in the centre with seating for ten around the perimeter. Elmwood's team, save for the pilot who stayed in the Falcon Two, sat around the edge of the odd shuttle.

"Will you be journeying with us, Marisa?"

"Yes. I need to guide you to where King Bennett lives, advise you on how not to attract attention on our world, and help you address any concerns he may have about the Alliance worlds."

The departure from the space station ended with a clunking sound, and a few minutes later the space shuttle entered the atmosphere of Proelium. Elmwood felt shaken briefly as the shuttle entered the atmosphere. The Star Hawk personnel were given different garments to wear; a heavy, dark material that covered their bodies along with a hood. Spelling mentioned she had never worn so much clothing before.

"The skirt goes right to the ground. I find it rather confining."

"Women are expected to be covered at all times." Marisa frowned. "Your uniform made you look half naked. I believe women should be modest in their appearance."

"I wasn't naked, just comfortable," Spelling responded.

The space shuttle shook again, jostling everyone in their seats.

Elmwood, sensing the tension between Spelling and Marisa, asked, "Is there a problem with the artificial gravity?"

"Likely." Geora shrugged. "We fix what we can, but the truth is that we don't know how these things are supposed to work. We don't have much spare parts either. Mostly we cannibalize the other shuttles for what we need."

The shuttle landed on top of a tower. Marisa explained it was part of the five stone towers with this one being in the centre. Elmwood and the others exited the shuttle. The roof had a trap door that led to a spiral staircase made of stone. They didn't stop at the ground floor as he expected, but continued on another level below. From there, they followed a tunnel going beyond the perimeter of the four other towers.

They finally climbed another set of stairs, this one straight, and emerged in a stone and wood dwelling. An elderly couple watched them silently as they appeared through a trap door. Marisa held up a hand in greeting.

"We arrive to aid in the Reform. I'm sorry for the disturbance." She led the shuttle group out of the home to a barn. "We will rest here until morning."

"Where did we land exactly?" Elmwood asked.

"The Towers of the Guard. It is a place where meetings are held to celebrate religious events."

"Yet you land the shuttle on top of centre tower."

"The New Guard never goes to the top of the tower, as that is reserved for their god. Second, the staircase we use goes to the tunnel. Another staircase winds around the opposite side and goes from the main floor to the top. It has not been used in decades."

Elmwood and the others made themselves as comfortable as they could in the upper loft of the barn. The straw made for sitting and lying comfortably, but between the farm animals on the main floor and the loose straw, the air was not pleasant to inhale. He sent a message to the ship, informing them of what they were planning to do in the morning.

"We will travel to see King Bennett and try to gain his trust so we can establish an Alliance world's presence."

"Please be careful," Morgan Regan replied. "We know little about the people or their beliefs."

The light from the rising sun stirred them from a light sleep. Marisa went to the farmhouse and obtained a meal of dark, heavy bread, cheese, eggs, and meat. Everything was placed on a large wood platter and everyone took what they wanted, washed down by warm tea served in metal mugs.

The morning was cool, although the clear skies promised the sun would warm the air soon. Marisa led the group from the farmyard to a dirt road, giving a lecture as they walked.

"Speak as little as possible. Your accent and manner of speaking may draw attention. Whenever you are near a tower, and these towers are generally the height of a man's reach, remember it is a sign of the New Guard. Slow your walk, lower your head and pull on your hood. Speak only in whispers. You may receive a blessing from the New Guard advocates. Respond by saying the Tower protects us."

"May I assume it is best we avoid such areas?" Elmwood asked.

"Yes, but the Towers are often along the main road to the kingdom ruled by King Bennett."

Spelling walked alongside of Elmwood for a short distance. "I find these clothes very uncomfortable. They are heavy and confining. I will not complain again about the ship's female uniforms being too revealing. There is something to be said about freedom of movement."

"You're aware men have to wear long sleeves and full coverage on board the ship, don't you?" Elmwood smiled. "What we wear on Proelium is not much different."

"But you don't have to wear a collar and cuffs. Don't get me started."

"I will leave that alone."

The road became firmer and wider as they travelled. They encountered more travellers, horses and horse drawn wagons. They came across a Tower, a small stone made structure slightly higher than Elmwood. Several people stopped to kneel around the tower before continuing their journey.

"Kneel by the Tower and cover your head," Marisa whispered.

The group did as she instructed. After the minute of kneeling, they continued their journey.

"That was the proper way to do it," Marisa commented. "Cover your head and remain quiet. I hope we can avoid other Towers."

"Don't you know if they are up ahead? Aren't they in fixed locations?" Elmwood asked.

"No, they are placed on wood blocks and are dragged by horses to different locations. The New Guards believe the Towers must go where evil may be hiding."

"All knowing and all seeing?"

"Yes, except know nothing and being blind." Marisa laughed.

The density of the travellers increased, and various vendors set up tables alongside of the road. Taverns and inns were spaced along the way. Near noon the group stopped at an inn in a town. The food for lunch consisted of a choice of stew with bread or nothing else. Ale was the beverage of choice, although tea was available.

"How I miss coffee right now," Elmwood commented to himself.

The entourage continued down a main street. In the distance, they could make the castle belonging to King Bennett out as a dark structure. Marisa pointed out the journey was less than an hour away.

"That's providing we don't run into any problems, such as a New Guard rally. All citizens have to stop and listen to the sermon. Many are annoyed to have to stop what they're doing to hear the New Guard's message but are scared what may happen if they don't."

"Compliance by intimidation." Spelling replied to Marisa.

"I suppose it is. I believe if we can convince King Bennett to agree to begin talks with the Alliance worlds, the New Guard will lose their influence rapidly. The New Guard claim their God has forbidden any visitors from other worlds because they are all demons. We have had no visitors for decades, and the New Guard has prohibited anyone from using any technology that would allow us to return to space. We have to be very careful when we use the shuttle and try to manufacture parts for the space station and shuttle."

"Star Hawk to Elmwood. Come in please."

Elmwood heard the quiet buzz of words in his earpiece of Morgan Regan's voice. "Elmwood here."

"What is the prognosis? Will you be able to have an audience with King Bennett?"

"I believe so," he whispered. "We're about an hour away from his castle. We have to tread carefully. A religious group here called the New Guard is against other world visitors and technology."

"Understood. Let us know if you require our help. I have a shuttle on standby with military personnel."

"I hope that won't be necessary. Could you study the shuttles the Proelium people use and see if we can determine what type of technology they use? I'm wondering if we can provide some critical parts to ensure they continue to operate."

"I'll investigate."

They neared the stone wall that marked the boundary of the castle property, although it was still a long walk to the castle itself. The largest difference was the lack of commercial buildings and only manicured gardens with tree-lined brick walkways beyond the wall.

"Praise the New Guard of the Tower! Praise the Tower! Gather around to hear our message from God."

Elmwood heard Marisa quietly curse as they moved to where a Tower had been placed. A tall bearded man bellowed out his message.

Elmwood and the others used their hoods to cover their heads and faced the speaker.

"The demons look for weakness, look for those who would use magic to make their lives easier. It is a sin! A sin, I tell you, to avoid honest work. We of the New Guard do not ask for special favours in bringing you messages from God. But know if you give generously to the Tower, we can spread the message of truth faster and easier. Be aware..."

Spelling looked up at Elmwood, caught his attention and rolled her eyes upward.

The speech continued and finally ended with a further plea to give to the New Guard and, by extension, the teachings of the Tower.

Two women moved among the crowd, giving a blessing of the Tower and seeking a donation for the cause. Each visitor received a hand on each shoulder, and a quiet plea to give so he or she would feel contentment.

Elmwood observed a woman bless Marisa, then Thomas Redding and finally step toward himself.

Suddenly his earpiece came to life. "Captain, we have diagnosed the shuttle craft and space station and determined that we can supply elementary parts to keep their equipment running."

As Elmwood heard Morgan's communication, the woman giving him a blessing heard the thin voice coming from Elmwood's earpiece. She stepped back and pointed at him.

"Demon!" she screamed.

[37]

MORGAN LISTENED to the shouting and the sound of people fighting, garbled sounds and suddenly nothing.

"Spelling, what's happening?"

"Mute."

Morgan understood mute would prevent voice both in receiving and sending. She spoke to the communication officer. "Janice, override mute to listening mode. I need to know what's going on." She turned to Walling. "Kelly, please launch Eagle One for orbit around Proelium, with armed personnel. We may need to intervene on this mission." The Eagle shuttles were lightly armed and could carry ten personnel. She turned her attention to the sounds from the earpieces on the planet surface. She listened to voices and the commotion, still uncertain of what was happening.

Finally, she heard from Spelling.

"I'm not sure what is going to happen next. They took the captain to a kind of a temple. He's been punched a few times, although he looks okay. It all started when someone heard a voice from his earpiece. They think he's a kind of demon. They stomped on the earpiece and roughed him up, as I said."

Morgan considered her options. *Not much I can do until Eagle One is in position.* She walked over to the steermaster. "Nicole, I want you to prepare a course for one kilometre above where our team is on the planet surface."

"Will do. Do you want me to execute the course immediately?"

"No, just be ready on my order."

━━

Elmwood was dragged to the Tower temple. He tried to see past the double doors he was pulled through. He had a glimpse of the wood interior that contained bench seating and a large space in front of a pedestal. Despite being daytime, torches were needed along the walls to help provide light. They pushed him to his knees with knives held at his neck, forced to look up at a woman dressed in black standing behind the pedestal.

"Demon. The New Guard has captured you and you will now meet your fate."

"I am not a demon, merely a traveler from far away."

"You may have come from far away, but you had the tools of a demon on you. Thus, you were in the company of demons."

"The device was only a tool for communication. There's no evil in it, nor do I wish ill will on anyone on Proelium."

"So you claim. Lock him up, and I will decide how to deal with him later."

"Kill the demon! Kill the demon!" A chant began in the temple from those that followed Elmwood's arrest.

"Silence! I will determine if it is best to kill the demon. Remember, if we kill him, the demon spirit would be set free to infect someone else. We need to contain the evil spirit if we kill him."

Elmwood was relieved she held off his execution, at least temporally. He was strong-armed out of the room through a set of doors behind the podium. The exit led to a courtyard of sorts, where several wood poles in an L shape stood along with pillories. A shirtless man hung from his wrists from one L shaped beam. His body showed whip marks as he hung as if unconscious. A naked man watched from a pillory as Elmwood was pulled by. He was placed in one of the ten cells that looked to be at one time a barn. There was nothing in the cell, and the walls were made of wood, save for the door made of iron bars. Two men stood in front of the cells.

Elmwood sat on the floor, avoiding the area where he saw a rat-like creature run by. He looked at the courtyard, occasionally seeing members of the New Guard march by. A few citizens stood at the boundary of the courtyard, looking at the unfortunate people being punished. He observed a woman approach one of the New Guards, pleading with him as she passed over something to his hand. Shortly later, he escorted her to where the unconscious man hung by his wrists. A few minutes passed, and he was released from his bonds and he crumbled to the ground. Water from a bucket was poured on his head to wake him. Gradually he sat, and the woman helped him stand. With an arm around her shoulder, he staggered out of the courtyard.

I wonder if I have anything to bribe the New Guards with.

A little while later, Marisa came to the same boundary of the courtyard carrying a basket. He watched as she spoke briefly to a guard at the perimeter of the courtyard, and he eventually gave her permission to enter. Marisa walked with purpose toward the cell doors. She spoke briefly with one of the guards and was permitted to approach the cell doors. She stopped by one cell door, peering at the prisoner inside, calling out a blessing. She passed over a small piece of bread and cheese. To another prisoner, she pleaded for him to return to the teachings of the Tower before passing him food. She stopped in front of Elmwood. In a loud voice she called out, "Demon. Repent your ways." In a quieter voice she added, "I have told the others in your group to be careful around here in case they are suspected of being demons. Despite the clothing I gave your group, you and the others look different. You speak with an accent and you look too healthy." She smiled. "Fear not. Your trial won't occur before tomorrow, and even then, the punishment is rarely immediate. I will take your members to see King Bennett and perhaps he can order your release." She passed him bread and cheese.

"Thank you. Do you think a bribe will help?"

"Not in your case. The New Guards believe you to be a demon and would be scared to accept your gifts."

Elmwood watched her walk away. *All I can do now is wait and trust King Bennett can be convinced to help us.*

Spelling had to decide whether to stay and see if they could aid Elmwood or continue on their journey to King Bennett. With Elmwood indisposed, she had taken over as the mission leader. She conferred with Morgan Regan concerning her choice. Morgan agreed that if freeing the captain was unlikely, then the next best option was to see if King Bennett could help.

Once they had crossed the stone wall that identified the boundary of the kingdom, the presence of New Guards and the Towers diminished. They increased their pace, less worried about being questioned by the Tower followers.

They reached the castle where they were stopped from entering inside by royal guards. Marisa passed a sealed note to the royal messenger.

"For his majesty's eyes only." She passed him a coin. "This is of great urgency." She held up another coin. "If we can see him immediately."

The messenger bowed and hurried off. They waited and Spelling asked, "What does your note say?"

"One word. Reform."

Almost an hour passed when the messenger returned, receiving another coin from Marisa. "King Bennett will see you now. Please follow me."

"I guess urgent and immediately has a different meaning here," Spelling commented.

They climbed a marble staircase that gently curved to the second level and were ushered into a study where King Bennett sat in a large chair. Next to him sat a woman Spelling presumed to be the queen. Both were older looking and appeared to be well fed over their lives. A table separated them from the others.

King Bennett spoke after the door to the room closed. "Your note. Do you have news of change?"

"I do." Marisa bowed her head briefly. "I present these visitors from worlds beyond Proelium. Diplomat Tiffany Harris, I present you King Bennett and Queen Charlene."

"It is an honour to meet you King Bennett, Queen Charlene," Harris responded. "I represent the Alliance worlds and invite Proelium to discuss trade and other matters with us."

"Do you have proof you come from beyond our world?" Queen Charlene asked.

"I only have this with me, but you can use it to speak to our ship." Harris passed over her earpiece across the table. "If you wish, we can send a shuttle craft to the planet surface to prove we come from another world."

The queen picked up the earpiece. "Hello? Is anyone there? Speak." She almost dropped the earpiece when a voice responded from the device. The queen pointed her finger at Harris. "Just one shuttle? Can you bring more than one? How about a spaceship?"

"Yes, we can if you want."

"Tell them to bring that spaceship." The queen returned the earpiece and looked at the king. "We can finally eliminate the Tower from suppressing our people."

The king hesitated. He licked his lips as his fingers clutched together at the top of his stomach.

The queen glared at him. "What are you waiting for?"

"I agree to start trade negotiations with the Alliance worlds." The king scratched his chin. "To avoid panic among the population, I need to send messengers to the neighbouring kingdoms prior to your ship's arrival. We must not underestimate the resolve of the Tower and the New Guards to try to maintain control. I need to have our soldiers ready to protect our interests. I suggest we have a formal meeting in two days time. Noon would be a convenient time."

"We agree to this." Harris added a request. "May I ask a favour? One of our companions is being held by the New Guard, accused of being a demon. Can you order his release?"

"No, I cannot." The king shook his head. "If I were to do that, the Tower might be suspicious of my intervention. I don't want them to believe anything unusual is about to happen."

"Please, I believe he is in danger of facing death."

"That is unfortunate, but I cannot risk helping you on this."

As they left the castle, Spelling asked Marisa what they should do. "How can we help the captain?"

"It would be suspicious if I were to visit him again. I suggest we stay at an inn close by. I need to contact other Reformers to prepare for possible changes. I believe your friend will be okay for a while longer."

Harris frowned. "You better hope he is, otherwise, I'll be withdrawing my support for diplomatic relations with Proelium."

"He is just one man." Marisa raised her eyebrows.

"He is the captain of our ship." Spelling raised her voice. "If he dies, the New Guard will be the least of your concerns. Our ship, the Star Hawk, is designed for battle. If we should choose to do so, we could obliterate all human life on Proelium."

Marisa bit her lower lip. "I'll see what I can do."

Spelling heard Regan's voice through her earpiece. "You do know that we would never seek revenge, don't you?"

"I know that, but they don't."

<hr />

Elmwood was taken from his cell the next day. His wrists were placed in wide, thick iron cuffs and chained in front of him. He was marched to stand in front of the same woman who had ordered him to be placed in a cell. This time, she waited for him in a building that faced the courtyard, a single room used strictly for trials. Elmwood stood in front of a table where the blonde woman sat.

"I am Priestess Alana and I will determine if you live or die. If you live, I'll be in charge of any punishment you deserve." She stood. Tall with slim features, she walked around him. "You say you are not a demon. Can you prove it?"

"A demon would do evil. I have not. How does anyone prove they are not a demon? No matter what I say, you could counter a demon would lie."

"Tell me this then. Is technology evil?"

"Only if it is used that way."

"A clever retort, but the answer is technology is inherently evil unless its purpose is to increase the efficiency of work. An example is the horse drawn carriage. It allows for faster transportation of goods. On the other hand, a tool that takes away from a person doing the actual work is to be avoided. So your answer is incorrect. Technology is more likely to be evil than good."

"I will respectfully disagree. I have seen great things done by technology."

"Demon words." She pointed at him. "Take off his shirt."

Two men used a knife to cut and rip his shirt off him.

Alana approached him, placing a hand on his chest. "I can feel your heartbeat, so you are at least human. However, you don't have any marks on your chest or back. There is a belief that demons are not born, but suddenly come into existence. That would explain your perfect skin."

"I hardly have perfect skin."

"You likely won't after we finish with you." She pointed at two of the men. "Strip him of his clothes and let's see if the rest of him is perfect."

The remainder of Elmwood's clothes were pulled and ripped off, leaving him naked as he stood in front of her. Alana slowly circled him, inspecting his body.

"I don't see any flaws with your body. But perhaps that will change. Do you still refuse to admit you are a demon?"

"I am no more a demon than you are."

"Then you shall be tested to see if you tell the truth."

Spelling watched from just outside the courtyard. She was shocked to see Elmwood naked. She felt uncomfortable staring at him as he hung by his wrists from an overhead beam. She also didn't want to look away.

Damn good looking. Muscular chest with just enough hair without looking like an animal. Flat stomach with a hint of a six pack. And he looks more than big enough too.

She watched as one of the New Guards used a whip to strike Elmwood's back. The whip had a single strand, and the muscular man took his time between strikes. The whip was long enough to wrap around his back and strike part of his chest. Harris saw Elmwood grimace from each strike, and red marks appeared at his stomach and chest.

She looked at the others, who were all staring at Elmwood. There wasn't anything they could do, other than hope the whipping wouldn't be too long or severe. Then she saw the blonde woman who ordered him to be locked up approach him. She raised a hand to stop the whipping and spoke to Elmwood.

Harris couldn't guess what was said, but shortly later the woman left Elmwood. He remained with his arms secured above his head, but it appeared the whipping had ended, at least for now.

Well, there are worse things to look at than the captain. I'm sure glad the whipping has ended. Her earpiece buzzed with a voice from Morgan Regan.

"We have a shuttle ten minutes away from your location and are prepared to use armed force to free the captain. What say you?"

[38]

"HOLD OFF ON THE SHUTTLE. The captain does not appear to be in immediate danger," Spelling replied.

"What is his situation?" asked Morgan.

"He is naked in a public courtyard with his arms secured above him to a beam. He has been whipped, but it appears that has been halted."

There was a moment of silence. "Naked, in public?"

"Yes." She checked him once again. "But he's okay right now."

"I'm not so sure about that. How are the negotiations going with King Bennett?"

"We're waiting to hear from Marisa concerning a meeting tomorrow at noon, local time. We asked the king to order his release, but he refused. He was worried such action would alert the New Guard that the Reformers were about to strike."

"Is diplomat Harris with you?"

"Yes, she is."

"Then I suggest it might be prudent for the two of you to initiate the conversation with Marisa rather than staring at our captain."

"Understood." Spelling took one more glance at Elmwood, touched the sleeve of Harris to get her attention for her to follow her. She found Thomas Vice standing nearby, instructing him to keep watch on Elmwood, and be prepared to intervene if necessary. "You may have to contact the Star Hawk if the situation becomes life threatening. They have a shuttle on standby."

"Understood. I'll maintain a presence here."

Spelling and Harris made their way back to the inn.

Spelling found Marisa in the dining area of the inn, sipping tea. Harris went with her and stood behind her. An empty plate sat on the rough wood table in front of Marisa. Spelling sat on the wood chair. "Is there any news on the negotiations?"

"Yes, King Bennett wants your Alliance world spaceship and shuttle to make an appearance above here tomorrow morning, just after sunrise. He doesn't want the spaceships to land. Just make an appearance. Then King Bennett will negotiate with you."

"Good. And our captain?"

"I have spread the word through our Reform members that your captain must not be harmed under any circumstances. I hope that will spare him too much punishment."

"Thank you. I noticed the whipping had stopped."

"Yes. Priestess Alana, the one in charge of his sentencing is actually a Reform member who had infiltrated the New Guard. Occasionally she has spared citizens from worse punishments. She has been asked to ensure his life will be spared, but I must warn you her authority may be questioned if she tries to save him from punishment."

━━

Elmwood felt his strength return after the whipping stopped. He was surprised when the Priestess Alana stepped up to him and told him to be patient, that the Reform was getting ready to take control. After she left, he looked at the perimeter where the crowd stood, recalling seeing Harris and Spelling. *I wish I had some clothes on.*

The exposure caused him to become thirsty and weak. Two men took him back to his cell, marching him at sword point across the courtyard. At his cell he received water to drink from a pail that was passed on to the next prisoner. He waited, feeling hungry, but conserved his energy by sitting quietly as he heard rodents scurry around.

Just after sunset, his cell door opened, and he was escorted back to the temple. From there he was taken to a side door that opened to a small room, consisting of a desk and three simple wood chairs. Alana waited inside.

"Sit down." She looked at the two men. "You may leave. Keep this to yourself."

"Should I say thank you for getting me out of the cell?" Elmwood sat on one of the chairs. "Or is something else going to happen that I won't like?"

"You can say thank you." She smiled. "I'm part of the Reform, and one of those that has infiltrated the Tower. Understand, as my role as a priestess, I have to punish those breaking the law. That has included even ordering the execution of some offenders. When I ordered you to be whipped, I was trying to delay a possible death sentence for you. So far, it has worked."

"Then I do thank you. What is happening now?"

"It is dark and your disappearance from the cell will unlikely draw attention. I decided you can hide here until morning when your spaceship is supposed to appear. When that happens, the Reform shall rise to overthrow the Tower."

"That's good to hear. Is it possible to get clothes to wear?"

She lifted her eyebrows. "Why? Are you shy?"

"No, but perhaps being naked in front of a lady is something to be avoided."

"I'm a priestess, so your nudity is all right. But to come to the heart of your question, if you were to be discovered, it would be best if you appeared to be in the same condition as you were in your cell. I could claim I was interrogating you." She paused. "Unless you're chilled. I could get you a blanket."

"I'm not cold, but perhaps I could use food and drink."

Alana opened the door and called out. "Bring some food and tea in here. Quietly." She closed the door and stared at him. "You're one of the few men I've met that look good naked."

"Tell me more what's happening tomorrow morning."

"I know little more than what I've told you. In the morning your ship arrives, and we become free of the New Guards and the Tower."

"Okay, but how do I figure in this?"

"You are returning to the spaceship."

"Naked?"

"Possibly. I don't have any clothes to give you, and it is risky to try to get you any. I'm risking my life as it is by hiding you here." She paused. "I will try later to get something for you to wear."

When the door opened again, Alana accepted a plate of food and mug. She passed them to Elmwood. "Here. I shall leave you now and return in the morning. Don't leave this room. If you are discovered, it will probably mean your death."

Elmwood woke up with a start as he lay on the floor. He saw the door to the side room open, and Alana entered carrying a lantern, a pair of pants draped over her arm and a mug.

"Good morning." She held the mug toward him.

Elmwood slowly rose, stretched, and reached for the mug. The tea had a strong smell to it, and he hoped it would help him wake up. "What's happening now?"

"It will be dawn soon. I hope your spaceship and shuttle will arrive as promised." She handed over the dark brown pants.

"I as well. So, we just wait for the ship to arrive, and then I go when the shuttle lands?" He pulled on the pants. The pants were loose fitting on the legs, but too short. The pants didn't quite reach around his waist and had a side closure secure by a leather drawstring.

"Sorry, it was all I could find. We will both go to the shuttle because once the New Guard sees you escaping in the shuttle, I won't be safe. Even though the Reform will probably win the day with your ship's arrival, the remaining New Guard will seek revenge on others who aided them. I would certainly be a target." She reached for the door. "Please remain here and be quiet. I will return for you when it's time to leave."

Elmwood was thankful she left the lantern behind, giving light into the small room. He sipped the tea, hoping the shuttle would arrive soon.

Janice Madison relayed the message to Morgan Regan from Spelling. "It's nearing dawn where they are. They're ready for when the shuttle and Star Hawk arrive."

"Anything more about our captain?" She waited as Madison contacted Spelling again.

"Yes, it appears the captain is all right, and has been taken from his cell. He is hiding inside a temple by the courtyard where he was seen last. Nothing else is known."

"Steermaster, you have command." Morgan considered the information. "I want the Star Hawk and Eagle One to arrive over the courtyard in thirty minutes. I will pilot Falcon One and will land on the courtyard to retrieve the captain."

She left the command centre, stopping at the captain's quarters to obtain clothing for him. *It's good he still left permission for me to enter his room. It wouldn't be good for the captain to board the ship naked.* She smiled. *But it would be good to see him that way.*

She had a ship's medical officer meet her at the shuttle, plus a soldier in case of danger. She decided against adding more personnel in the event they had to pick up more members of the mission.

She reached Falcon One. and saw the medical officer and a soldier waiting for her. She wasn't surprised both were women, knowing the Star Hawk was required to operate with a large contingent of women.

The medical officer gave her a brief smile. "First Officer Regan, I hope you don't expect a serious medical issue. It's worrisome when we have our people on a strange world."

"Yes, but that's why we're here." She glanced at the medical officer's nametag, Tricia Maddan, pinned on her uniform. The medical personnel wore the ship's uniform except in two areas. One was that females were not required to wear chains with the reasoning that it might hamper them in case of a medical emergency. The other modification was that the uniforms were white, with a degree of transparency.

Morgan looked at the military officer, a tall brunette with a name tag of Corporal Mandi Karmel. "Officer Karmel, I'm hoping we won't need your expertise either, but it's nice to have you here." She saw the soldier had long hair and suspected she was originally from Praxton. Praxton didn't have many female members of the military, but many who were, applied to work on the Star Hawk.

"Thank you."

Falcon One dropped out of the Star Hawk, and Morgan took a quick visual of the ground below before piloting the spacecraft down toward the courtyard below. Above, the enormous black shape of the Star Hawk slowly drifted by with Eagle One following at a lower altitude.

"People are running away from the ship," Tricia commented.

"I can't say I blame them. It'll make our landing in the courtyard and picking up the captain easier."

The shuttle landed, and Morgan opened the door, looking for Elmwood. She saw him and a blonde woman run to the shuttle. *At least he's wearing something, although those pants look like they're ready to fall off. And who the hell is that woman?*

Elmwood entered the shuttle first, followed by Alana.

"This is Priestess Alana. She has helped me escape and we need to protect her until things settle down here."

"Sit here." Morgan pointed at one of the seats in the shuttle. She looked at Elmwood. "Are you all right, captain?"

"Yes, I'm okay now."

Morgan shook her head and grinned. "You look terrible."

Medical officer Maddan approached him. "I better check your wounds."

Elmwood made his way to the rear of the shuttle normally used to haul cargo. He stood as the medical officer examined him. A flexible cuff went around his arm. Besides measuring his blood pressure and heart rate, it used a needle to take a small blood sample, plus readings from the moisture on the skin. It wasn't long before it gave readouts to Madden.

Morgan observed Elmwood being treated for a moment and turned to Karmel. "Hey, eyes up front. You're from Praxton, and you know a female is not supposed to be staring at an undressed male. Especially our captain."

Karmel's jaw dropped. "Sorry. I forgot." She reluctantly turned her gaze away from the back of the shuttle where Elmwood was being attended to.

"That goes for you too." Morgan looked at Alana. "If you want to stay on this shuttle, give the captain some privacy."

"Very well." Alana smiled and turned to the front.

"I'm done," Maddan announced. "He will need those wounds to be treated again, but he's fine for now." She moved to the front of the shuttle and sat next to Karmel.

Morgan carried Elmwood's new uniform to him. "I picked up these for you."

"Thanks." Elmwood took the clothes.

"That was quite a first mission for you." She saw him hesitate before removing his borrowed pants. For a moment he stood naked before pulling on his new pants. She knew she should have turned her back as he dressed, especially after scolding Karmel for staring at him. But he didn't look uncomfortable undressing in front of her, and she reasoned that they were friends who weren't shy in front of one another.

Morgan watched him ease on his shirt. "Do you need help with your shirt?"

"No. I'm fine." He tucked in his shirt and fastened his pant closure. "You do realize that watching me get dressed will result in you being disciplined later." He gave her a wink.

Morgan smiled. "I'm counting on it."

"You neglected my underwear."

"I'm sorry, there wasn't any time to look for them." She grinned.

"You're going to be in so much trouble later." He laughed.

I sure hope so.

[39]

PRIESTESS ALANA GRIPPED the armrests of the seat as the shuttle lifted off. The engine gave only a small vibration and the journey to the large, black monolith of a spaceship was smooth. Her fear was not of the flight itself, but the destination. Whereas before the captain was at her mercy, suddenly the roles were reversed. She didn't believe demons occupied outside worlds, but she wasn't sure of the visitors' intentions.

It surprised Alana when Elmwood stopped by her seat and inquired how she was doing. "Fine, thank you. I'm nervous about what will happen to me when we arrive at your spaceship."

"I believe you will find our accommodation a bit better than the one I was treated to." He smiled. "After you have rested, we will need your help in approaching King Bennett in negotiations."

"I will be glad to help." She looked at the captain, looking taller and more powerful than when he was her prisoner. "I'm sorry for any discomfort you had. I didn't want to cause you any pain, but if I didn't punish you, the New Guards might have become suspicious."

"I understand. In the end, we are all safe."

Alana breathed a sigh of relief. She saw how the others on the ship reacted to him and believed him when he said everyone was safe. She was curious about the difference between the female and male uniforms. The male uniforms made the men look large and powerful. The women, to her point of view, were underdressed. Bare legs and the top showed there wasn't much in the way of any secondary garments underneath. She decided it was best not to be judgemental, as her own world was critical of any supposed deviate behaviour. Alana was curious about the relationship of Elmwood and one of the female officers. The officer was very protective of him, giving sharp looks to any of the other female personnel on board who stared at him.

I suspect they are in a relationship, or at least she wants one with him.

The shuttle moved inside the Star Hawk and Alana felt her calmness evaporating.

I'm in the belly of the black beast.

After the shuttle stopped moving, Morgan spoke to her. "I'm sure you're a bit apprehensive. Come with me, and I'll find a place for you to relax."

"Thank you." Alana stood and followed Morgan. "How long will I be here?"

"Hopefully not long. I believe the turmoil will die down soon. Perhaps tomorrow we can return you to Proelium."

Morgan reviewed the reports from the planet surface with the captain. There were pockets of riots and fighting as the supporters of the New Guards of Tower resisted the overthrow of their control. Led by the armies of King Bennett and the other kingdoms, order was restored. The Reformers seized the opportunity to form a coalition with the kings to rule the land. Within a day, many of the symbols of the Tower were destroyed.

The captain deemed it safe to return to the Proelium. The rest of the team that first landed on Proelium returned on a second shuttle, including Morgan, to resume negotiations.

At Elmwood's request, she used her mobile to call for a meeting in one hour in the boardroom. She followed him as Elmwood went to the command centre to confirm everything was in order.

"We have made headway in restoring their shuttles to full operation." Morgan checked her tablet. "We have completed repair work on the space stations as well. We have supplied parts and technical manuals. All in all, I believe we have given them everything they need to return to space."

"That's great to hear. I would like to leave educational material on the ground surface. If we can include the general population in the instruction of technology and science, then it may help improve their economy and reduce conflicts."

"I can arrange for that to be done." She made a note on her tablet. "I'm glad to see you've recovered from your ordeal on Proelium."

"Thank you. My injuries weren't severe, mostly superficial. However, that reminds me we have a situation. We are moving the culture of this ship to be more in alignment with that of Praxton. There will be several deviations from that, however, there are other aspects we should not ignore. On our mission to Proelium, I was put in a state of undress and was observed by the female crew members, including yourself. On Praxton, a female observing a naked male who is not their guardian, is normally disciplined."

"Yes sir, I understand that, sir."

"Good. I will deal with you about this issue when this mission is completed."

"Yes sir." Morgan let out a long breath of air. *I hope he isn't just going to reprimand me with a verbal warning. This ship uses Praxton customs, and I hope what he uses is more along the line of a firm hand when he reviews the situation with me.*

Elmwood sat at the head of the table as he reviewed the procedure for returning to Proelium. "We will use two shuttles this time. We will need one of the Falcon shuttles to transport our negotiation team to the surface, near the entrance to King Bennett's castle. One of the Eagle shuttles will accompany us and will remain in the air above in case of any threats. On this visit we will be representing the Alliance worlds and thus will wear our uniforms. I am aware the citizens of Proelium may be startled by the style of our uniforms, and particular, the women. However, we need them to understand this is how other worlds do things. Our manner of dress is something they must get used to."

Diplomat Tiffany Harris walked into the great hall of King Bennett's castle. She was accompanied by Marisa, John Geora, Weapons Officer Spelling, Captain Elmwood and Charter of Conduct Officer Paul Thyssen, who was warned he was an observer only, and not permitted to enter into the negotiations.

Priestess Alana accompanied the Alliance team into the castle. She mentioned to Elmwood that when she is seen leaving the shuttle, there may be some who may want to do her harm. The population may see her as a possible demon since she came from the shuttle. Others would recognize her as a priestess who worked for the New Guard. Tiffany Harris thought she should join them for the negotiations and inform the kings of what she saw on the Star Hawk. Alana had expressed her amazement of what she had seen on the ship, including the observation of Proelium and the space stations. She said the lamb stew was the best she had ever eaten.

The group entered the castle and were escorted with horns sounding their arrival. Honour guards stood along the walkway to where King Bennett and the other kings waited their arrival.

Already seated at a long table were King Bennett, Queen Charlene and several other kings from other kingdoms. They stood as they entered and allowed them to sit first.

King Bennett looked at Captain Elmwood. "I understand that the Alliance worlds are offering to trade with Proelium, although I'm not certain what we have that you will find of value."

"Material goods are only part of the equation. I will pass the negotiations over to Diplomat Harris as she has the authority to make an agreement with Alliance worlds and Proelium." Elmwood saw the queen give a brief smile, obviously pleased a woman could make important decisions during the negotiations.

A few hours later they left the great hall, returning to the Star Hawk via the shuttle Falcon One.

Elmwood spoke to Morgan using his earpiece. "The negotiations are concluded. It went well, as far as I could gather."

"What are we giving them and what do we receive in return?"

"We are going to repair and upgrade their space stations and shuttle craft. In addition, we will provide education material so they can learn about technology, and how to do their own repair work. In return, they will keep us informed of any rebel world activity."

"A bit one sided for them."

"Yes, but they are now part of the Alliance world territory of influence. We hope they will eventually become full Alliance world members."

"What about Priestess Alana? Is she safe?"

"Yes. King Bennett has placed her on his staff for consultations for the integration of the Alliance education material."

"That's great to hear. We'll see you back on the ship soon."

Elmwood eased back into his seat, pleased at the conclusion of the mission.

Time to relax and have a coffee.

Paul Thyssen approached him. "Captain, I understand this was just the beginning of the relationship with Proelium. However, I have concerns with potential conflicts with the Charter of Conduct policies. For example..."

On the other hand, I think it's time for a drink instead. Maybe a double.

[40]

DIANA TRIED to concentrate on the food formula for tomato paste, wanting to increase the spice level, and make the texture less smooth so it resembled closer to the original product.

The spanking she received a few days ago left an impression long past the physical reminder. Diana sighed and saved her work for later review. She headed to the kitchen in the processing area and made two cups of coffee. She carried them to Derik's office and saw him working behind his desk. Then she saw a woman kneeling on a cushion by the wall. Her hands were behind her back and her knees a few inches apart. She looked up at Diana and gave a soft smile.

"Diana." Holton looked up in surprise at her entrance.

"Hello, Master Derik." Diana placed his coffee on the desk and stood in front of his desk. "Who is she?"

"She just decided to keep me company for a bit."

"By kneeling on the floor?"

"It is the Praxton way." Derik suggested.

"The Praxton way?"

"On Praxton, females will often kneel on the floor next to a male during a quiet time. It is common for them to be nude or topless, but in this case, she is wearing her uniform."

"I see. To be clear, if you find this situation okay, you need to be aware I most certainly do not."

He sat, slack jawed. "I don't understand."

"On Praxton, it may be fine for a man to have more than one female, but I have an Alliance background where men and women have one partner each."

"But Venessa is merely keeping me company. Nothing more than that."

"Company in a very submissive pose."

"It is how females often wait for males. It means nothing more than that."

"Then let me be clear about this. I believe relationships are a two-way street. I've already given in to you by having you over for breakfast. I even gave in to your request to wear shorter skirts and have followed other of your wants. Now I want something from you to show that you care for me."

"I don't know what you want."

"I suspected that." She looked at Vanessa. "Could you give us some privacy?" Diana waited until she left. Diana took a drink of her coffee. "Master Derik, I'm willing to follow aspects of Praxton customs because they are important to you. Providing you want to accommodate my needs."

"What would be that be?"

"That our relationship is monogamous. Master Derik, I'm puzzled. You have not yet asked to be my guardian, and I have a lot of questions about that, yet you have established control over me. I'm not sure what freedom I have. You removed my panties. Does that mean I'm not permitted to wear any after that? You have stated I cannot pleasure myself. How long is that for? Then I come in here and see another woman kneeling near you. If you want a woman to be kneeling by your side, it better be me."

"I see your point. On Praxton this is quite normal to have a female kneeling."

"Maybe on Praxton, but we're on the Star Hawk. I believe the rules may be different. In any case, I want you to make an effort in using Alliance world customs as part of our relationship."

"What would be the Alliance world customs that you want?"

Taking a sip of her coffee, Diana thought of how she should respond. "When I first arrived on the Star Hawk, I had to learn very quickly what

Praxton customs were with no help from you. Now I'm going to do the same to you. If you want me, then figure it out."

"I do not believe you are being reasonable. I shall remind you that Praxton customs dictate relationships on the Star Hawk."

"Do enlighten me. Where exactly does that put us? Are you declaring you're my guardian? Don't I get a say in this? I have needs too."

"On Praxton, before the war, contracts were always used to establish the conditions between a female and guardian." He frowned. "In the war's aftermath between Alliance worlds and Praxton, the Charter of Conduct Office declared that some provisions of those contracts were not legal and binding. It has made for a rather messy situation on Praxton. On the Star Hawk, it has been decided that while the role of a guardian shall continue, contracts will not be used. When a female agrees to have a male as her guardian, he reports that arrangement to the captain. The captain has the power to void it if he thinks it's not in the best interests of the ship."

"Okay, but where does that put us? Do you have control over me?"

"I have control over you only if you accept it."

"And if I refuse to accept your orders?"

He smiled. "Then under Praxton customs I have the right to discipline you."

Diana placed her empty coffee mug on his desk. "So, I don't have any rights?"

"You have the right to refuse my orders. In that case, under Praxton customs, you should have a guardian, or at the very least, a male to protect your interests."

"So where does that put me on a spaceship? What male can protect me? And why would I need one to protect me?"

Derik leaned back in his chair as he peered at her. "I have work to finish and you have presented a problem to me I didn't anticipate. However, in the meantime, I shall have Chiela Bently escort you to dinner, and then to your suite. I believe you will recall meeting her as one of the technicians." He held up a hand to prevent her from speaking and used his mobile to contact Chiela, requesting her to come to his office.

Diana took a few seconds to try to relax before speaking. "Master Derik, I am not happy with our present relationship. It seems you are enjoying all the benefits, and delight in giving me orders. If we are to continue to see one another, I need something in return from you, namely a recognition of my Alliance background."

"I don't understand." Derik looked exasperated at her comment. "What do you want from me?"

"That's for you to figure out. You weren't happy with me when I first arrived on the Star Hawk, and I had to figure out what you wanted. Now I'm unhappy and you need to figure what you're doing wrong."

"Do you want me to offer you protection like a guardian?"

"No. We're on a spaceship, filled with military personnel. Exactly how do I need more protection than that?"

Derik stared at her blankly when Chiela entered the office.

Derik sighed and addressed her. "Could you take Diana to dinner and later return her to her suite?"

"Of course, Master Derik."

Diana started to cross her arms and stopped, deciding to keep her body posture neutral. "Do I have to go to dinner with her?"

"You don't. You can refuse to do so. But I'm asking you this time to follow my instructions."

Diana frowned and finally nodded. She followed Chiela.

Chiela asked, "You weren't going to refuse his order, were you?"

"I considered it."

"I don't understand. He really likes you. Don't you like him too?"

"I do. But I need a man to do more than just give me orders."

———

Diana finished her dessert after a meal almost devoid of conversation. She overcame her apprehension of sitting with Chiela, although saw her as an extension of Derik's authority over her. There were other women in the large dining room, and Diana noticed that some of them were acting under the control of their male guardian and were sitting topless.

I know that sometimes he will have me topless in the public areas of the ship if we continue our present relationship. I have to admit it would be freeing, like when I sat around naked at that vacation resort.

"You look deep in thought." Chiela peered at her.

"Sorry, I'm thinking about Master Derik and what it would be like to be under his full control. He's already ordering me around and I wonder how far he would extend that."

"Do you like when he orders you to do things? On Praxton we consider it a sign the guardian likes you."

"That seems odd to me." Diana pushed her fork around on the empty dessert plate.

"Praxton males always assume they have the right to order females that don't have a guardian. Master Derik is acting normal in that way. He likes you, so he is paying more attention to you. Don't you enjoy it when he orders you to something?"

"I guess it depends on what the order is, and how he presents it. It seems I have little choice but to obey him. If I make a mistake, he is rather quick to administer punishment."

"A spanking is the Praxton way of establishing a relationship. He is declaring his ownership over you." Chiela spread out her hands over the table.

"I guess I sort of knew that. I would've liked a say in that. So, what happens when a male becomes a guardian for you? Is there a sort of announcement?"

"On Praxton when a female accepts a guardian, it is normal for the guardian to host a party where the female is stripped and disciplined in front of the others. It is a traditional way to introduce a female to the guardian's household. On the Star Hawk, I believe Master Derik would punish you publicly while you're naked to establish that he is your guardian. He would give you a new collar at the time. They're usually the fancy kind."

"Seriously?" Diana sighed. "Couldn't that be done privately?"

"Oh no. The more people watching your discipline, the better. It's the Praxton way."

"This Praxton way of doing things takes time to get used to."

I wonder if he's the right one for me. She looked around the dining room, noticing the women looked relaxed and sharing conversation.

Diana left the dining room with Chiela, walking toward Diana's suite.

They reached Diana's suite and Chiela expressed her admiration for its size and decor. "Wow, this is really nice. It's big enough to hold your acceptance of Master Derik as your guardian party." She removed her shoes and walked around the living room.

"Yeah, the one where I'm naked and disciplined. I can honestly say I'm not looking forward to anything like that." Diana crossed her arms briefly and uncrossed them. *I best not show how annoyed I am. She'll be telling Derik everything.*

"I understand your apprehension. But after a few drinks, it'll become less scary. I doubt Master Derik would hurt you. The floggers we use now barely sting."

"But I'll be naked."

"You will. You need to understand female nudity is very common on Praxton. I think you'll enjoy the experience." She looked up at the second level of the suite. "Can I look at what the upstairs is like?"

Diana agreed and the two women went upstairs. Chiela made positive comments about the bedroom and shower.

"And I like the restraints on the clear wall facing the living room." She looked at Diana. "You're very pretty. No wonder Master Derik wants to have you."

"Thank you, but I wish he also liked me for my intelligence and personality." Diana blushed. *Does she really like everything about me and my suite, or is just all flattery?*

"I'm sure he does. On Praxton, we show off the female body. Males must show a forceful personality and a physical stature. Those outside of Praxton believe it's just the physical attributes that make a difference. That's simply not true. One could make robots that look like humans if that was the case. While looks are important, personality and intelligence make for the sexy human being."

"I see your point."

"How about we have a drink and relax a bit?"

"Sure." Diana led the way downstairs. "Just have a seat. I'll make the cocktails."

Diana made cocktails and relaxed on the couch. "Would I be wrong to guess that Master Derik asked for you to talk to me about being a Praxton female?"

"He did." Chiela nodded. "He asked me to help you understand Praxton customs."

Diana lifted her arm and pointed to her wrist cuff and chain dangling from it. "So I'm supposed to wear this stuff to please him."

"To make you feel good too." She sighed. "It's the Praxton way. Females wear restraints and males protect them. It's not complicated."

"Maybe for you. But I lived in Alliance space. I am used to wine and dinner for seduction, not chains and whips."

"I hear you." Chiela nodded. "But try to accept the Praxton way of doing things. Compared to other worlds, we have very little conflict. Females are protected from harassment from other males and are generally happy with living on Praxton."

"Okay, let's say I follow the Praxton custom of letting Master Derik control me. Right now, he has it all his way. He even ordered me not to pleasure myself. I'm certainly not allowed to go after other men. That doesn't seem fair."

"On Praxton females will often seek comfort from other females. It is considered normal, especially in households of two or more females. If you're frustrated in that area, perhaps I can help you there."

Diana was shocked for a moment at the proposition. "Oh, thank you, but no. I'm strictly into men."

"Okay." Chiela smiled. "But if you change your mind, I'm available. I don't have a guardian and get lonely too. Maybe we can just go for a few drinks sometime."

"Sure, that sounds great. I'm still making my way around this ship and the nuances of the Praxton culture. New friends will be good."

"Yes, more friends are always good. If you accept Master Derik as your guardian, there will be more friends to watch your acceptance of him."

Diana frowned. "Yeah, more people watch me being whipped while naked."

"I best be going." Chiela finished her drink. "I have work tomorrow morning."

"I suspect Master Derik will ask you about our dinner together. You can tell him I still want him to show an understanding of what an Alliance female expects in terms of romance. Otherwise there will be problems between us."

Chiela gasped. "He won't like to hear that."

[41]

JULIUS ELMWOOD ENTERED the executive officer lounge, ready to relax after their successful mission. He saw a few familiar faces, Janice Madison, Nicole Redding, Kelly Walling and Khloe Levit, and joined their table.

"Everyone looks to be in good spirits," Elmwood commented.

"I believe it has a lot to do with making it through our first mission," Walling answered as he lifted his whisky glass. "We are now officially doing work for the Alliance forces and are not just a pretty face."

Elmwood ordered a drink as the conversation continued around the table. He glanced about the room and saw the Charter of Conduct Officer Paul Thyssen sitting by himself. He asked Janice, who sat next to him, if Thyssen was sitting by himself when she arrived.

"No, I was sitting with Kelly when he came in. He walked by us and sat by himself. Every time I've seen him, he has been by himself. I guess representing the Charter of Conduct Office is not the most popular position."

"I agree with you there." He picked up his rum and cola glass. "I'm going over and say hello to him."

⊏⊐

Thyssen looked surprised at Elmwood's appearance.

"May I join you?"

"Of course. Please sit down."

"I couldn't help but notice you were by yourself. Is everything all right?" Elmwood sat and focused his attention on Thyssen.

"Yes, it is what I expected. Being the Charter of Conduct officer is a responsibility I accepted, knowing that meant having few acquaintances." He frowned. "It goes without saying I may not be the most popular person on the ship since my job is to help ensure the Charter's laws are being adhered to." He turned his beer glass around, studying the rising bubbles.

"Understood. However, let me give you my perspective of doing things. I'm responsible for the operation of the Star Hawk every hour it is out in space. To be effective at being the captain, I need to correct deviations of proper behaviour of the crew when I see them. I cannot do that every minute of the day. Rather, I will act when it is appropriate to do so." He raised a finger. "If I went after every infraction, I would have a crew that disliked me, and that would cause problems on the ship."

"Are you saying I'm too zealous in looking for infractions of the Charter laws?"

"Partly." Elmwood folded his hands on the table. "Consider this. If you want to change the attitude and behaviour of the crew, you need to approach them as someone they respect because you respect who they are."

"How can I do that?"

"You need to stop being the Charter of Conduct Officer every minute and just be a human being. Find mutual ground."

"I hear what you're saying, but my mandate is to ensure the Charter Laws are being followed."

"Tell me if I'm wrong. Wasn't the Charter of Conduct established to help prevent conflict among people?" He leaned forward in his chair.

"Yes, that was the original intent."

"Well, we're not having conflicts on the Star Hawk, so I would say you're doing a good job."

"But not because the Charter of Conduct laws are being followed." Thyssen frowned.

"Paul, at least some laws are being followed, otherwise we would have chaos on this ship."

"That's true," Thyssen conceded.

"If you want to extend your influence, then you need for others to know and respect you. I suggest you join me and establish a friendship with the others. I believe you will find common ground."

"To be honest, I'm under the impression they don't care for me or the Charter of Conduct laws very much."

"That may be true. But sitting here by yourself will not change that. May I ask where you are from originally?"

"Yes, the planet Heimat. It's in the star system Doppelt."

Elmwood stood. "Pick up your drink and come with me."

Thyssen hesitated and followed Elmwood back to the other table.

The others at the table made room for Thyssen, shifting to allow for six people to sit around the table.

Elmwood renewed the conversation. "Paul just told me he originally came from Heimat."

"Isn't that one of the human planets circling a double star?" Walling asked.

"Indeed, it is." Thyssen gave a nervous smile. "A dwarf star around a large yellow sun."

"I heard Heimat has a rather warm climate but subject to severe storms." Redding added.

Thyssen nodded. "Indeed, it is an interesting world."

Elmwood nursed his drink, pleased at the interaction of Thyssen with the others at the table. *If he's more comfortable with the others, then perhaps he'll be less prone to push the Charter of Conduct laws at every chance he can get.*

He took another small drink, deciding to have only one drink before his video conference with his direct superior, General Noreen Howler. He hoped she didn't ask too many details on how he ended up naked and whipped on Proelium and focused more on the Star Hawk's next mission.

One thing I've learned is that even a well-planned mission can take a surprising turn of events.

He stood, advising the others he had business to attend to. "Time to find out about our next adventure."

End of Book Five of the Praxton Series

Don't miss out on your next favorite book!

Join the Melange Books mailing list at
www.melange-books.com/mail.html